Danger Wears White

Emperors of London Series

Lynne Connolly

LYRICAL PRESS
Kensington Publishing Corp.
www.kensingtonbooks.com

Lyrical Press books are published by
Kensington Publishing Corp. 119 West 40th Street New York, NY 10018

All Kensington titles, imprints, and distributed lines are available at special quantity discounts for bulk purchases for sales promotion, premiums, fund-raising, and educational or institutional use.

Special book excerpts or customized printings can also be created to fit specific needs. For details, write or phone the office of the Kensington Special Sales Manager:
Kensington Publishing Corp.
119 West 40th Street
New York, NY 10018
Attn. Special Sales Department. Phone: 1-800-221-2647.

Kensington and the K logo Reg. U.S. Pat. & TM Off.
Lyrical Press and the L logo are trademarks of Kensington Publishing Corp.

First Electronic Edition: July 2015
eISBN-13: 978-1-61650-571-4
eISBN-10: 1-61650-571-0

First Print Edition: July 2015
ISBN-13: 978-1-61650-595-0
ISBN-10: 1-61650-609-1

Printed in the United States of America

Hoping to live down her family's connections to the traitorous Jacobite cause, Imogen wants nothing more than a quiet life in the country. When she stumbles upon a wounded man, the white cockade in his coat tells her he's a Jacobite, and a danger to the crown. Yet there's something about him she can't resist . . .

In search of a document on behalf of his powerful family, Tony is shot and left for dead. Secreted away to a hidden chamber, he finds himself both a guest and prisoner of a beautiful but mysterious woman. What she wants and who she serves, he cannot know. But what he does understand is the desire burning strongly between them. And that neither of them will be spared until their lust is sated.

When the action moves to London, suddenly it's Tony who has to act to save Imogen. Forced to become a lady in waiting to Princess Amelia, she is in peril from the Jacobites, who are convinced she is their salvation. Only the strength of Tony and Imogen's love can save them now.

Visit us at www.kensingtonbooks.com

Books by Lynne Connolly

Emperors of London Series
Rogue In Red Velvet
Temptation Has Green Eyes
Danger Wears White

Published by Kensington Publishing Corporation

Chapter 1

Imogen hunched her shoulders against the drizzly rain and patted her horse's neck, but he was far too used to the inclement weather for it to make any difference to him. The white stone of the boundary marker stood starkly against the green of the hedge, in its rightful place. She breathed a sigh of relief.

Sir Toby had left them alone. He'd become so persistent, insisting the lush Lower Meadow belonged to him, that she'd taken him to court, but they'd conducted the case in as cordial a spirit as possible, and now Sir Toby appeared content. He was probably off harassing another neighbor.

Satisfied with her discoveries, Imogen turned to head for home. A stumble from her horse gave her pause. Had Blackie picked up a stone, or just skidded on the slick grass?

She'd had the gelding since he was a foal, hence the childish name the poor animal still bore. Imogen would rather have a stone in her own shoe than cause him pain. He was retired from most duties these days, but he'd stamped around his stall this morning, clearly restless, so she'd taken him on the relatively easy task she assigned herself today. That was before it had started raining.

A hut stood at the bottom of the field. Or rather, it teetered. It had suffered from the recent dispute, neither party wanting to go to the expense of repairing it until the courts decided on the boundaries. The roof was held on by a promise and let in more than it kept out. Any creature with nowhere else to stay might find a modicum of protection there. It would have to be a small creature, though.

Imogen climbed down from her saddle and led Blackie to the hut. Her cocked riding hat protected her head from the drizzle, but this kind of persistent rain tended to penetrate after a time, and she'd been out an hour already. Her practical close-woven brown wool riding habit kept out the rest, but it wouldn't have passed muster in the more fashionable areas of Lancashire. Not that she cared.

Blackie seemed steadier now she'd climbed down, but when she walked him, she spotted that slight stumble again.

When she reached the hut, she sighed. Usually she tried to ignore this tumbledown structure. Maybe she should get Young George to pull it down completely. Some aristocrats built ruins on purpose to make their estates appear more picturesque; they were welcome to this one.

Fumbling in her pocket, she found the hooked piece of metal she used to help scrape hooves. Blackie bent his head and started cropping the grass, hardly noticing when she tapped his hock for him to lift his foot.

Ah yes, there it was. A couple of scrapes and she had it. A small, though sharp, piece of stone. It hadn't done any significant damage, but if she'd ignored it, it would probably have eased his shoe loose by the time they got home and dug into him painfully.

Worth getting wet for. Her leather gloves were soaked and now grimy from the dirt Blackie had picked up—probably ruined.

Still, this was the north boundary, and the house was only a mile or so away. Her mother would murder her if she wasn't in the drawing room at half past three, ready to greet whatever guests she'd invited for dinner. Mother had mentioned guests at breakfast, but Imogen hadn't listened properly, so she wasn't sure who they would be.

Imogen tucked the hook back in her pocket and urged Blackie to lift his head. "I'll give you oats with your feed," she promised him, giving him a pat. "You've been a good boy."

About to lead him to a nearby tree stump so she could mount, she heard a groan. Was it her imagination, or perhaps some creature lurking nearby? Rabbits and foxes could make the oddest sounds.

The groan came again—low, soft, and…male.

She glanced around but saw nothing. Hearing another sound, she spun around and stared into the dimness of the rickety hut. She stepped closer, caution ruling her. A miasma of rotting vegetation and something else she couldn't identify rose to give her pause. Wrinkling her nose, she pressed on.

It had no door, and grass grew sparsely inside. A pile of forgotten hay lay in one corner, sodden and useless. That would account for the stink.

As her eyes became used to the gloom, a glint in the corner of the hut caught her attention. A large shape—hulking, the smell of old clothes and something tangy and metallic. Heavens, a man!

She raced back to Blackie, unfastened the saddlebag, and grabbed her father's old pistol. She never went out alone without it, but more for foxes and vermin than protection. She dragged back the hammer. Old the weapon might be, but she kept it in excellent working order.

She stepped forward. "Who's there? Come out at once!" If it was a beggar, she'd give him short shrift and send him on his way. A beggar was highly unlikely to be armed with more than a knife, so as long as she kept her distance, she'd be fine.

The pistol wavered in her grip. She brought her other hand up and braced her hold on it. "Answer me!"

All she got was another groan. Daring to move closer, she peered into the darkness.

He moved, and a shot of alarm arced through her. His body went on forever, and his bulk wasn't entirely due to his heavy clothes.

The rain had lessened and the sun had come out, giving her better light.

Something sticky and dark glimmered on the floor of the hut. The straw had absorbed some of it, but not all. That accounted for the rest of the smell she'd detected when she'd approached this place. It was the smell of the cobbled yard at the back of the pigsty after the slaughterman had paid his autumn visit.

Imogen uncocked her pistol and crept forward. When he stirred, blood seeped from a wound somewhere on his body, and the fresh red stain was easily visible, even in this gloom.

This man was no vagabond. He didn't wear rags but a sturdy overcoat covering a coat that, while not the height of fashion, was well made—and currently stained with his blood. Her heart missed a beat. How much had he lost? More than a man should, that was for sure.

Imogen dropped to her knees next to him, doing her best to avoid the sticky pool. She needed to discover the source of the blood, so she could try to stop it. He rolled on to his back.

He wasn't conscious, but a slit of blue showed from beneath his lids. If he'd ever had a wig and hat, he'd lost them long since. His short dark hair was clammy, either with rain or sweat, clinging to his skull. His hands, bare of gloves, were pale, and his nails broken. Had he had a horse? Horse thieves were rife around here. If thieves had set upon him, why hadn't they taken his clothes as well as his horse? And left a perfectly good pair of riding boots?

While she considered the situation, she pulled at his clothes, dragging them aside to discover the wound. Either she'd have to ride for help, in which case he might bleed to death, or she might find a way of stopping the bleeding long enough to get him to a place of safety. It didn't pass her understanding that she could be in danger here too, if the attackers were still lurking nearby. She laid the pistol down by her side and remained alert to any untoward sound or a whinny from Blackie.

His side was clear of wounds. The damage was to his arm. She breathed a sigh of relief that it wasn't near a vital organ. After taking her knife, she cut up the sleeve of the man's overcoat, and then, with more effort, the coat he wore beneath. She had to deal with the shirt. This man had dressed far too well.

There it was. A deep wound on the upper flesh of his left arm bled sluggishly. When he changed position he'd caused the fresh flow. Imogen breathed out slowly in relief. She had uncovered no mortal wound. He would most likely live.

Now to find something she could use to bind his wounds and prevent them opening up again when she moved him. The solution lay before her in the creamy white of his linen. She cut away the sleeve of his shirt, taking great care not to cut his skin. Busy about her work and planning her next move, she started so violently at the sound of his voice that she nearly leaped three feet in the air like a startled cat.

"Are you planning to hurt me again?" His deep and rich tones were tinged with amusement.

Imogen shrieked. Gripping the shirt sleeve, she sat back on her heels and glared at him. "How long have you been awake?"

"I keep drifting," he said. "I hit my head when I was shot. Didn't you realize that's what happened?" He closed his eyes and groaned. "Please tell me the bullet passed through and didn't shatter the bone."

"You're a doctor?"

When he shook his head, he winced. "What about my head?"

"Your head's hurt?"

He took a couple of deep breaths. "My horse bolted and threw me off. That's when I hit my head. I'm a damned idiot for letting the landlord talk me into hiring the beast. But perhaps if somebody hadn't shot at me, the beast wouldn't have run off. My head hurts like the devil. Somehow I found this place, I'm not sure how."

The road was at least half a mile away. "The bullet went through you. It's not inside you."

He closed his eyes and bit his lip. "Would you mind binding that wound before I bleed to death?"

Thus admonished, she returned to her task. After she ripped the shirt down its seam and split it in half with her knife, she had plenty of linen to bandage the wound. She bound it loosely to start, but gentleness wasn't the best way. Blood oozed through the fabric. Gritting her teeth, she started again. This time she pulled it tight.

He sucked a harsh breath between his teeth, but bade her, "Don't mind me. Keep going."

She did as he said because she had no choice. Only a tight bandage would work.

When she'd finished, she ripped the end of the makeshift bandage down to make two ties and fastened it off with an efficient knot.

Only then did she realize her calves were screaming at her to move. They ached with a deep, agonizing cramp. Trying not to whimper, she sat back, ignoring the damp ground under her backside. With little consideration to modesty, she lifted her skirts and rubbed her calves.

He glanced at her, and to her amazement, a smile flicked at the corners of his full mouth. A strained one to be sure, but it was there. "When you've recovered, would you mind taking a look at my head? Then I'll be on my way."

She could hardly believe he'd said that. "Where will you go?"

"I may still have my purse. Did you not look?"

"I was too busy saving your life."

He chuckled low in his throat before he groaned again.

Her legs tingling with pins and needles, Imogen strove to move. Despite the blood and dirt smears on his face, his powerful attraction pierced her awareness.

He was tall, or at the moment, long. When she spread her hands over his head to feel for any wounds or blows, she found nothing life-threatening, as far as she could tell. Touching him like this felt far too intimate.

He glanced up at her without moving his head. "Do you feel anything?"

Yes, a man. She'd never expected to get this close to a man, having long given up the prospect of marriage.

Better to give up the idea entirely than lose her land. But now, with her hands on this man's head, she realized exactly what she was giving up.

Intimacy. She would never be close to anyone. She had been an only child with an undemonstrative mother. Only her body servants would touch her. In any case, she took care of most of her personal needs herself, so that would be rarely. No man, and never in the act of love.

Her thoughts came to a halt. "You have a lump as big as a pigeon's egg." She gentled her touch.

"Anything else?"

Wasn't that enough? "A cut. Not a deep one." At least, it wouldn't be when the bump had subsided. The wound had begun to clot, and soon it would have a substantial scab. His only problem would be dirt. But she couldn't wash either of his wounds or any she hadn't yet discovered because there was no pond or stream close by. The rain had helped, but he needed proper care.

"I'll do. Help me up, and I'll leave you in peace."

"You're mad," she said before she could control her thoughts. Come back to my house and I'll make sure you're well. I'll even lend you a horse."

He tilted his head. "What's your name?"

"Immie." Her childhood name.

"Emmy. Very nice. My name's Tony."

So he'd heard wrong. It didn't matter. His head must be buzzing after receiving a bump like that. "Where do you live?"

"In a big house about a mile away." Better if he didn't know she was the mistress of the house. After all, she was a property owner, if not a great one, and if he was, despite appearances, a ruffian, he might attempt to abduct her or hold her to ransom. It happened a great deal in society, and while she wasn't a prime target, she could prove a convenient one for a man in need of money.

He clapped his uninjured hand to his side. "As I thought. My purse has gone."

"You think they were thieves?"

"What else could they be?"

He stared at her and she caught her breath. He had beautiful eyes, expressive and well-shaped with sweeping black lashes. They'd appear even better if they weren't bloodshot, but that was to be expected after an experience like his.

Nothing more. Except they were a shade of heavenly blue she'd rarely seen before. When their eyes met, an emotion stirred deep inside, one she didn't immediately understand. She recognized it with astonishment. Desire.

That didn't happen to her. She identified it by instinct alone, not experience. And with a man who was half-dead and filthy to boot? Oh yes. She wouldn't deny the inconvenient heat swamping her body. However she would conceal it, being a civilized woman.

He held up his relatively uninjured arm. "Would you help me up? I hate to ask you, but I don't think I can do it on my own."

He was right. He had to stand if she was to help him. She spread her feet on the floor, bent her knees, and gripped his arm with both hands. It was a strain, but once he was sitting, he planted his feet on the ground and pushed himself up.

He released her hand to prop his arm on the wall nearest him. It swayed alarmingly, creaking loudly. He sprang upright with a curse, and the movement dislodged something from what remained of his coat.

A bunch of white satin ribbon formed into a shape Imogen knew well. A white cockade, the symbol of the Jacobites.

* * * *

Tony let the cockade fall to the ground. Emmy paled, and immediately he felt sorry for his subterfuge. She'd done everything she could to help him. "I'll accept your kind offer, thank you." His head swam alarmingly, and he would give a great deal for a soft bed and a glass of brandy.

He'd suffered injuries before, and seen worse. In his profession, he could hardly avoid it. His *old* profession.

Recollecting his usual life helped to keep the dizziness at bay. The only big house this close was the one he'd headed for with a particular aim in mind, so although he hadn't banked for someone shooting at him, he had achieved his objective of getting inside the house. Even worse that he'd enter it as a guest, when he'd planned to enter it as a thief. He tried to smile, but feared it turned into a grimace. "What's wrong?"

"You're a Jacobite," she whispered, dread in her tones.

Tony fixed all his attention on her face. She'd gone white, and she was staring wide-eyed at him. He couldn't tell if she was appalled or awed. Which? Was she a loyalist to the Crown or a rebel? He wouldn't agree to or deny her statement. Since he'd hoped the cockade would get him into the house via the servants' entrance, he couldn't be sorry she had seen it. "Does that give you a problem?"

"The magistrates will hang you if they find you with one of those things." She nudged the piece of white ribbon with her foot.

"You've seen a lot of these hereabouts, haven't you?"

"Yes."

At least she didn't deny it. Jacobites riddled this part of Lancashire. Most of them were licking their wounds after the defeat of the 'Forty-five. Others considered it a setback and carried on with their plotting.

By inserting himself in their midst, Tony anticipated discovering more about the plot that threatened his family, irritatingly known as the Emperors of London. His own name explained the reason for the sobriquet. Antoninus. Damn stupid name. His brother, Nicephorus, was another example of their mother's warped sense of humor.

For the first time in months, Tony felt alive. The edge of danger in this self-imposed assignment gave him a thrill he thought he'd left behind.

Not to mention a pretty servant girl.

But Emmy was more than pretty. She was stunningly beautiful. An appropriate description, considering the circumstances. He didn't know if she was aware of the effect of her exquisitely pointed chin and her liquid brown eyes. If anything, the cloud of dark hair at present untidily straggling down in tails and curls only acted as a frame. And he wasn't being partial, even though when he'd first opened his eyes to see her he'd wondered if angels had brown eyes. If he'd said it, she'd probably have left him, and he didn't fool himself. He'd come close with this one.

He glared at the blood he'd left on the floor. Weakness filled his bones. He could use a good night's sleep before he got to work.

Emmy took his elbow, and he felt the same jolt of awareness that he had when she'd touched his head. That had come as a profound shock. Women had a place in his world, but here and now, he didn't have time for that. Unless he'd found an ally.

Hurting someone who'd done nothing but help him went against the grain. From the way she was dressed, in a drab riding habit that had seen better days, and her attitude, with no maidenly modesty, he'd guessed she was a servant at the house.

Tiredness swept over him in a swamping wave. He still couldn't believe he'd nearly ended here, in the English countryside instead of one of the battlefields of Europe. The vagaries of fate never failed to amaze him.

When he moved, he staggered, and he decided against picking up the cockade. Instead, he scuffed it into the ground with the toe of his boot. His valet would probably faint dead away if he saw what Tony was doing with the boots meant to grace Hyde Park. Well, they were good boots, and they deserved a better fate than prancing around town.

"In truth, I don't think I could go much farther today," he said, passing a hand over his forehead. The dramatic gesture wasn't altogether undeserved. Heat washed over him and he knew from experience that was part of his condition. A soak in a bathtub to get all the dirt out of his wounds and a good night's sleep would see him right. If he was fortunate, he'd get one of those.

He was damned lucky not to have suffered a broken bone. That bullet had come out of nowhere and he'd only had time to jerk to one side before it struck. The retort and the pain weren't that far apart, so his attacker must have been close. A footpad? Maybe, but he hadn't been robbed, and the ruffian had every opportunity to do so. He'd lost the contents of his saddlebags, but only because the horse had bolted.

No, someone had shot him for a different reason. The devil was, he didn't know which one. Either because he was a Jacobite, or because he wasn't. At the last inn, he'd ensured the landlord had seen the cockade when he'd asked for directions, so maybe the innkeepers weren't pleased to see him. Certainly, the nag he'd allowed the landlord to fob him off with wasn't the sprightly mount the landlord had promised. A lively mount, but only when a bullet zipped past its ear.

A mile wasn't too far. Not when he'd been lying in that run-down hut for the best part of a day, blood seeping out of him. He'd been unconscious for half of it, and when he'd woken, one movement had told him his head was broken and he'd swum in and out of consciousness.

He had to get to shelter, whatever that was. Now he pushed away from the wall that threatened to collapse under his weight and took a step toward Emmy. "Shall we go?"

Unfortunately, he'd lost his practiced manner. He stumbled, and his words came out as a definite drawl. Like he'd been drinking French brandy all night. His head felt the same, full of heavy syrup.

Cursing to himself, he let her lead him out into the sunshine.

When had it stopped raining? During his ordeal, part of him had welcomed the rain as a way to irrigate the wound, but it had turned chilly, and he feared he might shiver himself to death. A horse stood outside, calmly cropping the grass. It had good bones but signs of age. Black with a white blaze on its forehead that vaguely resembled a white cockade. Appropriate. It was probably called Charles or James.

"I think you should ride the mile to the house," she said.

"Dear lady, I wouldn't dream of depriving you of your gallant steed."

She turned to face him, studying him with a frankness that in other circumstances he'd enjoy. "I fear that if you don't use the horse, you will fall over. I can't pick you up. You are far too heavy for me."

Yes, he was, and she was right. But she'd patched him up, so he wasn't in danger of bleeding to death. A mile, she'd said. Hardly any distance at all.

But every step felt like he was lifting a ton of weight.

She walked toward a tree stump at the corner of the field. "You can mount here."

"I don't need a tree stump." At times in his life, he'd lived on horses. Slept on them too. He could mount an average-sized docile gelding.

Besides, the walk seemed too far. Grabbing the reins, he put his foot in the stirrup and prepared to swing his other leg over the saddle.

Except when he pushed up, something happened to his head, and while he gave his free leg the order to lift, it didn't want to obey him.

The dizziness overwhelmed him, the grass becoming even greener, spinning, as if the horse had taken off and was cantering in circles. Just a rest, and then he'd complete the action.

Black edges at the corners of his eyes warned him what would happen next. With a silent prayer that he wouldn't be unconscious for long, he fell forward, slumping over the saddle.

Chapter 2

"Miss Imogen, your lady mother will be expecting you. Shall I take the…" Young George's voice trailed off when he saw the burden Blackie was bearing.

Silently, Imogen opened her hand to reveal the scuffed, filthy white cockade. "I found him in that run-down hut near the highway. He's been shot, George." She wasn't above using the loyalty of the Georges, young and old, especially now. She'd waited until the stable lad had run from the yard, probably, considering the hour, in search of his dinner, before she'd led Blackie around the corner and into Young George's view. "Quick, George, help me get him out of sight."

Young George touched his forelock. "Yes'm.'"

Not for the first time, Imogen had cause to be glad of Young George's towering height and overpowering strength. Over six feet with a huge frame, he nevertheless could be quick when the occasion demanded it.

She knew exactly where she would take her captive, and she headed for a corner of her house, key in hand. Unlocking the small door, she waited impatiently for her servant to catch up.

Young George lifted Tony off the horse as if he weighed no more than a lamb. Tony flopped over Young George's shoulder. All the way home, Imogen had paused to check the pulse in Tony's wrist, terrified that utter collapse meant he would never wake.

He might be a Jacobite, but she meant him no harm, and if she'd left him there or informed someone in authority, they'd have locked him up. He'd have taken prison fever in a week. She couldn't have lived with herself if that happened.

Imogen opened the door and waited for Young George to step through before she relocked it and dropped the key in her pocket. She followed him up the narrow wooden staircase that led to the highest room in the house, the Long Gallery that stretched across the front of the main building.

Imogen had avoided the courtyard, because the parlor overlooked it and her mother might be already there, foot tapping, waiting for her daughter's tardy presence. What Imogen had imagined as a leisurely hour to wash and ready herself for dinner would turn into a frantic ten minutes with cold water from that morning and the first gown she could lay her hands on.

But she had rescued someone.

The Long Gallery was of a piece with the rest of the house. One of the Thanes in the past, when they'd been country squires with not a title in sight, had seen an elegant long gallery in one of the large aristocratic houses being built at the time and decided he wanted one, too. But not as long and not as high.

She kept the gallery free of all but a few pieces of furniture, something she was glad of now, because Young George had less to trip him. A shame her sixteenth-century ancestor hadn't used weathered wood because this place didn't have one straight line in it. Successive owners had to practice constant make do and mend as the timbers had warped and twisted, and now the Long Gallery resembled the deck of a ship, one that had seen more than a little action. The warped boards were patched and the worst places covered with rugs, but every spot of the long room shone and gleamed with careful polishing. If Young George hadn't known the vagaries of the gallery, he'd have stumbled. As it was, he carried his burden carefully around the more prominent of the gaps and jutting floorboards.

Halfway down the gallery, they paused. Young George shifted Tony's weight, but not because it bothered him. Imogen had seen him carry a heifer five miles with no discomfort, so he could manage a man. It was to prepare them for the next part of their journey.

Very few people knew this secret. When Imogen had discovered it, she'd stood amazed.

Now she pushed open a panel, revealing a room, the upper half abutting onto the gallery. When the owner had built the Long Gallery, a room from the old part of the building, the wing leading up to the gatehouse, had inconveniently abutted at the wrong height. So instead of demolishing or reconstructing, he'd merely blocked it off. Although it had formed a secret room, it wasn't meant that way when first built.

Imogen used to jump down the four feet to the floor of the secret room, but Old George, Young George's father, had discovered her playing one day, and later he'd made her a set of stairs, so she didn't have to jump and risk breaking her ankle. At the time she'd scoffed, but secretly warmed to the old man's concern.

Now she was profoundly glad of the rudimentary steps. She went down first, waiting for Young George to pass his burden to her. He didn't, but held Tony in his arms as he scrambled through.

The bed here must have been blocked in with the room. It was too large to have passed through the small opening. Not as large as the one in her room, but not a narrow cot, either. Big enough for a man. She'd stored some old sheets in the chest pushed against the wall, ones she had darned instead of throwing out. While Young George stood patiently, head bowed because of the low ceiling, holding the still unconscious Tony, she hastily made the bed and threw a blanket and quilt over it.

"Can you strip him, George? All but his shirt and drawers," she added. "His clothes are filthy and his wounds need bathing."

"Best to leave him awhile, miss," Young George said. "I'll strip him all right and put him to bed. Best you get off and change. Your lady mother will be sending for you if you don't go."

She'd return later. "Can you bring some water up?"

"I'll do that for you, miss."

Ah yes, the cockade. Imogen pulled it out of her pocket and tossed it on the chest where she kept the blankets and sheets. It was grubby now, since he'd ground it into the dirt, creased but still recognizable as the symbol of the Jacobite. What a stupid man to carry this about his person! But they did, so they could recognize each other. Young George would tell nobody.

Reluctantly, she left the room and scurried along the Long Gallery in the direction of the passageway that led to the main part of the house, and her bedroom.

After a perfunctory wash, she brushed her hair and twined it into a knot at the top of her head. After she had dropped her wet riding habit and boots on to the floor and scrambled into hoops, petticoat, gown and satin shoes, Imogen considered herself ready for dinner. Powdering her hair and applying the face paint her mother considered proper would have to wait. She only remembered to snatch up her fan and lace-edged handkerchief as she was leaving the room.

A London lady would consider her gown hopelessly outdated, but Imogen couldn't help that. She hadn't visited Lancaster in—goodness, nearly a year!

Maybe she should think about visiting her dressmaker and ordering a gown or two. Hurtling downstairs, she nearly came a cropper on the narrow wooden staircase at the end of her corridor and had to grab the worn banister rail to steady herself. With a silent prayer that nobody had heard the clatter, she crossed the hall to the drawing-room.

More people than she had expected turned to watch her entry. Covered with confusion, Imogen settled for a curtsey. "Good afternoon," she said.

"Good afternoon," a stranger said in a softly cultured voice. She lifted her chin and stared into a pair of gray eyes crinkled at the corners with amusement.

Damn, they'd heard her. The only thing she could do was pretend it hadn't happened.

She rose as gracefully as she could manage and held out her hand. He bowed over it, far too deeply for comfort. The depth of the bow indicated the rank of the person being addressed, and he'd almost touched the polished wooden floor when he performed his obeisance. Of course he might be demonstrating his poise.

He was dressed in velvet and brocade, dark red the main color. He looked magnificent, especially compared to her well-worn apple-green silk. No awareness of her admittedly dowdy appearance showed in his face, and his fine eyes showed nothing but warm regard. He straightened. He was six feet or just over, and handsome, with smooth skin and a well-shaped face.

Her mother drifted forward, her silks rustling. Imogen suppressed a sigh when she recognized another new gown. Unlike Imogen, her mother visited Lancaster on a regular basis. This pretty embroidered pale blue had probably cost a field's worth of barley. She'd ensure the carriage lost a wheel so her mother could not get into town for the next month or two. Her mother had a room full of gowns she'd worn perhaps once.

"My dear, may I introduce you to the son of an old friend of your father's?"

Imogen released another inward sigh as her heart plummeted to her shoes. Goodness, she'd turn into a gust of wind if she sighed much more. She forced a smile of welcome.

"My dear, this is Lord William Dankworth, the son of the Duke of Northwich. Your father knew his father in Italy. Your lordship, I have the pleasure of introducing my daughter, Imogen."

Oh, yes, Italy, where her father had given away every penny of his inheritance that he could get his hands on. All for a man who didn't care about them, would probably not remember their names if repeated back to him. For her father was a devotee of James Stuart, known in some quarters as the Old Pretender and in others as King James III. And, of course, his sons.

Imogen refused to have anything to do with any of it. She had little left to give, and she was determined to keep hold of it.

Keeping the smile fixed on her face, she led the way to the fire and greeted her neighbor, Sir Paul Reeves, and his sister, Amelia. Paul had long been a suitor of hers, but she suspected he was more interested in her land than her body.

For it was hers. Her father had been forced to leave it to her, because of the terms in her grandfather's will. Otherwise, she'd be sleeping in a ditch somewhere, Thane Hall gone with everything else. Her house was all that was left of a once considerable inheritance and respected title. Now, the title in disgrace and most of the property gone, Imogen remained determined to hold on to what she had left.

Receiving an exalted person like the son of the Duke of Northwich meant one of a few possibilities. Either he was breaking a journey, as he claimed, or he'd come with some other purpose. If he tried to recruit her to the Cause, she'd send him away with little more than a flea in his ear.

That determination made her greet Paul with more than her usual friendliness. And Amelia, a shy woman in her early twenties who enjoyed nothing more than a quiet dinner at a friend's house, was always welcome.

"I have ventured to invite Lord Bartlett to join us," her mother said. "He will be here directly."

Lord Bartlett had a much tidier fortune and clearly adored Imogen's mother, but she wouldn't have him.

The man in question arrived on the heels of her mother's announcement, so Imogen greeted him with her customary kiss on the cheek, ignoring Paul's disapproving stare.

Lord William led her in to dinner, and they followed her mother. By rank, he should have escorted her mother, but she had given a tinkling laugh and announced that they didn't stand on ceremony here.

Once in the dining room, Lord William helped her to sit and took the chair next to her. "This house is charming. How do you keep it so unspoiled?"

By "unspoiled," he probably meant "old-fashioned." Still, he seemed interested, leaning forward, a half-smile on his face.

"The house was built when my ancestors were wealthy farmers, in the fifteenth and early sixteenth centuries. They gained favor under King Henry the Eighth, and in two generations they had become nobility. They abandoned this house and built a grander structure a few miles further south."

"And you do not live there?"

"We no longer own it," she said smoothly.

At the head of the table, her mother winced, the movement nearly imperceptible, but Imogen had expected it.

"But we still have a comfortable competence," her mother murmured very softly, but loud enough for his lordship to hear, just in case he had any doubts.

Imogen doubted her modest portion would attract a duke's son.

"I have told my daughter I don't know how many times that she should go to London for a season," her mother said. "She would cause a sensation. I have no doubt about it, although I do have to admit a certain partiality."

"I'm glad to hear it," his lordship said dryly. "May I help you to some buttered parsnips, my lady?"

Imogen hated the title. She preferred her first name, or "Miss," or even "Madam," but anyone using the title she was born with made her edgy. She took the buttered parsnips. "But I have to correct you, sir. I'm not a 'my lady.'"

"There are different ways of looking at that." Lord Dankworth took the opportunity to lean close enough to murmur softly, "Your mother is quite right about the other observance. You will indeed cause a sensation."

She wanted to scoff, but when she met his gaze, sincerity was all she could read. "I doubt it, for I have no town polish. But thank you, sir." She didn't want to appear curmudgeonly in her acceptance of a compliment. At least she knew not to do that, even if compliments made her uncomfortable.

He moved back before anyone could remark on the intimacy. "Think nothing of it," he said, as if she'd just thanked him for the vegetables he'd placed carefully on her plate.

By the time they'd finished the repast—a single course which her mother apologized profoundly for, even though she'd managed to scrape eight removes together—Imogen had become aware of two things. That Lord William was a charming man and that he was undoubtedly interested in her.

How interested, she had no way of knowing. He might have decided to flirt with her as a way of passing the time. She could only hope so, because she had no intention of allying herself with Jacobites. He didn't wait in the dining room with the gentlemen after dinner, even though Lord Bartlett insisted on his glass of port, but followed the ladies into the drawing room.

Unlike the other rooms in the house, which boldly proclaimed their Tudor origins with linenfold paneling or timber-studded walls, the drawing room was paneled in the modern style and painted a light ivory. A fire glowed in the grate, and the maid must have found every beeswax candle in the house that she hadn't used in the dining room, because the drawing room was aglow.

Lord William took her to the harpsichord. "Do you play?"

"Indifferently."

He turned his back on it. "Let us not bore ourselves with such things. I would rather talk to you. I decided to let the carriage continue while I rode. Just myself and a footman. Charmingly rustic."

"So only your footman is with you? No valet?" Did that mean his visit would be short?

He gestured to his appearance. "Indeed, can you not tell? This is the poor effort I make on my own."

His coat of olive-green watered silk and cream embroidered waistcoat did not seem at all poor to Imogen, but she held her tongue and smiled.

"At least I had a change of clothes. The carriage will catch up with us, if it has not done so already."

With alarm, Imogen recalled her charge. She was harboring a Jacobite fugitive with a guest in the house. And the guest's servants.

"I was too anxious to meet a lady I have heard so much about."

He gave her a look she couldn't misconstrue. He was interested in her. She couldn't imagine why. He must have access to any number of sophisticated London beauties.

"I trust I'm not discommoding you with my precipitous arrival."

While she couldn't help but be charmed by his address and attention, Imogen wanted him gone. She knew a little of their history from the gossip-sheets her mother enjoyed and she professed to despise, although she sneaked a look from time to time.

The Dankworths had fared better than the Thanes. The old Duke of Northwich, the present duke's father, had gone abroad with the old king, and his son had continued his loyalty to the Pretender but had carefully forbore to break the law and make his adherence into a traitorous activity. So the Northwich family had escaped much of the punishment meted out to others.

"I am delighted you chose to visit us, but a little surprised."

He raised a brow. "How so?"

Her mother was at the other end of the room, sitting by the fire chatting to Amelia and her brother while she made tea from the tray the maid had brought in. She couldn't hear what Imogen had to say. "I cannot see us visiting London any time in the future. We are happy here, in the country." In for a penny, in for a pound. "I prefer 'Miss' to 'my lady.' My father was attainted."

"You may use the titles," he said with a careless shrug. "It makes no difference to who you are. Your mother is still a dowager countess and you, as her daughter, may use the honorific."

"I prefer not."

"Use it," he said firmly. "Claim it. When you marry, you'll carry a different title, in any case."

"What if I marry a mister?"

He gave a half smile, a charming effect that made her respond with a smile of her own. "I don't think that will happen. You will attract a man of quality."

"I rarely go anywhere I can meet people of quality." And her neighbors suited her very well.

He glanced down and then back up at her. "You should amend that. You have your fortune and the friendship of my father. He is a widower, but I'm sure your mother is capable of chaperoning you, should you choose to make him a visit."

Why in the world would she do that? Her astonishment must have shown, because he continued.

"Our fathers were once close, or didn't you know that?"

"Only that they supported the same cause." Her mouth twisted bitterly. "A lost cause."

"Not so." He spoke so quietly she couldn't be sure she heard him right. "I daresay you are right. But not about visiting London. The season proper starts just after Easter. You should consider visiting this year. My father would welcome you. And I would deeply appreciate a chance to further our acquaintance."

But Imogen had decided she'd had enough of his disturbing presence and used the pretext of helping her mother hand around the dishes of tea. After she'd finished, she strolled toward the fire, where the more comfortable presence of Sir Paul and Amelia awaited her.

Her tiring day had made her imagine things that weren't there, but she couldn't deny that Lord William's presence formed an inconvenience she could well do without. Meeting two men in one day was two too many. That both stirred her was an even bigger complication.

Chapter 3

At midnight, Imogen could finally leave her room. She'd retired an hour before, after seeing Sir Paul and Amelia to the front door and promising Amelia that she'd call on her soon. How she would do that she had no notion. She needed to rid the house of the inconveniences that plagued it before she could think of setting foot outside her boundaries.

She spent her time making a list of things her patient might need. Anyone finding it might think it was an ordinary household list, and the aide-memoire helped her to steady her thoughts.

Her covert guest must be starving by now. She hadn't thought of providing food or asking the Georges to do so, but Tony was a strapping man, and he'd need sustenance to aid his recovery. Once she'd washed, braided her hair, and donned her night rail and robe, she took her candlestick and crept downstairs.

The house was quiet now, the fires banked down, doors and windows firmly closed. Most nights she liked to check the fires were safe and the windows properly bolted. She would use that as an excuse now if anyone caught her.

Lord Dankworth would be in the best guest room near her mother's chamber. Imogen's room was on the other side of the house. The building ranged around a courtyard, with the main body of the building at one end. The Long Gallery sat above the gatehouse and Imogen had a bedroom in one of the wings.

She tiptoed along the corridor, shielding her candle with her hand until she reached the stairs at the end. These led right down to the kitchens, and the other way up to the attic. They were set in a building to one side of the gatehouse in the old style. She'd been going down these stairs since she could walk, so she knew all the creaky parts of the worn timber treads. She achieved the descent with barely a sound.

Moonlight filtered in through the kitchen window, just enough to see by. Imogen snuffed her candle and went about her tasks as soundlessly as she could. When the scullery maid stirred in her nest of blankets by the fire, Imogen murmured, "Quiet, Aggie. It's only me. I'm hungry so I came down for something to eat."

Imogen filled the capacious pockets of her robe. Apples from last year's crop, wrinkled but still good because of the careful storage, half a loaf of bread, and several other items. She grabbed a pewter plate and filled it with the remnants of their dinner, all that could be eaten cold. Roast beef, boiled potatoes, carrots.

Finally, she found a pewter mug and filled it with small beer from the barrel near the door. She should probably find some barley-water. She'd talk to one of the Georges and ask them to provide boiled water for her patient. Perhaps Young George could manage to heave a small cask of beer up there.

On her way out, she grabbed a handful of candles. Not the best beeswax, because they were carefully counted, but the tallow ones. She had oil lamps somewhere. Perhaps she could find one for him. But with fire an ever-present danger, oil lamps were probably not a good idea.

During the day, light filtered in through slits in the floor and the walls. She knew, because once she'd hidden there for a whole day when her mother had threatened her with a beating after she'd climbed the big oak tree in the Lower Field. That was when she realized her mother didn't know about the rooms.

Grabbing up everything that wouldn't fit in her pockets in her arms, she balanced the candlestick on top and headed for the Long Gallery.

Imogen could traverse the whole of it almost soundlessly, but tonight, every creak and crack broadcast like a gunshot to her, ratcheting her nerves to screaming point. Just as she reached the panel that slid aside, she dropped the fork. It fell with a metallic clatter, like one of the bells of hell calling the damned to their doom.

Imogen stood perfectly still, hardly daring to breathe, frantically devising a reason why she would be standing in the Long Gallery at midnight with several days' supply of food.

But nothing happened. Nobody came. Not a whisper disturbed the silence of the night, not even an owl hooting or a rabbit screaming in the jaws of a fox.

Breathing more easily, Imogen carefully laid her burdens on the floor and slid the panel aside. She slipped into the opening, drawing the food behind her, taking two journeys down the steps to carry it in. She closed the panel.

Only then did she turn around.

He lay watching her. He was sitting up, one hand curled behind his head, and he was naked, as far as she could see, blatantly displaying the firm lines of his chest. The bandage was a stark white reminder on his arm, his dark head a clean silhouette behind the soft creamy white of the wall behind him. A beam of light fell directly on him. His eyes glinted.

She faltered. "I brought you food," she said. At the same time, his stomach rumbled and she stifled a laugh.

"Who can hear us?" He kept his voice low.

It sounded intimate rather than born of necessity, and something deep inside her, long repressed, stretched and smiled, as if waking up from a long sleep. "No one. I don't have a regular maid, and only my room is on this side of the house. The kitchen is too far below for anyone to hear anything. The other side is where the guest rooms and the main rooms are situated. The south side."

"You chose the cold side of the house?"

"It's worth it for my privacy." She dared to raise her voice to near normal level. Only someone sitting outside in the Long Gallery would hear them speaking once she'd closed the panel. As long as he didn't scream. "How are you feeling?"

"Bewildered, bored."

His face was not smoothly handsome like Lord William's, but she couldn't deny the feelings rioting inside her when she saw it. The ones she had to ignore or push back into the box they'd escaped from. She must concentrate on being practical, as she always did.

"Do you hurt much?"

He shook his head and belied his denial by wincing. "Only the bump. My arm is sore, but I've suffered worse. I'm a little hot, but this room is hardly conducive to coolness, is it? It must be hell in winter."

They shared a smile. "It is."

She felt strangely at ease talking like this. Apart from Amelia, Imogen confided in few people, and even Amelia didn't know everything about her. She just didn't feel happy sharing with anyone.

Her cheeks flaming, she picked up the plate and took it to him, together with the mug of beer. With a word of thanks, he took it from her, and before she could protest, drank it down in one. His throat worked as he gulped, a strong column of muscle, and she could examine his body without him seeing her do it.

Flat slabs of pure muscle defined his chest, which was sprinkled with dark hair, concentrating on the center. A line below his navel disappeared to his groin, but the bedclothes covered all but the first inch.

She wondered if he was wearing anything at all and decided she was better not knowing. "I couldn't bring more to drink, but I'll ask Young George to bring up a cask tomorrow."

He frowned. "Young George?"

With an effort, she forced her scrutiny back to his face. "He carried you here."

His thick black brows shot up. "He did? I remember the horse, but not a man."

"He's built like an ox. Without him, we wouldn't have got here. I would have had to confess your presence and put you in a guest room."

"Would that have been so bad?"

She gaped in disbelief. "After what I found in your coat? Do you have an explanation for that?" Flinging out her hand, she indicated the dirty cockade, which she'd left on the chest against the wall.

He'd picked up the plate and spoon and was busy shoveling food into his mouth, but he spared the bunch of ribbon a glance. He shook his head. No explanation. After he cleared his mouth, he picked up the mug and made a sound of frustration.

"I brought apples," she said.

He nodded. "You did very well. Thank you. Tomorrow I'll leave."

"No!" The idea filled her with revulsion. "Someone will hear you, or see you. Then what will we say?"

"That I'm an intruder?" He didn't seem concerned. He filled his mouth again.

For all his evident hunger, he ate like a gentleman, keeping his mouth closed and eating over the plate. That and the clothes she'd discovered him in pointed to the fact that he wasn't a common man.

"If they think you're a traitor, they'll arrest you and throw you in jail. You're in no condition to cope with that."

"I have no choice but to stay here." He didn't seem sorry, giving her an easy smile. "I will be well enough to leave soon, though."

"Will your people miss you?" If he were gentle-born, someone would miss him, surely.

He shook his head. "I told them I'd be away for a while." He looked around, grabbed his shirt, which lay on the floor, and found a clean part to wipe his mouth. He picked up the loaf and started on that, tearing off pieces instead of ripping into it with his teeth. He'd finished the food on the plate as if it were an appetizer.

Imogen sat on the floor, curling her arms around her upraised knees. "I brought candles, but it wouldn't be a good idea to use them all the time."

He nodded. "Enough light comes through the cracks in the floor and ceiling." He glanced at the timbered ceiling above them. "This is an old house, isn't it?"

"Yes. Built in the fifteenth and sixteenth centuries. Some parts are even earlier." She paused, wondering how much to tell him, but cast concern to the winds. He had probably shared some of her experiences, being a Jacobite. "I was born abroad, in Rome, but I came here as a child, barely a baby."

"Your father supported the—King James?"

The pause before he said the last word was strange, but she understood the reason for it. Not many people in Britain talked openly about James Stuart in those terms. To do so in the wrong quarters would mean death.

"Yes he did. The loss of the 'forty-five broke his heart. But he sent my mother and me back when I was a baby to keep us safe."

"With the people here," he suggested.

So he still thought she was a maid. Best he carried on thinking that way. If his enemies caught him, he could only point at a serving girl and not the mistress of the house as his savior. "Yes. With them. And you?"

"I became a soldier," he said.

The competence, the casual treatment of his wounds, and his practical but good clothes made sense in that context. "With which army?"

He gave her a secretive smile that she returned, aware he was teasing. "That would be telling, wouldn't it?"

So, the rebel army. "Were you on a mission here?"

"Yes, I was." He glanced down and leaned forward, reaching for an apple from the pile on the floor. He bit into it, the crisp sound assuring her it was good. "The parents' sins are visited on the children," he said softly, back into the intimate tones. So gentle, she wanted to tell him everything, all of it.

Not that she would, of course. That would be unthinkable.

"You must not go without telling me of your intention. I can get you a horse, as long as you leave it at an inn when you're done and send word. Young George can fetch it back. And some money. I can get you money."

"I have enough. The thief took my purse, but when I travel I keep a little elsewhere about my person."

This close, with him wearing so few clothes—it was too much. The vision of him kissing her closed in until she could feel his lips on hers, his breath warming her. Her face heated and she leaped to her feet. "I have to go."

"Then kiss me goodnight and leave. Will I see you tomorrow?"

She ignored his request. He was probably a natural flirt. "If I can. I'll tell Young George to bring you something to drink. Or it might be his father, Old George. But you have to be quiet during the day when people are about."

"George is a strange name for a Stuart adherent."

"Old George says that his family was always called that and he wasn't about to let some upstart prince take it away from him. He had it first, and he's keeping it."

His shout of surprised laughter made her step forward, arm outstretched. "Shhh!"

Near enough for him to grab her hand and overbalance her, so she fell into his lap.

Damn, he really didn't have any clothes on. His limbs hardened against her, and something else, something intimate.

She'd seen men naked before. After all, she was a country girl, but she had never come so close to a cock in its tumescent state. The heat of it burned through the blankets, and hotter than ever, she tried to lever herself up.

He wrapped his good arm around her and hauled her up so she sat sideways on his lap. Her robe and night rail covered her decently, but without her stays she felt bare, vulnerable.

Even more when he kissed her.

Sparks and tingles shot from her fingertips to the most intimate parts of her, and she fought an urge to squirm. All that from a closed-mouth kiss of friendship and their close proximity. He didn't mean it.

He thought her a poor servant girl. He probably thought she'd done this before, kissed a man so intimately, because servant girls did. At least hers did, the impertinent madams.

Now she knew why. His lips were warm on hers but with an underlying tenderness that revealed his true nature. His chest, hard yet so secure, was a wall she could rest against. The temptation was too great not to do so.

With a sigh she gave in, and as if she'd given him some kind of signal, he opened his mouth and touched his tongue to her lips.

Hesitantly, she opened and let him in. Gently he traced the edges of her mouth and licked inside with quick forays, like a bee collecting nectar from between the delicate petals of a flower. He tasted of apples and beer, an intoxicating combination.

He shifted her so she lay more securely against his chest, his uninjured arm holding her safe, while he explored her mouth with an abandon that was anything but safe.

His caresses grew more daring. He licked the roof of her mouth, then her tongue, teasing it with his until she responded, moving it to stroke him back. They played, and when he moaned into her mouth, the vibrations pulsed all the way to her toes, pausing at the place between her legs that began to throb. Innocent she might be, but she recognized arousal. The speed of it floored her. Her capacity for reason went on holiday.

As if he sensed the beat, he thrust his tongue into her mouth, darting it in and out with an insistence she found instinctive to follow. Accepting him, she responded in like mode, daring to dart her tongue between his lips. He sucked on it gently, like a special treat.

She was lost. She nestled into him and feasted.

His shaft burned into her backside, a hard rod that reminded her of his essential masculinity, and she responded, softening and heating, her body preparing itself for his possession.

When she shifted to move closer to him, she must have moved something under her because he moaned and finished the kiss, but kept her cradled close.

He gazed into her eyes. The darker blue lay around the outside, and the brightest color was at the center, surrounding the pupil. He had eyes the color of the sky on a summer night.

"I never meant to do that," he murmured, his voice rumbling through his chest. "I meant it to tease, or as a kiss of friendship. Not this."

He kissed her again. This time he kept it light, but it still affected her.

He gave her a crooked smile. "What is it? You've never been kissed before?"

"Not like that." Maybe she shouldn't have said it, but it was true. Paul had kissed her, and she'd enjoyed it, although he hadn't used his tongue and he'd kept it much less—lavish. Another man had kissed her, grabbing her in a corner at a ball when she wasn't prepared for it, and he'd bestowed a wet and sloppy kiss on her mouth. Horrid. She'd shoved him away, ensuring he wouldn't come near her again.

Nothing like this, but then, what could be? How could she have imagined anything like this?

When she stretched up and curled her arm around his neck, he held her off, firmly but gently.

"No, I won't do that to you."

"Even if I want you to?"

His smile turned rueful. "Don't tempt me, sweetness."

With a shock, rationality returned, slamming back into her brain.

She sat up, making him groan again, but this time with an edge of pain. Scrambling off the bed, she stammered her apology. "I'm sorry, so sorry!"

He cupped his tender parts over the blanket. "It's what I deserve, to have an elbow in the balls. I'm only surprised you didn't do it earlier. Please accept my apology."

She still wanted to do it again. That was why she kept her distance. Instead of going closer, she busied herself sorting out the fruit so he could reach it from the bed and stacking the rest of the food on the chest, covering it with a linen cloth. She should really have brought more to drink. Her fumbling covered the few minutes she needed to get some semblance of calm into her ravished senses.

"Don't worry. I've foraged and found worse," he said, as if he'd forgotten her kiss already. "I have the juice from the apples and plenty to eat. You're not imprisoning me, are you?"

She lifted her head from her self-imposed task and stared at him in alarm. "No, but don't try to get out. The gallery outside is all timber, and if you don't know which board to tread on it creaks like a ship at sea. During the day people use the gallery to cross from one side of the house to another."

"I see. So I am in effect a prisoner?" He shot her a sudden grin. "No matter. I'm in no state to go far for a day or two."

"I must get back." Unable to stay another moment in this room with the man who had become overwhelmingly attractive, Imogen turned and left.

* * * *

The rustle at the door jolted Tony out of sleep. He sat up in bed, suppressing his groan as pain shot through his arm. He'd slept fitfully, but better than in many campaigns, and should have felt able to cope, but weakness still excoriated him, turning every part of his body to leaden lethargy.

Despite that, he reached for the knife she'd left behind, which he'd shoved under his pillow. He felt uneasy without a weapon, and his would-be assassin had taken his pistol and sword, but he had this table knife. At least it had a sharp point, and he could do a great deal with it, even in this state.

The panel moved, letting in a blinding shaft of light. He'd become used to the dim light in here.

He half closed his eyes until something blocked the source of it. The shape of a man, bent and shuffling.

Tony cleared the sleep from his throat. "And who might you be?"

"Old George." The man scrambled down the ladder and turned to grab a small cask. "I brought your beer. Miss Emmy must be mad, doing this."

"I think so too, but I'm grateful for the madness."

"My boy says we should keep your secret," Old George continued.

He didn't look that old to Tony, probably around fifty.

He heaved the cask across the room as if it weighed nothing and set it up in the corner. "I put a tap in it but wait for it to settle before you 'ave anything. Listen."

He turned to face Tony. "This 'ouse 'as suffered because of the Cause. I don't want that 'appennin' again, clear?"

Tony tended to agree, though he could hardly say that. He was supposed to be a Jacobite spy. If he confessed otherwise, Emmy might not feel the same way about him. She might betray him, and in his current state, he couldn't fight very effectively. After that he could probably get out of the tangle, but not without scandal and not without his powerful family becoming involved. He'd rather confess his failure privately and slink away in the night. Perhaps he'd even get the chance to achieve his mission and find the documents he'd come for. "I understand. Once I'm well enough, I'll leave."

Old George grunted. He put his hands on his hips, increasing his girth impressively. Although he could stand upright in this cramped space, he filled it with little to spare. "Good. I'll come and get you. I don't want 'er involved any more than she 'as to. And don't come back."

"You're not a loyalist?" He forced a smile he feared was more of a grimace.

"Depends. I used t' be. I could see the sense. And Gawd knows we need something. But as things turned out, it's time to start again. Especially the people 'ere. We need a bit of peace. Not all that hurly burly again."

By which Tony assumed he meant the 'forty-five. The Young Pretender had mustered forces from the Catholic peers in this area. Lancashire had been as hot for the would-be prince as Scotland, but it hadn't done either the Pretender or the county any good. Many old families were ruined. This one had come close.

"I promise I will leave quietly as soon as I can. Your friend even offered me a horse. Is that possible?"

Old George gave him a considering stare. "Yes."

That was succinct. "Another day, perhaps two."

"I'll 'ave a coat for you too."

"Just as well. I might get taken up for a madman if I rode around the countryside with half a coat. What made you do it?"

"I wouldn't have brung you 'ere. I'd 'ave told somebody, but you was 'urt and she always did 'ave a soft spot for the wounded."

He couldn't deny that. He'd been in danger of bleeding to death. That must be why he felt so weak now.

With one final "humph," Old George left and settled the panel back into place.

Tony had little to do other than sleep, eat, and think. Ponder on his failures, perhaps. Bored with the social round in London, which never stopped, only peaked at certain times of the year, he'd leaped on this opportunity to act with all the enthusiasm of the barracks-bound soldier. Jolted into action by yet another argument with his brother, he'd only wanted to escape from London. That was how it felt when he'd first reached the open road. Freedom.

A strange place, this. The creaks and groans of a timber-built house disconcerted him. It was like existing inside a living thing, not a building. The timbers on the floor here weren't straight. Neither were the walls. His bed was set in a corner of the room, but while the bed had right angles, the walls did not.

He loved it. All his life he'd lived in regimented circumstances. Either the family seat or a military tent, with everything where it should be. This appealed to his long-dormant sense of the ridiculous. It made him smile. God knew he needed a reason to smile. He picked up the prosaic list she'd made, the one she'd obviously forgotten, and smiled down at it like a loon. Shoving it under his pillow as if it were a love letter, he determined to keep it. She had a firm, steady hand, with few flourishes and loops. Like herself. He liked her the better for it.

Her kiss had given him reason, shocking him with its instant sensuality. He had nevertheless recalled that he was, nominally at least, a gentleman. He could not return the kindness she had bestowed on him by seducing her. Those were the actions of a cad, and he'd tried very hard not to be a cad. But oh, she was sweet, and she'd felt so good in his arms!

His wound throbbed, but he decided to leave it for now. He was too tired to concern himself with a little pain. He'd known worse.

* * * *

Imogen's mother expected her to entertain her noble guests. Imogen guessed the visit wasn't as unexpected as it had first appeared. The Holland covers were off the furniture in the summer parlor. Usually they didn't come off before Easter. The paintings and furniture gleamed with extra polishing.

Was her mother matchmaking? Of course she was, but even if the Duke of Northwich was a known Jacobite, he wouldn't want his son to marry the daughter of a person who'd had his title removed by Act of Attainder. Imogen still cringed at the memory.

They'd received a letter from her father, who loftily ordered them to ignore the edict, since it was imposed by an illegal government. A government that had the power to take everything they had. If not for this house, she and her mother would be living in a hovel somewhere.

A fact that her mother was blithely unconcerned about, or so it appeared when she arrived in the parlor in her best white lustring gown, as if preparing to take the salons of London by storm.

Lord Dankworth arrived shortly afterward, and from his dress Imogen concluded that he planned to take the air. She forced a smile. "It is cold today, sir. The rain turned into a hard frost this morning."

He slanted her a smiling glance. "Lady Imogen, I am perfectly aware of that. I've been out already. I must compliment you on the excellent condition of the estate. I believe you manage it?"

"It is my estate, sir, so yes, you guess right." He used her courtesy title but to correct him would be churlish. Besides, her mother would object if she did that.

He raised a dark brow. "Indeed, ma'am. You are to be commended. I find a woman who does more than sit in front of the fire and sew a fine seam far more interesting."

Why should she care? Perhaps her lack of sleep had made her irritable. She ameliorated the sharp retort she'd originally planned in favor of a smile. "My mother sews far better than I. I could never keep the line entirely straight." She glanced at her mother who gave her best gracious nod.

"Perhaps, madam, you would give me a tour later. I noticed a particularly run-down hut at the edge of your estate when I was riding here. Surely it must belong to someone else? But it could prove a hazard in a storm."

Her heart pounded against her ribcage and she had to take a couple of deep breaths in order to remain in control. "The hut was part of a boundary dispute which has fortunately concluded in my favor. Unfortunately, the hut belongs to me. I will either have it repaired or demolished soon."

"It is remarkable in a beautifully kept estate." He favored her with a warm smile she was hard put not to turn her back on. She didn't cultivate the estate to please some passing lord. She did it purely for herself, and to keep the house in food and fuel.

She murmured a "Thank you, sir," and attempted to pass on to other matters, but she was to be disappointed.

"I would appreciate a tour of the grounds, if that is not too much trouble." He came closer, with that smile fixed on his face, although something else lurked behind his eyes.

She saw no humor there.

Fear clutched at her heart. What was this? Did he know her secret, the man in the hidden room? Was he privy to his identity? This man was a Jacobite, so surely he was on the same side as Tony?

Even Jacobites had factions. *Especially* Jacobites. Probably inevitable when a group of plotters gathered together. Maybe they wanted different things. Perhaps one was an adherent of the father, the Old Pretender, and the other of his son.

Imogen didn't know. She didn't care, other than getting Tony out of the house as soon as she possibly could. The circumstances had become too dangerous for him here with this man prying.

Consequently, she gave a sweet smile and told him she would show him around with pleasure. If she kept an eye on him, he was less likely to try to seek out secrets for himself. He'd been to the hut; he could have found something there. That blood, perhaps some of the rags. She had hardly attended to tidying up afterward, more concerned with getting Tony to safety. She should have returned, except she hadn't had the time.

When she excused herself to change, she wished she could visit him. During the day, servants scurried up and down the Long Gallery on their way from one side of the house to the other. She didn't employ many indoor servants, as few as she could get away with, but they would be working in the bedrooms this morning and then moving to the parlors. Her mother had probably given extra orders, engendering more activity.

No, she couldn't go. Instead, she changed into her best riding habit, disdaining the help of the maid she used on those rare occasions when she had to dress to make an impression. "I will manage while Lord Dankworth is here." She stood before the mirror, pinning on her hat. Not the everyday one but the one with the gold braid. "Concentrate on my mother."

"But, my lady, your mother told me to concentrate on you."

With an exasperated exclamation, Imogen spun around. "Please get it into your head that I am not to be addressed as 'my lady.' Not under any circumstances and particularly while Lord Dankworth is here. The title doesn't belong to us anymore. It's presumptuous to use it. Miss Thane is my name."

The maid flushed red and stammered her understanding, which made Imogen feel like a bully and immediately regret the vehemence of her denial. "As long as it doesn't happen again. I'd appreciate your reminding the other servants."

The servant scurried off, leaving Imogen to sweep downstairs to meet Lord Dankworth, who was waiting for her in the main hall. He wore a riding habit of scarlet cloth, his blue waistcoat bringing out the gray shade of his eyes. His black knee length boots were highly polished and furnished with shiny spurs. Anything less like Tony's practical wear was hard to imagine.

They left, and at least she could provide a decent mount for him, since he had only carriage horses with him. He approved of the choices. Today she'd left old faithful Blackie to his oats and straw and had chosen Jessie, a sweet-tempered mare she'd raised herself.

Lord Dankworth proved knowledgeable about horses, and they walked the first part of the estate in relative amity. "My father owns many such, but few are so well tended as this. You will prove any man a formidable wife."

Imogen forced her fingers to relax on the reins. "I don't have any plans to marry, sir."

"I can see why." He turned his head and fixed a charming smile on her. "Anyone lucky enough to win your hand would find himself in possession of a neat estate and a perfectly unusual house." Without looking away, he corrected his horse's natural urge to move faster, only a slight ripple disturbing his perfect seat.

As a younger son with no estate, he would be looking for a wife with some property. Had he put her in the picture? She didn't know how many children the Duke of Northwich had, but if he had a quiverful he'd be hard put to settle all of them creditably.

"I am over twenty-one, my lord. Nobody may order me to marry."

He inclined his head in acknowledgement. "Except for the king, naturally."

Startled, she widened her eyes.

He responded before she could say anything. "We must temper our ideals with practicality. The de facto king, I should have said. I forget

I'm amongst friends. In London, a whisper of dissent from our quarters is pounced on and called treason."

His shame-faced expression made her laugh, and he joined in.

"There, I'm glad we are back to our cordiality of last night. I do like you, Imogen, if I may address you as such?"

"It's better than 'my lady.'"

"You are wise," he said. "But many people in London will call you that."

"Will?"

She took him along the lower field, on the other side of the estate from the hut, but they were heading in that direction now. She planned to suggest they return to the house, having no desire to examine the place with him.

"I would like to see you in London." He glanced at the path ahead of them. "You deserve a season."

"I have neither the fortune nor the looks to attract attention there. One day I may go purely for amusement." She paused, loath to reveal her dearest wishes. Because if she admitted it, she did want to see London. The theatres and great buildings appealed to her, and while she didn't relish the ballrooms and salons of society, she could easily avoid them. Routs and balls didn't obsess the entirety of the population of London.

"You should enter society," he said, his face serious now. "I am convinced you would take very well. You have enough fortune to satisfy all but the most particular, and you should not hide your beauty away in the country."

That was the second man to tell her she was beautiful in as many days. What had brought on this flattery? She'd managed five-and-twenty years without attracting too much scrutiny.

She could only assume that the men were deluded or they had other motives for trying to coax her to town. "I have never considered myself anything above the ordinary." When he would have protested, she held up one hand. "Please, sir, I cannot think I would outshine the society ladies."

A note of alarm entered her thoughts. If Lord Dankworth spoke that way to her mother, who knew what maggots would get into her head? When Imogen turned eighteen, her mother had insisted she make her debut in Lancaster, a precursor to her London debut. Imogen had barely escaped the great waste of money that would have been. The hire of a house and suitable clothes were far beyond her budget, she'd protested, although even then she knew she wasn't a pauper. But neither was she a wealthy heiress, and the scourge of Jacobitism tainted her name.

At least they weren't Catholics. She had found it too wearing to combat the local vicar, preferring to have him on her side, and had received confirmation into the Protestant faith at the same time as the Young Pretender. The Dankworths were a prominent Catholic family. Perhaps that would put him off, if nothing else would. She would save that weapon for when she needed it.

"I am flattered, but not persuaded." She spurred her horse to a trot.

They were getting too close to the hut. But he rode before her and led the way, damn him. She had to follow.

Chapter 4

He rode unerringly to the hut where she'd found Tony yesterday and dismounted with ease, tossing the horse's reins over the outstretched branch of a nearby tree. She left her mare by the fence and trudged across the field in boots definitely meant for riding and not walking. "I know this place, sir," she said when she reached him. "There's nothing to see here but ruin. I may have it rebuilt, because we use this field for summer pasture."

When he showed every indication of going inside, she tried one final time. "It's probably dangerous in there."

"I'll take my chances." He ventured inside, stepping cautiously.

Damn. Her throat tightened. Would he say something? She had no choice but to follow him inside.

She had to wait for her eyes to adjust to the gloom.

Nothing. Nothing that shouldn't be there. Fresh straw was strewn on the floor. She breathed out slowly, releasing her sigh of relief.

Lord Dankworth kicked the straw, gaining nothing but a few wisps that stuck to his shiny boot. Served him right.

One of the Georges must have been here. Thank God for that. They'd cleaned up the blood and taken the rags away. There really was nothing to see.

Had this man suspected something? But he turned to her, his smile as charming as ever and his eyes warm, for a change. "We should not linger. You're right, this place is dangerous. Whatever you plan to do next, I'd have it demolished."

"You're right, sir." She felt like adding something sarcastic along the lines of informing him that she didn't know how she'd have managed without him. But she forbore. He might take it seriously.

He followed her to her horse and kindly threw her up into the saddle so she didn't have to lead the mare over to the tree stump. He mounted with an ease that spoke of hours spent riding. But a mite showy for her taste, even though he didn't appear to think about it. Like his riding habit. Perfectly fashionable, slightly flamboyant, but it made her uncomfortable, as if she weren't good enough in some way.

Imogen didn't like feeling like that in her own place, but she did him the courtesy of believing he might not mean it. It was probably his way, but if she threw in her lot with him, he would be forever challenging her to match him.

She caught herself short. What was she thinking? This man had gently hinted, that was all. Probably had no intention of putting himself in the picture, but giving her some guidance. After all, he'd been on the town all his life.

Why had her mind turned to something she'd determinedly put out of it? Nothing had changed, except two handsome men had come into her life. Temporarily. Nothing else. In a few days, they'd move on, both of them, and she'd settle back into her everyday life. Maybe she should practice on him. Or maybe she should continue as she was and not try to add any airs and graces to something she was not.

They turned back to the house, but she had no chance to visit either of the Georges, who were outside servants, before it was time to change for dinner.

She chose a different gown from the night before. Unusual in itself. Once she chose a dinner gown, she wore it for a week before she sent it to the laundry. But she felt she owed their guest something.

Her mother had asked the vicar tonight, alongside the squire. A perfect country gathering and a perfect bore. Just as she liked it, she assured herself. Lord Dankworth was perfectly affable, although at times he showed a little impatience with the entrenched attitudes of the guests. The squire's daughter showed an alarming propensity to flutter her fan and giggle, something she'd never done before.

Lord Dankworth responded with cool pleasantries and once exchanged a speaking glance with Imogen that told her he preferred her company. She shifted uncomfortably in her seat and forced a stiff smile to her face.

The squire showed no desire to join the ladies immediately after the meal, so she had a reason to excuse herself. Pleading a headache, she ignored her mother's disapproving frowns and made her escape.

Hurrying upstairs, she got to her room without anyone stopping her. Laughter echoed from the dining room and up the stairs as she scurried along the corridor to her room.

She wouldn't pause to change, but dropped her hooped petticoat, fan, shoes, and stockings in her room and went straight to the Long Gallery. She could see him and get back to the safety of her bedroom.

But she had to see him. Had one of the Georges brought the small beer she'd requested? She couldn't provide tea or barley-water. People would ask what she wanted it for, and she could hardly tell them.

Even before she slid the panel aside she heard muttering. When she had it open and had slid through, she wasted little time replacing the piece of wood before she leaped down the short flight of steps and ran across the room to his side.

His eyes were half closed, and he'd been thrashing around, twisting the sheets into tangled knots. As she approached, he flung an arm out, barely missing her. It skimmed past her body, sending a breeze across her cheek.

Sweat bedewed his brow, and he'd torn his shirt in his efforts to remove it. Each muscle tensed when he turned. It shouldn't be like that.

Dark blood stained the bandage that last night had been clear.

Leaning over him, she captured the arm. The knot was too tight, the flesh of his arm bulging top and bottom. The pulse in his throat throbbed, and he didn't seem to be aware of her until she caught his wrist.

"No!"

He fought back. She was no match for him. He pushed her away.

The panel slid aside with a scrape of wood, and Imogen held her breath. "Miss?"

She sighed in relief when she saw Young George's anxious face. "It's the wound. He's taken a fever. We need to drain it. Can you get water, a knife?"

Turning, she spotted the table knife sticking out from under the pillow and seized it.

"No, miss, he's too strong for you." Young George scrambled down the steps and crossed to her side, taking Tony's wrist. "Now do it."

She sliced through the knot she'd been so proud of last night and unwrapped the bandage.

The stink filtered through the room before she got off the last part. The wound was swollen and red. Pus seeped from it. "It's gone wrong."

"It's not too bad, miss. I've seen men recover from worse."

"Can we manage it between us?"

Young George grunted. "I don't know, miss. If we don't manage it tonight, we'll 'ave to call for help."

He was right. "So you'll stay with me?"

He stared, his brows raised. "Of course. Now you mop up this mess but keep out of 'is way if he moves around too much. I'll get what we need."

As good as his word, George was back within twenty minutes with supplies. Those twenty minutes had been the longest in Imogen's life.

Tony turned restlessly, muttering incomprehensible half-words. Once he shouted, "Julius!" and she had to stop him before someone came.

She said his name, "Tony," and immediately he quietened and opened his eyes, gazing at her. For a moment, he appeared perfectly lucid, cupping her cheek softly, and then he was off again.

"I know," he said then, and panted as if he'd run for miles.

She used the old sheet to wipe some of the sweat from his chest and face, but she daren't touch the wound. The suppurating mess had become so bad so fast that she could hardly believe it, but they didn't clean bullets before they fired them.

When Young George returned, he carried a bucket of fresh water, clean rags for bandages, and another cask of small beer. "Best 'e drinks, miss," he said. "'E's sweatin' it out too fast." He'd also brought another tankard. "We need to keep 'im clean. Listen, miss, if I 'old him down, can you clean him up?"

She swallowed. She too had seen her share of injuries, but never had they affected her in this way. Fearing for his life, she grabbed a rag, soaked it in the water bucket, and wrung it out.

By then, Young George had Tony pinioned by the simple expedient of climbing on the bed, straddling and clamping Tony's lower body between his thighs, and grasping Tony's elbows. That held the wound rigid enough for Imogen to work on.

Before she joined the scramble, she paused to unhook and remove her gown, leaving her in her fancy petticoat, stays, and shift. Plenty for modesty. She'd worn as little when she'd labored in the fields when they were short of hands. She had no time for embarrassment.

If her bosom fell out of her stays completely, she wouldn't care. She only concentrated on cleaning the wound, eliminating every trace of the evil liquid that had risen like a demon from hell to plague them

After the first few passes of her cloth, Tony tensed and arched up. He'd have cried out if Young George hadn't had his hand clamped firmly over his mouth. She only shot a terse glance at Young George and nodded.

The flesh around the wound was reddened and risen, forcing the edges apart. A good thing in a way because they couldn't let the wound close until all the badness had gone. Putting everything else out of her mind, Imogen swabbed, tossing the soiled rags to the floor, and scrambled back to get fresh. More seeped out, and she put her fingers either side of the hole and squeezed. Evil yellow liquid spurted out, and if she hadn't had a cloth ready, it would have struck her. She ignored the mess, snatched another cloth, and kept going.

Without warning, Tony's body went lax and he slumped back, unconscious. Pain or delirium had the better of him. Young George released Tony, and Imogen worked on him more efficiently, now Young George was free to pass the damp cloths and dispose of the old ones.

Tony's chest moved up and down in a regular rhythm, and Imogen straightened up, pressed her hands to her aching back, and examined her handiwork.

Although the wound was red, it was a healthy red. She'd done it, removed all traces of corruption. She wanted to thrust her fist into the air in triumph, yell her victory. At one point, she'd feared she'd have to cut away the flesh, but the infection hadn't taken hold that deeply. They'd got to it before it had a chance to form the red lines that signified the poison was spreading around his body. She'd cleaned and cleaned until pure blood had welled up, and then she'd concentrated on cleaning and waiting until the bleeding had lessened enough for her to bind it loosely. They weren't out of the woods yet.

"You should get to bed, Miss Imogen. The maids'll be up soon."

She glanced at her servant, her friend, the man she'd grown up with. His mid-brown hair was plastered to his skull and his broad face was pale, but triumph shone in his eyes, an emotion that must be reflected in hers.

"We did it, George."

"We did, miss. Now get going, or someone will see you. I'll stay with him today, if you would be so kind as to tell my da' where I am."

"Yes, of course." They could say Young George was ill, or busy somewhere else on the estate. That would work fine, especially since the house was busy with its exalted guest.

Damn, the guest! She'd have to rise, be pleasant, *entertain* him. Although none of this was his fault, she resented Lord Dankworth for being here. Without that, she could have told her mother she was needed on the estate and disappear for the day.

She ran a few plans through her head, but none of them worked. If she pleaded illness, maids would check on her through the day and she'd have no opportunity to check on Tony. She trusted her maids, but all staff gossiped, except for the Georges.

She couldn't bear the thought of leaving him there while she entertained Lord Dankworth. On her way back to her room, she considered bringing

Tony out of hiding and installing him in a bedroom. But her mother would probably talk, and she didn't know if she could trust Lord Dankworth. He was a prominent Jacobite, but that could mean anything. As many factions lay inside as out, and she didn't know him well enough.

No, Tony was safer where he was, although if his condition worsened, Imogen wouldn't hesitate to bring him out of hiding and call a physician.

Her mind still racing, she ripped off her clothes and threw them in the corner of the room, ready for the laundry. Her gown was reasonable, but the petticoats and stomacher were probably ruined, soiled with blood and pus as well as heavily creased. She shoved them in a corner of the clothes press. She'd have to deal with them herself if she didn't want questions asked. Scrambling into her night rail, she made her preparations and then waited.

She must have fallen asleep, because when the knock came at the door, she glanced at the clock on the mantelpiece, and to her shock, it was ten in the morning. She had never lain in that long before. Startled, she jerked awake and put a hand to her tousled hair.

A maid put her head around the door. "Madam, your lady mother asks if you are ill?"

She laughed. "No, indeed. Tell her I am well, and I will be in the parlor in twenty minutes."

Her mother must have roused early to greet their guest, because she rarely left her rooms before noon, as if she were living in the middle of fashionable London. Not that she'd ever managed to do so. They'd come straight here from Rome when Imogen was a baby. York was the farthest they'd managed, and Imogen had gone there under protest, concerned the laborers wouldn't plant the barley straight.

The expense of the visit and the attendant costumes her mother insisted she needed still made her blench.

Finding something a little above her usual day wear proved easy because of that trip to York and the occasional ones to Lancaster. Although the petticoat to the apricot silk was somewhat creased, if she turned it around it wasn't too bad. Her hair, brushed out and wound up into a bun, made a reasonable show, and she even found a string of amber beads to wear. She had to tack a ruffle to the edges of her shift. She didn't usually bother with lace elbow ruffles but her mother would notice if she sported her usual linen ones. Good lace could cost a king's ransom, but it was pretty.

Standing before the spotted mirror propped up by her linen chest, she made a reasonable show. Probably not enough for a London drawing room but perfectly adequate for her mama.

Instead of using the Long Gallery, she went the proper way, down the big stairs to the great hall and through the door at the end to the main rooms of the house. Big mullioned windows let the March sunlight in, and it cast the breakfast parlor—now, sadly, cleared of viands—into a bright, welcoming place. This was one of her favorite rooms in the house, together with the library.

Voices came from the half-open door of the downstairs drawing room, a grand name for a jewel of a room. The upholstered chairs and the decoration were her mother's improvements. Modern paneling painted a pretty pale blue covering the old timbers. A harpsichord, usually a dust-gatherer, stood in one corner, but today it was being used. The painted top and sides were opened, and Amelia posed there, playing something pretty.

Lord Dankworth sat on the big sofa, holding court. The news that the son of a duke must have raced around the district faster than a carrier-pigeon could have managed, because most of their neighbors sat in Imogen's parlor, drinking tea and consuming dainty little cakes and bread and butter.

In town, visitors usually restricted visits to half an hour. In the country not so, because people came farther. Never had Imogen longed more for the half-hour rule.

After greeting everyone, she went to sit with Amelia, to turn pages or some such excuse, but his lordship called her back.

That was the start of her ordeal. She sat next to him for most of the day, either here or walking slowly around the part of the house her mother considered presentable. She had little option for her mother blatantly pushed them together.

Nobody commented on her tardy arrival, and when she tried to excuse herself to check on various household tasks, her mother gave a tinkling laugh and declared that the servants were quite good, considering they had such a small pool of available staff to choose from.

At one point her parent suggested a stroll along the Long Gallery. "For while it cannot rival the glories of a house like Chatsworth, we are tolerably pleased with our poor effort."

Climbing up the stairs to reach it, Imogen made as much noise as she dared, raising her voice and stamping her feet, just in case Young George was asleep or Tony was delirious again.

But all was silent, and she could explain the portraits to his lordship. "This is my Elizabethan ancestor," she remarked, coming to stand in front of the gloomiest picture, of a man standing against a black background dressed in a dark brown suit. The only light parts of the painting were the man's lugubrious face and his huge ruff that presented his head like a pig's head on a plate. Why nobody had painted an apple in his mouth she'd never know, except the face was too high to easily reach. If his lordship stretched, he could manage it. He paused outside the painting, which unfortunately was situated right next to the panel that led to the secret rooms.

Imogen heated, and her breath caught in her throat. Panic invaded her stomach, tying it into knots. She had to say something, shuffle her feet, something. Oh why didn't he walk on? This was a terrible portrait. The other guests chatted quietly. Too quietly.

"You wouldn't know that the man in this painting created all this." She waved around, indicating the gallery. "Of course when he built it, most of the lines were straight, but by the time he died they'd begun to warp. They used green wood."

"It looks brown to me." He smiled and some of the company tittered. The highly polished timber was indeed that color.

"It refers to the state of the wood. There was too much moisture in it. That meant that it dried unevenly." Oh, stupid, she shouldn't have explained his lordship's sally.

He listened gravely and then smiled. And she hated him. He'd been teasing her. Of course he knew what green wood was, and he'd led her on. She'd always hated people teasing her and now she flushed to the roots of her hair. "I'm sorry."

His smile softened and he moved closer. "Don't be. I find you refreshingly charming. And I agree. It's strange that the stern man of this portrait was responsible for this. Don't you ever want to live in a house with parallel lines occasionally displayed?"

"No," she answered distinctly, but realized he probably did, so that would be impertinent. "That is, I don't miss it, and there are some in the newer part of the house. Parallel lines, that is."

"Of course. Perhaps one day you'd grace my father's house with your presence. We would be charmed to greet you."

While Imogen took that as a general politeness, her mother exclaimed with obvious eagerness, "Indeed, we would be delighted!" thus turning a vague wish into an invitation. She didn't want it. She wouldn't go.

"London first," Lord Dankworth said. "I have a longing to see you in the ballrooms of Mayfair. Do say you'll make an appearance this season."

She'd say anything if he would just move on. Thankfully, when she stepped forward, so did he, although his tread wasn't as heavy as hers. Carefully she kept her head away from the panel, holding her pose stiffly so she should not be tempted. Except that she was. Beyond that piece of wood was one man who could be dying, and his attendant who was probably holding his breath while he waited for them to pass.

Just as they walked past, she heard something. A muffled thump. Had Young George dropped something?

Imogen cleared her throat and stamped, offering a weak smile to Lord Dankworth. "I should get my shoes attended to. I think they're too big." He probably thought she was demented because she delivered her words of wisdom far too loudly.

"Indeed, my lady. You doubtless have a dainty foot." His smiling glance said he wanted to see it, but she saw more than amusement in his slumberous gaze. Oh hell, had he noticed? And her reaction might have made her culpable. But what would he make of such a sound? It could be a mouse, or something shifting.

"Timbers move all the time in these old buildings," she said.

"I noticed," he replied drily. "My sleep was punctuated by a series of cracks so sharp that at first I thought someone had opened fire on us."

Imogen's mother joined in the complaints. "Indeed, I have never accustomed myself to the odd noises old buildings make. My sleep is frequently disturbed by the sounds. I do not know why my late husband didn't have the whole house demolished and a new, modern house built. I constantly requested it of him, but he took no notice."

"I will build you one somewhere else." Imogen swore she would if it killed her. Or she would buy one of those boxes people were so fond of these days, a square-shaped house with square-shaped rooms.

Any man she married might take it into his head to demolish this house, and with it, her heart. She loved it, couldn't imagine living anywhere else. And when she was alone with her love, she'd be as happy as a person could be.

No more guests she couldn't abide, only those she liked. Spinsterhood? She couldn't wait.

Having affirmed her deepest desire, Imogen reached the end of the gallery and led them along her part of the house, the second oldest part. "The great hall was built first, of course," she told them, into her stride now, "and then the solar above it, which is now a bedroom." She could pass for a guide, the housekeeper who showed people around great houses for a gratuity.

Although Lord Dankworth expressed interest, his eyes glazed when she started talking about the different styles of half-timbering, and how the house could be dated by the different styles it used.

Good. Perhaps he'd go away.

Her ploy must have worked, because later, at dinner, he announced that he had to leave. "My father has sent a message, summoning my presence." He lifted his glass of wine, his fingers perfectly displayed against the sparkling crystal. "It is a great bore, but I must obey."

"You live at your father's whim?" Imogen couldn't resist asking, although relief speared through her at the knowledge.

He smiled, but it looked a bit tight at the corners of his mouth. "No, though I do respect his views. This time it appears he requires me for a favor. One should always obey one's parents. However, if I may, I would appreciate the opportunity to write to you." He leaned forward, although with a table of eight, everyone would be able to hear whatever he said. "I will speak to him of you. I confess, ma'am, I would greatly appreciate the chance to get to know you better. I would deem it a favor if you would consent to visit us sometime. Unfortunately, my lady mother has left this world, but I have a great many aunts anxious to act as my father's hostess. If I give them a reason, that is."

Damn. He was getting particular, and Imogen's mother was perking up far too much. She would make Imogen write, by dint of long and tedious complaining. Nobody complained better than her mother. Or with greater effect. And once a correspondence began, it would be far more difficult to escape the insidious and expensive clutches of London.

"Sir, I have my duties here, but it would be delightful to write to you." Perhaps she could space the letters out or just write terse replies. He'd probably become bored in a month. As long as a definite invitation wasn't issued or accepted, that should work, and Imogen would only have to bear her mother's complaints for a short while. With any luck, she'd blame Lord Dankworth for his fickleness.

The candles were guttering by the time her mother decided to leave the table. Once on the way to the drawing room, she hissed at Imogen, "Don't you dare leave early tonight! He is particularly interested in you, and you will show him every favor."

"*Every* favor?" Imogen turned a wide-eyed expression on her mother.

"Oh come, Imogen, you're no child. You know what I mean, and if you do not, it's time you learned."

Could her mother mean…? No, not that. She'd try other means to drive him away.

By the second sly look over the top of her fan, he merely smiled and remarked, "My dear, if I didn't know better, I'd think you were trying to deter me. It won't do. You're quite lovely and your figure is exquisite. If you come to London, I want it to be with my knowledge and friendship. I saw you first. Never forget that."

If she felt in the least attracted to him, that look of smoldering promise would have turned her to a melted puddle at his feet. But she didn't.

Someone else had indeed got to her first.

With a shock, she realized that yes, he had. Tony was far more than a stranger she'd taken in. Rough manner and all, his genuinely friendly demeanor—when he was in his right mind—and powerful form attracted her far more than this society lord. Infinitely more. Lord William might have all the appeal of Narcissus, but she was no Echo, to follow blindly and do as she was bid.

The evening dragged on. The six fortunate enough to receive an invitation to dinner left at ten, this being a night of the full moon, so they could see their way home. They would normally have left at nine, but the vicar's wife declared herself perfectly charmed by Imogen's harpsichord playing. She was either deaf or lying, because Imogen played tolerably, no more, and she had difficulty keeping time, so her pieces meandered more than the composer intended.

Imogen shuddered only to receive a solicitous query about her health. Her excuse. "My lord, I am perfectly well now, but I confess to feeling tired. We keep country hours here, and I'm not used to staying up so late."

Her mother trilled with laughter in an alarming way. From her perch next to Imogen on the large sofa, she tapped her daughter on the arm with her fan. "Really, Imogen, we are not quite the provincials his lordship will think us."

Lord Dankworth got to his feet. "Nevertheless, ma'am, I do believe Miss Thane has the right of it."

For once, her mother didn't remark on the lack of title, and Imogen liked him better for using the honorific she was entitled to.

"If I may escort you as far as the hall, I'd count it a pleasure."

She could say nothing, and truly, she didn't want to. He chatted comfortably as they traversed the corridor and then the morning parlor, which led into the medieval Great Hall. At the door that led to her part of the house, he paused, took the candlestick form her, and placed it on a nearby table. He took both her hands and turned her toward him.

"One kiss," he murmured in an intimate tone she would rather not hear. "That's all I ask."

"Sir, it's not proper—"

"Nobody is watching us. I will be gone in the morning, far too early for you to see me off, I fear. I want to assure you that if you give me cause, I'll stop here and my father can go to the devil."

"Don't you rely on him for a living?" The words were out too fast for her to stop them. If he wanted her for her fortune, even her house, she'd understand. Younger sons could have a hard time of it, even sons of dukes.

Smiling, he shook his head. "Not I. I inherited a tidy estate from my mother." He paused. "I don't rely on my father in any way. I do share his political leanings, and when in London I use the family home, but that is all." He gazed into her eyes and she couldn't look away. "I don't expect you to agree to everything right away, but my desire to see you in London is genuine. I would love to present you to the ton, but I want to do it with you by my side. You understand me?"

She did. He wanted to marry her, or at the least, to court her. "I-I do not think we shall suit."

"I think we will. Let me show you." Drawing her closer, he released her hands to slide his arms around her waist, and then he kissed her.

He didn't use his tongue, as Tony had. That utterly carnal kiss still haunted her, and through the day, she'd occasionally touched her lips in remembrance, but this was a kiss she'd find hard to remember. It was perfectly pleasant, perfectly placed, and utterly forgettable.

She endured, even let him draw her close, but when it was done she didn't linger.

"I will return," he said. His lips were reddened and for a change, he wasn't smiling, only gazing at her as if she could solve some problem.

He gave her the candlestick, and with one backward glance, went back to the south side of the house.

Imogen continued north.

Once in her room she changed out of her finery and into her usual clothes, plain but serviceable. A dark green skirt and one of the white shirts she wore with her riding habits. A little jacket in gray wool in case it got colder, although the little room rarely suffered from the chill, built as it was above the kitchens and with little space to actually get cold.

The day had been interminable, unbearable, and by the end of it, she'd been at screaming point, wanting to yell for everyone to go away and never come back. Didn't they know she had a sick man to visit?

Was he well? Better or worse? Because God help her, she'd move him into the main house if he were suffering, Lord Dankworth or no. Standing before the mirror, she stuffed her hair into a white cap that she used when undertaking dirty work, the kind dairymaids used for keeping hair out of the butter.

Finding a pair of soft shoes, she slipped them on and then bethought herself what she could find. Probably better leaving it to Young George to decide what to replenish. She would stay all night. Lord Dankworth was leaving early, and he had given her leave not to see him off, so she could stay with Tony all night.

The notion made her heart beat faster and her midsection tighten.

Chapter 5

When she slid aside the panel, the little room glimmered with soft light. Young George had lit the lantern, but pulled the shutter half way so that the light dimmed. Still, it was enough to see by. As she scrambled down the steps, the servant yawned and stretched. Disdaining the use of the single chair available, he'd stretched out on the floor, but he sat up, yawned, and stretched. "He's sleepin'," he said in a stage whisper.

"How is he?"

"He's much better," came a voice from the bed, soft but firm.

Her heart leaped to her throat. "You're recovered!"

"Not entirely, but I'm back to myself again."

She climbed over Young George to get to Tony. With a man of that size on the floor, Imogen had little option. Ignoring Young George's chuckle, she found the chair and used it, gazing at her patient.

The lamp was set on the linen chest, so when she leaned forward, she cast him in shadow. Young George mumbled something and moved the lamp. That was better.

Tony was bright-eyed and smiling at her. He wore a clean shirt, and the bed was made with clean, though darned and threadbare, sheets. In the corner of the room, a bundle sat. Young George touched it. "That's the laundry. I'll take it 'ome and get Ma to do it. That way none of the laundry maids will see it."

In common with other houses in the district, Imogen had one maid to do the washing and several others who came in once a month to do the "big" wash, the sheets and linens. That meant that one of the best sources of reliable gossip rested with the peripatetic laundry maids, who went from house to house. Sheets stained with pus and blood would keep them busy for a se'ennight.

She'd considered throwing everything away or tossing it on the fire, but the housekeeper in her rebelled. The rags could go, but the sheets were still useful. While she castigated herself for her unromantic practicality, Young George got to his feet, even though that meant he had to bend his head and crouch. "I'll take the linen and the empty cask and fetch you some more before I go. And my dad got my ma to pack extra food, so I've put it there." He indicated a willow basket on the chest. "It's cold, but it should keep you." He hefted the bundle. "Is there anybody about?"

"No. They've gone to bed."

Young George humphed. "About time. They've been gallivanting about all day. Clumping up and down until I thought I'd go mad. He sweated out the poison, then 'e slept most of the afternoon. All but when 'e turned over and nearly fell out of bed. Then 'e slept some more. 'E's been awake mebbe a couple of hours. Proper awake, that is."

Conscious. Imogen exchanged a laughing glance with Tony, but neither revealed their mirth outwardly. Young George had done her a favor she doubted she could ever repay. If her mother had caught him, she'd have dismissed him on the spot. "George—"He brushed aside her thanks before she could utter them. "I'll bring the stuff and then go. When 'e's ready to leave, bring word and I'll sort it out for you. Or my dad will."

He slid aside the panel and left, hardly needing the steps to get to the floor above them. Once he'd replaced the wood, Imogen turned to Tony, anxious to see how he was.

Only for him to roughly haul her close and kiss her. It was brief, but it spoke of a hunger she found hard to believe but easy to reciprocate. Hooking her arm around his neck, she opened for him, and when his tongue entered her mouth she knew this was right. Once again, the world seeped away. Only this was real.

A slow burn crept through her as he tasted her thoroughly. He explored her, touching the roof of her mouth and sending shivers through her. He caressed her tongue with his, so carefully and tenderly that a lump came to her throat.

She'd nearly missed this. Missed *him*. He could have died. Losing someone to an infection happened so fast and had devastated not a few families she knew.

He spread his big hands over her back, encompassing her body, and she strained up toward him, pressing her breasts against his chest, loving his body heat. If he surrounded her with that heat and never let go she could stand anything. She just needed to keep it there.

When he finished the kiss and gazed down at her, she whimpered and tried to pull him down for more. With a groan, he obliged, and she lost herself in him. He moved her, swinging her to the side to lie next to him, and then he rolled to lean over her, all the time with their mouths locked together, drinking each other in.

A jerk disturbed her, a tiny wince, but that served to bring her back down to earth. About to grip his biceps in an unthinking action she stopped. Shame swept through her and she pulled away. "I'm sorry."

"You have nothing to be sorry for." His voice was rough. "I'm the one who should be sorry. I didn't mean to pounce on you like that. I don't know what came over me."

"I do." With an instinct as old as time she cupped his cheek, melting when he turned his head and pressed a kiss into her palm.

"I'm sorry about the whiskers. There's little I can do about that at present."

When she rubbed her palm against his jaw, the bristles set up an abrasion that half-tickled, half aroused. These new sensations gave her new responses, but something deep inside her stirred and awoke. She could even put a name to it. Desire.

Imogen wanted this man with a desperation she couldn't have imagined before she met him. If she didn't have him, she'd regret it forever. She knew it. It was worth any price. Five minutes, ten, half an hour—she didn't care.

Spinsterhood stretched ahead like an empty wasteland. But she could have this, once, this one time. Nobody would know. Unless the unthinkable happened, but she could even cope with that.

"I like it." She smiled, letting her need show in her face, daring to open to him. He could reject her. She wouldn't blame him if he did. Or—her cheeks heated. She was forgetting far too much here, taking too much for granted. "Are you too tired to stay awake? Too weak?"

When he moved, something brushed her hip. His erection, hard and needy. Heat flooded her groin, and she shifted to ameliorate the desire to be touched.

"Does that feel weak? But you're my savior. I'd be a poor man if I thanked you in this way. I can't take advantage of you like that."

She took umbrage at that remark. As if she had no choice in the matter. "Take advantage? I should strike you for that. But you've suffered too much hurt already. I can't. How are you feeling?"

He tried to move away but she refused to release him. She pulled him back. His smile was rueful. "Sweetheart, if I don't let you go now, I don't think I will be doing it for some time."

"I don't want you to." She bit her lip. "But you should rest."

"I am resting. Here, with you. Don't tempt me, please."

The plea pushed her the rest of the way. She had to persuade him somehow or spend the rest of her life regretting it. "I want you."

This close she saw the way his pupils widened. "I want you too. Never doubt that. But I cannot. How can I despoil what isn't my right to take?"

"It's your right if I give it to you." She needed to tell him the truth. Well, not all of it. "I'm not married, nor am I likely to. I'm a maid, but I want you to take it as a gift. My virginity."

His shock was evident in the way he froze, every part of his body stilling. "You can't do that."

"It's mine. If I want to give it away, I will."

He swallowed. "Are you sure?"

"Are you up to the task?"

Her inadvertent *double entendre* gave him a smile, and his body relaxed against her when he laughed. All but one part. "Yes, I'd say so. I've suffered much worse in my time, and seen worse, too. Your prompt action saved me from harm, and Young George worked like a Trojan to reinforce what you started."

"What did he do?"

"Washed out the wound every hour. Every trace of infection is gone. He fetched some brandy last night that you're not supposed to know about, so don't go telling him that I told you."

Now he made her laugh, and on the heels of her laughter, he kissed her.

Mirth stopped, and passion took its place. At his taste, every part of her body strained up to him. Her yearning became undeniable.

Especially when he spread one hand over her waist and slid it up her body to touch that part of her breast that swelled above her stays. It felt so good, his warmth and the way he was stroking her, that she wanted more. She unfastened the first hook. He groaned. She kept going.

After brushing her hand away, he took over, rapidly unhooking her stays, and then broke their kiss at last. When he opened his eyes, the pupil was nearly all black. "Why don't all women have their stays made that way?"

"They do." He couldn't have seen many women in their everyday wear. For some reason that made her happy. With a wicked smile, she wriggled, and the stays fell away.

He touched her as if she were sacred, feathering his fingers down her breast to the edge of her shift. When he pulled the bow undone, nothing stopped him pushing it out of the way. He made careful work of it, his fingers shaking against her flesh.

Anticipation made her center dampen. She bit her lip, trying to push some control back into her wayward body, but he smiled and dropped a kiss on her mouth.

"Take off your shirt," she said.

"It's all I have on."

Seeing the justice in tit for tat when he sat up to pull his shirt over his head, she loosened the strings of her skirts and kicked them off, bending to remove her garters, stockings and shoes. She had a problem with one of the garters, her fingers trembling on the knot, but she took them off and turned back to him.

He was half-propped up against the wall behind the bed, his body on blatant display. Her attention went first to the white bandage bound over his upper arm. There was no sign of blood, no swelling or redness. She breathed out in relief, a deep sigh that he seemed clean of infection. And something else, that masculine gloriousness, all for her. He smiled. "Like what you see?"

He lay back, not reaching for her but letting her take the lead.

"May I touch?"

"Anything you like."

She spread her hand on his chest. It was covered in a light dusting of dark hair, abrasive to her palm. He shuddered, adding vibrations to the warmth.

His heart beat strongly, pounding against his chest. He wasn't unaffected by her touch and that pleased her.

"You're strong."

"Years of soldiering."

"Are you still a soldier?"

He shook his head. "I—no, I'm not."

"Are you looking for work?" An idea occurred to her. Why not have him working here?

"You could say that." He covered her hand with his. "Don't think about that now. We have much to talk about, but not yet. Please." He squeezed her hand warmly. "I should tell you so many things, but I can't. And if you don't take off that shift I'll rip it from you."

He said it in such a reasonable tone she nearly missed it, but then her attention flew to his face and she gasped.

"Let me see you, Emmy."

She loved the way he said that. Although not her real name, it was close enough to give her shivers. Without another word, she sat up and lifted the thigh-length garment, slowly revealing her body to him. She'd never shown a man her body before. She cast her gaze down, worried he wouldn't like her or that he'd change his mind.

He tucked his hand under her chin, urging her to lift it. "Look at me."

Heat rushing to her face, she acceded to his request.

"Emmy, you're beautiful. I'm humbled that you decided to let me make love to you. I don't deserve this honor, but I'll do my best."

Her subterfuge, letting him believe she was a servant, returned to plague her, but she couldn't tell him now, because he'd stop. Now she'd come so far she couldn't bear it. Desires invaded her usually rational mind. She wanted to taste him, lick him, and touch him. Claim him.

For the first time, she dared to look down. He'd shoved the sheet out of the way so his body was on blatant display.

She'd seen men's organs before, of course, but not in this state. It was long, hard, and thick, covered with fine skin, the tip appearing like sheared velvet, that most delicate of fabrics. A drop of clear liquid escaped from the tip. That would penetrate her soon. She'd seen the animals do it, and she knew the mechanics of the act, but had imagined she'd never learn how her kind did it. Certainly not as fiercely as horses or the bull on its mate. *Or so fast*, she thought with a rueful smile.

"You find it amusing?" He spoke softly, a smile in his voice.

"No, not that, but—" She shook her head. Impossible to explain. Emotions coursed through her, following each other faster than she could analyze them. Tension rose high, stopping her throat.

"Lie down, sweetheart. Let me pleasure you."

She nodded, and when he moved over, did as he asked, carefully shifting until she was lying on her back. The heat of his body radiated along her whole length as he rose on one elbow and leaned over her. She didn't feel overwhelmed, but spread her palm over his chest and smiled. She loved the heat and strength of him and the way he let her touch.

His shaft lay along her upper thigh, but she dared not touch it. Everything was too strange yet, and she wasn't ready to explore as fully as she yearned. Reticence still ruled her. She was afraid of what she might do wrong. This was foreign country.

With a smile as intimate as their naked bodies, he touched her. He appeared to have no problems from his injured arm, but spread his hand on her stomach and up to her breast, cupping it. She glanced down, astonished at the depth of feeling he evoked with that simple gesture. He stroked and tingles spread from her breast through her whole body, down her spine to her groin.

She gasped and he smiled. "Tell me when I do something you particularly like."

"I like it all."

He bent and kissed her, his tongue tickling her mouth, and he closed his hand over her nipple, pinched it. Her resulting yelp made him smile through their kiss, and he lifted his lips from hers. "You are sweet and lovely. I should call you honey."

"Please don't. Honey is sticky and cloying."

"I aim to make you sticky, but I don't think you could ever become cloying. Very well, I will call you Emmy and sweetheart and any other names that might occur to me. We'll see which ones you like. But I need to know what you taste like first."

For the instant it took him to turn away, she caught an expression in his face that looked very much like stark hunger. His eyes widened and his mouth opened as if he wanted to devour her.

Tony sucked her nipple deep. She cried out before she clapped her hand over her mouth, afraid someone would hear. But nobody did except the man torturing her. He grazed her breast with his tongue and licked the tip.

He broke away. "You taste so good. Strawberries and honey and you. Most of all you." Scattering kisses over her breasts, he continued lower, stroking her like she did when she was soothing an animal.

They had cats in the house, mostly to catch vermin, but occasionally she liked to have one purr on her lap while she riffled her fingers through its soft fur. He touched her in that way, but his fingertips shook.

Smoothing lower, he touched the hair at her groin. He lifted his head to gaze into her eyes as he insinuated his fingers lower, and finally along the crease that defined the area between her legs. He touched the extra-sensitive knot of flesh, and she jolted, shocked at the intensity of her response.

"That's it. Do you like that?"

"I-I don't know. I didn't know I could—it's almost hurting."

He touched the spot again, gently. She could bear it this time, respond by opening her legs so he could move easier between them.

"Good girl. More? You'll enjoy it, I swear you will. But if anything is too much, let me know."

"Do you like to be touched?"

"Yes." But when she reached for him, he moved away, just a little bit. "Not now. This is for you. We'll explore, I promise, but this time I want to make everything good for you. It's important, your first time. I want you to come."

"Come?"

"Orgasm. I want you to feel that peak of sensation. Many women don't, not their first time, but you will. I can help you like this."

And yes, he was moving his fingers against that—part of her. "What is it?" Every part of the body had a name. Some had several. Jagged shots of sensation arced through her, up her spine, and spread in her head and to her fingertips.

"It's your clitoris, and it's made for this. Wait, sweetheart. Let me try this."

He shuffled down the bed, a little awkward because he had to take all his weight on his right arm, but when he spread her to expose her clitoris, she let him, despite the flush of embarrassment that heated her all the way through. The prickly heat added to her arousal, but when he lay between her legs and put his mouth on her clitoris, she cried out in shock. This time her hand stayed over her mouth. As if acting on instinct, she slid her heels up and lifted her knees, making more room for his big body. He murmured his encouragement against her skin and then went back to his task. He sucked and licked. She twisted beneath him, but he held her steady, one big hand on her stomach.

The tingles sending her into a frenzy coalesced and then peaked. Afraid of losing control, she gritted her teeth and held on, until she recalled his words. He wouldn't do this to her if he thought she would come to harm. She had to trust him.

So she released all her control and gave it to him. Reaching down, she clutched his shoulder, holding on for dear life, letting the frissons build and collect, her whole body rippling in response to his actions.

He touched a finger to her opening and pushed inside, just a little. Shocked, she held on and let go.

Shivers racked her body, and she yelped. Powerful waves coursed through her and she arched her back, whimpering into her fist, biting down, her mind closing to rational thought. Sensation ruled her.

He licked and sucked until her shudders subsided, became controllable again so when he slid back up to her, still lying between her legs, she could smile at him. His mouth was swollen and wet with her juices. He'd tasted her as intimately as possible. She'd given him the freedom to take whatever he wanted, and there was more to come.

"I eased you open, but there might be some discomfort. Are you sure you want to do this?"

Of course. He hadn't penetrated her yet. "Yes." If he stopped now she might hurt him. "I want it all. I want to know what it feels like. Please, Tony."

"You never have to say please to me." He frowned, but the smile returned. "I want to kiss you, but I have your flavor all over me."

"I want to know what I taste like on your lips."

With a groan, he bent and kissed her. She opened eagerly for him, licking into his mouth to share her taste. Odd, but not unpleasant. And so arousing. She could smell herself, too. On him.

He lifted his head. "Don't close your eyes. I can see if I'm causing you too much distress." Taking his shaft in his hand, he guided it to her.

The smooth head of his cock nudged just outside, but with him watching her she knew no fear. Only eager anticipation. "Should I do anything?"

"Hold still. Push back against me, but don't tense. Try to relax as much as you can."

She laughed shakily. "Relax?"

He joined in her laughter and eased in a tiny bit more.

Her laughter ended in a gasp when he thrust in, stretching her. "Harder," she said. "One push."

Gazing into her eyes, he did as she bade him, driving into her in two relentless, hard thrusts. The first took her virginity. A sharp pain shot through her groin, making her cry out. But she knew it would hurt and the pain didn't shock her. She accepted it and absorbed it, as she did with other pains.

The second thrust took him deep into her. He stopped. Despite the coolness of the night sweat broke out on his forehead and his upper arms.

"Are you all right?"

He shook his head slightly. "You never fail to amaze me. Shouldn't I be asking you that question?" He dropped a gentle kiss on her lips. "Well, are you?"

Experimentally, she moved a little. "I'm fine. It feels odd, but I think I like it."

"Good." It was his turn to move, but he did it with more purpose, pulling out of her a little before pushing home again.

Warmth suffused her, not the heat of a moment ago, but a pleasant, stirring feeling, making her restless.

"Keep your legs open and your knees apart. Let me do all the work."

Giving herself up to someone was against her nature, but she did as he bade her, promising herself that if they did this again, no, *when* they did it again, she'd know how to participate. This was her first lesson in making love, and she'd make the most of it.

He eased out, and then in. The pain disappeared, replaced by a shifting, restless feeling and the need to push back against him. Instinct drove her now as he repeated his action. Her body responded, folding around him, accepting him, and the tension eased as he moved more, nearly out, and then deeply in.

He was gritting his teeth.

"Does it hurt you?" she asked.

"Too much." He dropped his forehead against hers and lifted it once more. "No, it doesn't hurt at all. But I want to do this more than I want to breathe. Forgive me, sweetheart, I must do this."

His thrusts grew harder, more forceful. Imogen let it happen, let her body respond to his, as if she'd been waiting for this. Waiting for him. This man, this time, this space. It belonged to them. She'd make a shrine of it, keep it to herself, her secret, as was what was happening here and now. Nobody would take this away from her, and she set her mind to remember every part of this, every touch, every sweet murmur, every lunge he made deep into her body.

Their flesh slapped together, and while she was sure such an intimate connection should embarrass her, it did not. "More," she gasped. "Do it more."

He laughed breathlessly. "My lady commands me." He moved down a little, and then thrust again.

Her clitoris touched his body with every stroke, and the heat and tingles inside her increased. Similar but different to previously, more encompassing and more difficult to resist.

She knew better than to fight against it this time. She embraced him, held on, his powerful back muscles bunching every time he drove inside her, increasing the wonderful intimacy. Surely people could not do this with people they didn't know or trust. But she'd read about such encounters and the devastation they could bring.

Not this time. Only pleasure coursed through her, until she gasped in surprise.

Her channel convulsed around his cock as she clamped her lips together on her cry. She wanted to scream his name, let him hear it on her lips, the result of his exertions.

But with a muffled cry of his own, he jerked out of her, grabbed his cock and lifted it free of her, pushing up on his elbow. Hot wetness flooded her stomach. He ejected his seed on her belly rather than inside her. Even at the peak of his arousal, he had thought of her.

She wished he had not. She wanted him as mindless as she felt. A foolish desire, when his precaution made it less likely that she'd have to face any consequences from this act, but while being grateful, she was also sorry.

He bent, kissed her, and swung out of the bed, keeping his injured arm away from bearing his weight. He did it with such athletic strength she wondered at it, and what it would be like to have him make love to her completely fit and well.

Likely she'd never know. She'd have to remain content with this.

He crossed the room to the basin, and the notion occurred to her that this was the first time she'd seen him walk freely, or as freely as he could with his head bent to avoid banging it on the rafters. After dipping a rag in the water, he came back to her and efficiently cleaned her, wiping between her legs first, and then her stomach. Although he was gentle, she still winced.

"You're sore." He made it a statement, not a query. "I'm sorry for that." He shot her a wicked smile. "If not for that, I'd keep you busy here all night." He said nothing else until he'd dropped the cloth on the floor and climbed back into bed with her.

The previously white cloth now bore red stains, the only evidence of her virginity that remained. Not much to show for it. All the riding she did had probably eased her way.

"Yes."

Propping himself on his good arm, he kissed her. "Thank you. We should not have done that, but for the rest of my days I'll be glad we did. Nothing will alter that. But whatever got into you? You're a respectable maid, so why do this?"

"I'm not a maid," she reminded him. "Not anymore. I wanted it, and with you. I haven't wanted this with anyone else."

"Young George admires you a great deal. Are you sweethearts?"

Shocked, she recalled that he thought her a servant. In that case, a match with Young George would be a natural conclusion. "No, we're not. We're good friends who grew up together."

He laced his fingers with hers, resting them on her stomach. She watched his arm carefully, but he seemed at ease.

"I swear all the poison has gone. You and Young George drove it all away. I'm still weak, but I could get up and leave."

She didn't want him to. If she had her way, she'd keep him prisoner here forever, or at least until she could bring him out. Which reminded her. "My unwanted guest is leaving tomorrow." Probably today now. It must be after midnight. "I could move you into a guest bedroom and claim you were a traveler I discovered. Which you were."

He shook his head. "No. I'll leave soon." Lifting their linked hands, he kissed her knuckles one by one, the softness of his lips a tender touch. "I swear, I'll come back."

"You will?" She couldn't quite believe him. "You must not if it means you'll be in danger."

"I'll find a way. "

When she gazed at him, she could believe him. His expression was entirely open.

A wave of fatigue swept over her. "I need to go," she said. "I'm tired."

Fortunately, he didn't argue. "Yes, you should go and rest. I will be with you. Imagine me holding you all night." He kissed her.

She loved his kisses, could become addicted to them. But he drew away.

"I want you here, but we can't risk it. And you need your sleep. Bathe yourself in the morning as I showed you. Hold a pad of cold water against yourself if you are uncomfortable. I took you as carefully as I could, but I don't make a habit of deflowering virgins, so I was acting mainly on instinct."

The knowledge warmed her, gave her the certainty that what they'd shared was special. "I'll come back as soon as I can tomorrow to see you. Either I or one of the Georges will bring you food."

"I have plenty. Young George brought bread, cheese, and apples. Good country fare."

The basket stood on the linen chest, testament to his statement.

He helped her to dress, but she left off her stays and stockings and only stuffed her hair into her cap in case she met anyone who might wonder why she was abroad so late. Or so early. With a few last kisses, all of which she entered into her mental inventory, she left, wishing with all her heart that she could stay with him and let him hold her, as he'd told her he wanted to do.

The clock in her room chimed the hour as she entered. One o'clock. And all was well.

Chapter 6

Tony lifted his arms, prepared to take up his usual thinking posture, hands tucked behind his head, but the twinge in his arm reminded him of the injury and he only lifted one hand. The infection might have gone but the wound still pained him. He'd had to grit his teeth a time or two when he'd been making love to Emmy, to stop her noticing the soreness. He hadn't told her that Young George had, at his instigation, slipped out for some brandy and used it to irrigate the wound. It had hurt like hell, but he'd seen it work in the field. It would help prevent further infection.

He was still shaking at the reminder of what they'd shared. He'd never known anything like it. She'd encompassed him with her beauty, humbled him with her generosity. But he couldn't help himself, couldn't stop the hot tide of desire that had swept over him, conquering him completely.

Stripping off the bandage, he reached for a rag and crossed the room to dip it in the water bowl. He would clean the wound and then get some sleep. Drowsiness invaded his limbs. It would be the best sleep he'd had for a long time.

While he worked methodically, careful to ensure he'd cleaned every part of the wound, front and back, he had time to deal with his guilt. Because, damn, he should have told her who and what he was. She thought him a rebel soldier. How would she feel when she knew that until recently he'd been an officer in His Majesty's Armed Forces? Working under the Duke of Cumberland, the man the Jacobites liked to call Butcher, no less.

Water dripped into the bowl as he held the cloth still. *Nobody knows who I am.* He'd rushed away from London without leaving much of a coherent message behind him. After he'd discovered a clue about the whereabouts of a document his family was hunting, he'd taken the initiative. If he died, his parents would mourn, even if his brother would not. If they knew where he was, to mourn for him.

He was on his own. Behind enemy lines, hunting down an elusive document that he now didn't have a hope of discovering. He'd wanted to present himself as a weary traveler, have them welcome him into the house as a fellow Jacobite, but it wasn't that simple.

At least he was well enough to move. That bout of fever had set him back. He'd have to get out of here and return to London with his tail between his legs. Let his almighty cousin Julius deal with it, as no doubt he planned. Tony was closer to Julius than he was to his brother, but that wasn't saying much. Every time he tried for a rapprochement with Nick, his brother pushed him away and provoked him into yet another argument. Not that Tony wasn't capable of causing a few of his own.

When he flexed his muscles, his arm still hurt like hell, but the wound was crusting over, a sure sign recovery was happening as it should now. She must have worked for hours, easing out all the noxious substances.

He took a fresh strip of linen and re-bandaged his arm, deftly fastening the end as he'd done for others in his time. As a soldier, he'd been lucky to escape serious injury. After he'd conquered his father's efforts to have him sent to the safest regiments, the most luxurious postings, he'd faced death, as soldiers do, and seen injuries to men who had fought by his side, but he'd come away relatively unscathed. Men had vied to join his regiment and serve under him, because they'd seen him as a talisman. He grimaced. Some talisman.

He'd have to tell Julius what he'd done and how close he'd come to death. Not his father though. He'd grieve him. He couldn't do that again. The remembrance of his father's face when he told him he'd joined the army would remain with him for the rest of his days. He'd sold out largely because of his father's urging.

One thing he was sure of. He would not, absolutely not, leave Emmy to suffer the consequences of what she'd done. One way or another, he'd take care of her. Doing his best to ignore the need to hold her close, he climbed into the narrow bed and forced himself to sleep.

* * * *

Tony was waiting eagerly when Emmy returned the next night. She brought food, a bundle of bread, cheese and ham, and that, added to the barrel of small beer Old George had delivered, was plenty. He watched her bustle about. Her movements made him strangely content, considering the beat prowling within him that urged him to throw her down and strip her of her practical clothing.

Old George was the first thing he mentioned. While she was stowing the food safely away out of the reach of the mice that scurried in the rafters, carefully covering it with cloths, he told her about his day, such as it was. "My wound is now well on the way to recovery. Old George brought me food and drink today. If he stood upright, he'd be as tall as his son."

Laughter lent a cadence to her voice. "Their family has worked for— the family here for generations. Their loyalty belongs to the Thanes, not any cause."

"Like in the middle ages, when one family gave their loyalty to another and another, right up to the crown."

Her head bobbed as she ensured the bread was tucked up and stowed. He liked this domesticity. More than liked it.

He began to consider the impossible. What if he could see her like this every day? After all, he wasn't too important in the scale of things. His estate wasn't likely to overwhelm her. She must be an upper servant here. Abruptly he asked the question. "What kind of maid are you?"

Her hands stilled and her head bowed. His hands itched to remove that white cap that covered most of her hair. He wanted to feel the strands against his fingers. "I'm the housekeeper," she said eventually.

A position of responsibility and some status, all of which she'd imperiled by bringing him here. "You must be very busy during the day. You can't do this. You must be exhausted." He determined to make her rest tonight. Nothing else.

That resolve dissolved into mush when she turned around, smiling. "Not too exhausted."

Her shy smile killed all his resolves stone dead. He crossed the room in two strides and wrapped his arms around her. When she lifted her face, he kissed her, tasting her with the avidity of a man dying of thirst, thrusting his tongue into her mouth, claiming her.

With considerable effort, he tore his lips away from hers. "You need to rest." He said it as much to remind himself as for her.

"I'll rest when you're gone." Melancholy laced her tones, her musical voice dipping.

"I'm not abandoning you."

She placed a hand on his chest in a way he was already anticipating with pleasure. He covered it with his own so she wouldn't pull it away. His heart thumped against their joined hands, hers now completely engulfed in his.

"You must."

"I will not. I'm retreating to regroup. I'll come back." He squeezed her hand. "There might be consequences from our actions. Pregnancy."

There, he'd said it.

Her eyes widened. "You were careful."

Of course a country girl would know, even a virgin. Virgin until last night, that was. Satisfaction filled him where shame should have taken its place, but the emotion was undeniable. It would have its way. "It's not infallible. I won't abandon you. Don't ask it of me."

"But I don't want to live abroad."

Of course. If he were a Jacobite he'd take her into exile, probably Rome, where the Jacobite court currently resided. "I don't want to take you there. Be assured, I won't leave you to your fate."

"That sounds ominous."

It did. He laughed and kissed her again, his heart lighter now he'd told her what he intended. He would make love to her now, and return to claim her as soon as he could. She was his, and the heat they engendered together in bed had no comparison. That would keep him warm for many nights to come.

She sighed, a gentle puff of air against his cheek when their lips parted. He led her to the bed and sat her down on it, taking the opportunity to do as he'd longed and unfastened the strings of her cap. He laid it aside on the chair, because she would need it and maids didn't have the resources their mistresses did.

After that, she found it easy to take off her jacket, loosen her stays, and help her take off her skirts. Going down on one knee, he unfastened her garter and gently rolled down her stockings. Her shoes were soft slippers, easy to remove. He pressed a kiss to the upper slope of her foot. Such a pretty foot, the nails little shells nestling on the soft pink skin. Damn, he was getting poetic. Just as well he hadn't articulated that aloud.

Except, when he glanced up at her face, she blushed. Oh God, he'd said it to her. Compared her toenails to shells, just like some blasted poet.

"That was sweet. Nobody has said anything like that to me before."

"They should." Stupid to say it but even worse to take it back. "You're very lovely, Emmy."

"Thank you." At least she didn't deny it this time. Who had told her she wasn't beautiful? Because she undoubtedly was. Beauty could be a problem for a maid. Especially with men like him around.

Guilt washed over him, and he moved away to put her stockings and garters on the pile. The garters were pretty ones, embroidered in silk thread with forget-me-nots. Fine for a servant. Perhaps she'd stitched them herself. Imagining her sitting by a fire in winter, plying a fine needle gave him yearnings so foreign that he didn't know how to define them. A sense of homecoming, something that had never concerned him before. He undressed, but only to his drawers. Old George had brought him a change of clothing, and while the garments were coarser than the ones he was used to, he was grateful for them. He laid his clothes on top of hers, just as carefully, as a humble soldier would.

Shaking off his strange mood, he turned and went back to her. "Only resting tonight," he said, but her knowing smile made him groan. "Emmy, don't do that."

She raised her brows. All she had to do was lie there, the sheet modestly tucked under her arms, covering her breasts, and desire flashed through him.

Unfortunately, the erection tenting his drawers didn't hide his state of arousal from her.

"I can't help it."

He drew back the covers and got in next to her, drawing her into his arms. "Sleep. I'll wake you before sunrise."

"In a while."

That throaty tone would be the death of him. Rising up, she straddled him. He was helpless to prevent her sliding her shift over her head.

He stared at her and moaned. "You're so beautiful. Lush. Your skin is poetry under my hands." He couldn't keep from touching her, cupping her breasts and lifting them to bring her nipples into prominence. They were already puckered at the tips, tempting him to taste.

"I'm not a saint," she said.

Surging up, he looped one arm around her waist and brought her to him, sucking her left nipple into his mouth, and bathing it with his tongue. Soft, sweet skin that tasted of her greeted him. Greedily he released that one and turned to the other, claiming that one too.

Why couldn't he marry her?

The notion appeared so quickly that he stilled, his mouth on her flesh.

No time to think about that now, except his mind whirred. He kissed his way down to her navel, and she leaned back, using her hands to support her. When he touched her cleft, she moaned. He reveled in her response. "You have to be ready for me," he said, finding enough sense to add, "Are you recovered? Can you take me?"

"Yes!"

Her emphatic reply made him chuckle, his lips reverberating against her skin. He licked her, relishing her responsive shiver. "You are so sensitive."

"To you."

He felt like a king. Yes, he could marry her. He really could. London wouldn't like it, but London could go hang. They need never go there, and from what she said she'd not miss it. Two days? Was that enough to make such an important decision?

Yes.

Once he'd made his decision, contentment settled deep inside him. After one last kiss to her stomach, he sat up and gazed into her eyes. "Take me, Emmy. I'm all yours. Whatever feels right to you."

While she was grasping his cock to keep it steady, he watched her blink and stare at him, while she processed what he'd just told her. "You mean I can…" She glanced down at him, and that adorable flush stained her breasts and throat.

"I burn for you. Take me any way you want me. Just do it, sweetheart."

Her smooth thighs whispered against his hairy ones when she lifted up, hovering over him, her heat kissing the tip of his cock. He nipped his lower lip, the wait unbearable.

She saw it and smiled, the light in her eyes wicked.

"You should do this more often. Like every night." The light fled and he cursed himself. He wasn't ready to broach his plans with her yet. He wanted to have this first. The possibility of her refusal lurked in the depths of his mind, although he didn't know why, just felt it. He wouldn't let her refuse.

She lifted farther and watched his face as she lowered herself onto him. He groaned. "Lord, you're tight! Slowly, my sweet, move carefully. Take your time."

His cockhead barely eased inside her before tension tightened the lines around her mouth. Placing a hand on her hip, he helped steady her. "You're doing fine." He crooned encouragement as slowly, so slowly, she eased her body down on to his.

This way he felt every fraction of an inch as she enveloped him in a torture so exquisite he never wanted it to stop. Her heat encompassed him. She didn't stop until she was resting on his balls. When he moved his hand out of the way, he curved it around her to cup her bottom. Like the rest of her it was beautifully formed, a delight to touch and hold.

Taking care, he guided her up, her channel gripping him as if it didn't want to let go. They had to pause for breath when he held her at the crest of his cock, her from effort, him because he would lose his control if he didn't. After fighting hard, he regained a measure of control and then guided her back down again.

Emmy was a quick study. Leaning forward, she planted her hands either side of his rib cage and moved again. The expression of wondering enjoyment on her face sent delight spiraling through him, pleasure in her pleasure. That was new to him, and he blessed her for gifting it.

He moved her up again, and then down. With a gurgle of delight, she did it again.

"Is that good?" he asked.

"Better than good." She moved again, this time easier, their juices lubricating them. By the next stroke she moved freely. Tony braced his body against the straw mattress, pushing up as she came down on him. She gasped, and he grunted, the sound involuntary.

"Don't stop."

"Why would I do that?" she said, breathless.

Watching her discover the extent of her control brought more pleasure, almost as good as coming. Almost. He gained a new ambition to come inside her, but not tonight. He wouldn't force pregnancy on her. Or himself for that matter. While he'd decided on his course, he wasn't sure yet about children. Of course if they came, the decision would be made, but he wouldn't force the issue.

When she leaned forward, her breasts dangled enticingly close to his face, something he took advantage of when she'd found her rhythm.

Catching one in his mouth, he licked and kissed it, the feel of her soft skin against his mouth adding to his pleasure. Her soft moan drove him to do more. Ignoring the twinge of pain from his arm, he leaned in and took more, nuzzling and kissing. The bristle on his chin abraded them, but she pushed the abundant swells against him, silently begging for more as she drove him up to madness and beyond.

Although he wanted to take care of her, to give her all and let her take from him, he could bear it no longer. Gripping her hips with new purpose, he took control, rammed her body on to his, and ground his hips up in a desperate attempt to take it all. His body took control, instinct driving him, and to the symphony of her moans and soft cries, he pushed them harder, until they found ecstasy together.

Just in time he pulled her off him, slapping her on his thighs as he came and came in hard, fast spurts. The sight of his seed on her body gave him a deep sense of satisfaction, warming him and quickening his desire to make her entirely his.

This time she cleaned them, wiping his cock, with a care that made him smile, and then herself. He'd have done it but she stood by the basin, teasing him as she swiped the wet cloth between her legs, sparing him glimpses of her pink inner crease and that pretty little clitoris.

"You take my breath," he told her, because it was true.

But she only laughed and turned to the chair where he'd left their clothes. Divining her intent, he threw back the bedcovers. "Come here. I want to hold you for a while."

Should he ask her now? But no, not yet. When she turned into him, he curved his arm around her, and she tucked herself against his side. He liked this. He'd never been good at intimacies, but with Emmy it was easy. She asked for nothing more than he could give, and what he had he gave freely, enjoying her to the fullest. His mind at peace, he kissed and petted her. "Sleep for a while. I want to take care of you for a change. I'll wake you before the servants get up, I promise."

With a sweet sigh she nestled in, and in a few moments she was asleep.

* * * *

"What was that?"

Emmy's sleepy murmur made Tony smile. He snuggled her closer. "Just somebody outside. Don't worry. You have hours yet."

She sat bolt upright in bed, and her nakedness made him groan.

"There shouldn't be anyone moving about, not at this time of night."

"Hush, sweetheart. It could be one of the Georges. I'll wake you in an hour."

Along with a few others of his military colleagues, Tony could wake himself when he wanted. He'd set his mental alarm for four, to give her time to dress and go back to her room, but not enough to make love again, because he didn't trust himself. She was new to this, and he should give her time to become accustomed to it. In time, they'd keep going all night, but not now.

She moaned when he pulled her back down, but she must be exhausted. Nights of lovemaking and before that, caring for him, hadn't given her much time to sleep. In seconds she'd fallen back to sleep, and after making a few pleasurable plans, he followed her, vowing to wake soon. He would at least have the pleasure of holding her before he had to send her on his way, and then make his own way out of the building. Young George would come at half past four with a horse and outer clothing for him, so he could get to the nearest inn. He could become himself again and return to claim Emmy for his own. He didn't plan to let the grass grow under his feet. Why a local lad hadn't claimed her before, he didn't know.

His eyes flicked open when a murmur of voices sounded close. Far too close for his liking. What the hell was going on? Tramping feet turned the room outside into a storm of cracks as the timbers adjusted to a multiplicity of feet.

The panel moved aside with a scrape. A flare of light temporarily blinded Tony, and he lifted his hand to shield his eyes in automatic reaction. Yells jolted him into action.

Rolling out of bed, he flung the sheet up to hide Emmy, praying she'd stay quiet and still. He'd had no time to warn her. What the hell was this?

Shouts of "There he is!" and "Traitor!" told him.

Hell and damnation, someone had betrayed them.

Chapter 7

"What is it?"

Tony's heart sank. Behind him Emmy had moved, and her voice had revealed her presence. The men crowding into the room, those who could fit, had a view of her glorious breasts before he dragged up the sheet to cover her, as much for his own sake as hers. He didn't want anyone seeing what he already regarded as his.

"Oh, biding his time with a maid!" Raucous jests followed, some of them fully as crude as any a soldier would make. Three men faced him. One pushed his good shoulder. Tony stood his ground. He shoved the other, on the bandage. Gritting his teeth, he kept his expression bland. Reaching out, he grabbed her shift and tossed it to her. Growling insults, the biggest man, a ruffian with a greasy wig and bad teeth, stepped forward and grasped Tony's arms. Hard.

The pain only exacerbated Tony's fury. "Get out of here. I'll come with you if you let her go."

Laughter echoed painfully around the room. At least he had the cramped conditions on his side. He stayed where he was, his body between theirs and hers. Behind him, a stifled sob told him all he wanted to know. Fabric rustled as she scrambled into her shift. He had no thought to his own nakedness, not caring, but she was a modest maid, until two nights ago a virgin. He would protect her as he'd promised.

"Bring 'em out here!" The shout came from outside. "As they are!"

The men chortled, but backed away and then went up the steps and out of the room. Tony grabbed the pile of clothes, swiftly finding hers, and tossed them to her. By the time they turned back to him, he had his drawers on, his other clothes in his hand. He loitered as long as he dared, but when a pistol appeared in the aperture, he knew his time was up and he stepped up to face it.

He climbed out, keeping hold of his clothes. They could be useful as weapons or shields. If she weren't with him, he'd toss the bundle at his would-be assailants and run for it.

Who were they? Should he reveal who he was? No. He didn't recognize any of them, and they wore no insignia nor made any effort to identify themselves.

His main concern remained with Emmy. She must not suffer for this. He'd take care of her if it was the last thing he did.

Rapidly he assessed the situation. A man with his sweetheart, meeting clandestinely. That would be the best answer. He could take her and make everything right for her. More than ever, he was convinced they should marry.

"What is this?" he said loudly, over the guffaws and sniggers. He threw his shirt over his head and thrust his arms into the sleeves. The fewer people who saw that bandage, the better. Nobody who saw it would doubt that it was a bullet wound, and a fresh one at that.

"We got word you'd be here." While the man spoke with a definite accent, he spoke quietly and the men around him fell silent.

"Someone told on us?" Grinning, he shrugged. "We're breaking no law."

"Who are you?"

"A soldier." He gave a version of his real name. "Tony Shaw." He borrowed the surname from his cousins. His was more distinctive, and he couldn't risk that they'd heard it, not until he knew who they were.

"Rank?"

He pretended not to hear and concentrated on pulling his breeches on. He had a pair of stockings, but no shoes.

As he unfolded the breeches, something fluttered from them and landed on the floor.

Oh damn, no. This couldn't be happening. Before he could step on the offending item, his interlocutor bent and swept it up. Maybe the cockade was so battered he wouldn't recognize it.

But the man spread the folds and creases and there it was; the bunch of ribbon with a specific meaning. The white cockade.

"You're a traitor," the man said softly. "A Jacobite."

And there it was. This was a Jacobite household, and its future fraught. How could he repay them by bringing this home to them? He couldn't do it. "I came at night," he said rapidly. Once he was away from this place he'd sort it out. "Nobody knew except for the maid."

"And we all know 'ow you know 'er!" a voice called out from the back and the six men facing him burst into laughter.

Tony welcomed it because it delayed them and gave Emmy time to make herself decent. He feared for her. If they separated them, the men would hurt her. He'd kill anyone who did, but that depended on him getting out of this mess and returning in force. By then she could be hurt beyond repair, her mind destroyed by the rough treatment meted out to her. He'd seen it. How he wished he hadn't.

He stayed by the door and let them taunt him, saying nothing, standing proud. Until she moved behind him and he bent to help her out of the room. Only then did he have time to take in the terrain.

They stood in an astonishing space. By the light of the flickering lanterns, this place looked like an insane person had built it. A long space, the floor highly polished boards of oak, timber-framed in the Elizabethan style, with timber beams over them. Mullioned sash windows looked out into the darkness, a small stone bridge just in view.

But every timber was bent, curved so the gallery wasn't straight at all, but appeared as nothing so much as the product of a twisted nightmare. He'd never seen anything like it before. The room where he'd spent the last few days was in a similar shape, but not so pronounced. How this place stood beat his understanding.

Next to him, Emmy moved and he curved his arm protectively around her shoulders. "She had nothing to do with this," he said. "Take me, and leave her. She's a maid, that's all—"

"Imogen!"

A woman's piercing voice screamed the name from his left. He'd concentrated on the men who'd come to take him, standing to his right, but now he spun around. An older lady hurried up the room, her feet rapping on the wood, uneven in her hurry. Someone followed her, a man. Tony couldn't see his face yet as it was cast into shadow. The lady carried a single candlestick, but her body blocked Tony's view. He walked much quieter and stopped, a few feet behind her as she rushed toward Emmy.

Shoving him out of the way, she smothered Emmy, dragging her into her arms. "What are you doing?"

From within the folds of the lady's voluminous wrapper, in what in other circumstances might be considered an interesting and unusual shade of green, Emmy's voice emerged. "Please, Mama, I was only caring for a wounded traveler. What would you have me do?"

Mama? Although the older lady's robe was a trifle worn, the heavily lavender-scented garment was made of fine silk. Emmy had a mother here?

This woman was no housekeeper. More like a house owner.

The truth hit Tony like a ton of bricks to the side of the head. Emmy—Immy—Imogen. He hadn't taken the housekeeper to bed. He'd had Imogen Thane, the daughter of the house. And its owner.

Everything grew ten times worse.

"She was doing more than caring for 'im when we caught her!" One of the men who'd crammed into the small room leered at her, his eyes bright.

"You will not speak of that to anyone," came a clear, crystalline voice, one without inflection or emphasis. There was no need because every syllable was stamped with authority.

The man previously in the shadows stepped forward. "It was a misunderstanding, and you saw nothing. I'm sure your commander will repeat that to you until you understand that simple fact. Surely even a yokel can come to grips with that concept."

Did he say ten times worse? Make that a hundred.

Standing calmly in the middle of the circle of men, dressed in an exquisite crimson coat and waistcoat, his breeches of a similar color, his cocked hat glittering with gold braid and a huge emerald ring a king would be proud to own on one finger, stood a figure Tony wouldn't have imagined standing here. Perhaps he should have done, because he and his cousin Julius had been after the same quarry.

Julius, Earl of Winterton, son and heir of the Duke of Kirkburton had come to the rescue. And Tony had never been less pleased to see him.

* * * *

Imogen gaped at the figure standing so calmly, staring at the man who'd appeared like a magician from a cloud of smoke. He was dressed for town, gold braid and jeweled buttons on his waistcoat and coat, his boots so highly polished she could've seen her face reflected in them had she wanted to.

Lace so fine spiders could have woven it protruded from beneath the large cuffs of his coat, and the perfectly tied white stock at his neck glittered when he breathed, the result of a diamond pin being used to hold the knot in place. He stood completely still, and while he wasn't looking at her, she couldn't take her attention from him.

The man he was fixing his attention on paled, his black stubble easily discernible. He nodded and swallowed. The man glanced away as if bored and turned his attention to the local constable. He wouldn't be too happy to be roused from his bed at this hour. When the newcomer fixed him with a gimlet stare, he glanced down sheepishly. He could have felled an ox with one blow of his meaty fist, and he was trembling before this dandy?

Except that when the dandy glanced at her, she knew why. That blue stare could have fixed a tiger into place. She dared not look away. His finely sculpted mouth twitched once, and then he swung his gaze back to the constable. "Take the traitor, not the woman he tricked into thinking he was a sad case. I have a warrant for her and her mother."

"I need to see it, my lord."

Who was this man? Beside her Tony breathed quietly, but didn't otherwise move a muscle. He stared at the newcomer, as they all did. She wanted to take his hand but dared not. Her mother stood on her other side, uncharacteristically silent.

With a curt nod, the man dipped a hand inside the capacious pocket of his coat and drew out documents. They looked official, and big red seals decorated one end. "Here." He handed them to the man.

"I can't read these."

He shrugged. "It is hardly my fault that you can't read Latin. It says that Mrs. Thane and her daughter are of interest to the King, and he wishes to see them." He glanced at Imogen when she gasped. "My dear, you can hardly continue here. Not now. Your unfortunate encounter will soon be forgotten." He flicked a glance at the man standing next to her. "Take him. Try and hang him for all I care. He's a traitor."

"Halt!"

This was another voice, this time from the left hand side. More feet, more men. Lord Dankworth came into view as the first lord tucked away his documents. Too many boots, too many men. She wanted to shrink away, hide herself. There were almost as many men here as at the last ball she'd attended in Lancaster Assembly Rooms, and none of the women who softened and ameliorated their presences.

"What is this?" Dankworth demanded. He sent a glare in the exquisite's direction.

The man met Dankworth's gaze blandly. "I had no idea Northwich and his progeny would take an interest in this case. How interesting."

"I have a warrant for this man's arrest." Dankworth jerked his head in Tony's direction.

"What a coincidence, so do we." The exquisitely dressed man stepped forward, addressing the captain of the guard, not Lord Dankworth, who evidently knew him. "Allow me to introduce myself, since nobody of suitable rank is here to do it."

Dankworth shot him a look of pure contempt, but jerked his head in a terse nod.

The exquisite smiled, slow and lethal. "I will, if you please, dispose of my lesser titles. I'm Julius Caesar, Earl of Winterton, heir to the Duke of Kirkburton." He turned slowly and executed an exquisite bow. "Dankworth."

Dankworth returned the bow, but his seemed jerkier, less practiced. "Winterton."

Lord Winterton—*Julius Caesar?*—curled his lip. "I fear your presence here is a trifle superfluous. The man is to enter the custody of the authorities, and the lady has a pressing appointment with His Majesty at St. James's."

Dankworth's eyes opened a little wider. "How does the king know about Lady Imogen?"

Lord Winterton's smile didn't waver. "I told him. She could prove a charming addition to his court. *Miss Thane* is wasted here in the country."

He shot her a quick glance, and although his perusal made her feel dowdy, Imogen caught something else in that blue gaze. A warning, perhaps. Her senses sharpened. All wasn't as it appeared here.

"I—I have no desire to go to London." She wanted everyone to leave her alone. Now Tony knew who she was, now everyone knew what she had done, how could she do anything else?

Lord Winterton's voice softened. "Nevertheless, a royal command is not one you may disobey with impunity."

How could her life change so fast, so suddenly? Imogen went back in her mind to when all this had started. The only chance she'd taken in her life had gone wrong so quickly. She lowered her head, unable to look at anyone any longer. Her face flooded with heat, and she clenched her fists in the skirts of her crumpled gown.

"Why are you dressed like that?" her mother demanded abruptly. "That's your housekeeping gown."

She didn't reply. Twice she'd known pure ecstasy. At the time it had seemed worth it. Was it still? Her body answered. *Yes, yes it was.*

With that knowledge, she lifted her chin and met the curious stares aimed at her. She would give no excuses. She had helped a wounded man, and she would do it again. She had made love with him and she'd do that again, too.

But the court? The king? Surely not. She was disgraced, her father an attainted traitor. Why would they want her?

Dankworth waved a piece of paper. "Here is my warrant. The scoundrel will die." His voice grew louder.

Winterton sent him a look of pure contempt, his blue eyes glittering slits and his mouth set in a hard line. Even though he spoke quietly, everybody listened. "He will suffer the penalties of the law. My compliments to your father." He nodded to the ruffians. His ruffians. "Take the prisoner, lock him up. I don't want to see any marks on him, are we clear? When he faces justice, I want him to do it unmarked. After…" He shrugged, the shoulders of his coat moving in a way to suggest powerful muscles beneath.

The men mumbled their assent. Clearly they'd been looking forward to a session of serious bullying. They'd have beaten Tony to a pulp. He would have been fortunate to get to court in one piece.

A king's court for her, a court of justice for Tony. It hardly seemed fair. It wasn't fair. How could she leave him? A sob rose in her throat. She swallowed it down.

At that moment Winterton came forward, smiling, his expression a shocking contrast to the one of a moment ago. To her he was all friendliness. He held out his arm. "We will, I believe, be better discussing your appearance at court in private. Perhaps at a more convenient hour. While I frequently keep to such hours in London, I confess that in the country it fatigues me. Do you have a guest chamber you can put at my disposal, or shall I rack up at the nearest inn?"

He waited for her reply, but truly, there was only one. "You are welcome to stay, sir."

When she glanced up at Tony, his expression was stony. Until he met her gaze, and then his brow creased and he moved his hand, but returned it to his side. She wanted to hold him, but they couldn't.

To say goodbye like this was agony. "I won't go, not until I know you're safe."

He shook his head. "No, go. You can trust this man." He shot a quick glance at Winterton. The men were of a height. Challenge flashed between them, so fast only she caught it. "If you harm one hair—"

"Why would I do that?" Winterton stepped back and held an embroidered lace handkerchief to his nose. "Faugh, the man stinks! Take him away."

After she shared one last lingering glance with her lover, his lordship led her away.

They walked to the end of the gallery, the only sound their feet on the boards and the tap of her mother's steps following them. For once her surviving parent had the sense to keep quiet.

In private she'd speak to him, beg him if she had to. Behind them, a scuffle began, but Winterton drew them inexorably on. "Looking back is a sign of weakness," he said unexpectedly. "Don't doubt that Dankworth will obey the king's command. He has lost this battle."

She wasn't aware there was a battle, and his softened tones startled her. Almost as if he were a real person.

Imogen had difficulty imagining this man doing anything normal, like, oh, having breakfast, or helping with a difficult delivery during lambing-time. He'd probably never spent time close to livestock. He smelled wonderful, a sort of spicy citrus scent. Men didn't usually wear perfume in her world.

"Careful, you're letting your prejudices show," the exquisite murmured so that only she could hear.

How did he do that? How could he possibly know what she was thinking?

They didn't stop until they reached a guest bedroom. While they didn't keep all the rooms ready, this one had lately contained Lord Dankworth, so it was freshly cleaned and prepared. Imogen opened the door.

"Did Dankworth sleep here?"

"Yes."

"I have a strange disinclination to use the same bed. Call it fastidiousness. I will sleep on a couch if that is all you have." He turned a laughing face to her. "What, you didn't think me capable of it? I assure you, ma'am, I've slept in worse places than a comfortable couch."

"There's another room," her mother said. She led the way to the next room along. "If you will give us half an hour, we can make this one comfortable for you." She opened the door.

The room wasn't as fine as the other. It had more old-fashioned furniture, but the bed was made up and although a fire didn't burn in the grate, at least one was laid.

"Thank you." His lordship turned away and took her arm. "I will be perfectly comfortable here. My man will make any changes necessary." A Superior Being glided along the hallway. Winterton spared him a glance.

"Ah, Moon. Do come in." Even his valet was better dressed than most people of her acquaintance. "I will sleep. You may deal with my wardrobe in the morning. Just ensure the dark blue is ready."

"My lord." He gave a small bow and as Imogen exited, he entered, no doubt to help his master prepare for bed. He wouldn't like the accommodation provided for servants here. She did her best, but the quarters he had with his master were no doubt palatial.

She held her tears back until she reached her room. While she stripped off her clothes and washed herself from the bowl of cold water on her washstand, she sobbed. She took a wrung-out cloth to bed with her and laid it over her eyes.

She wouldn't leave Tony to his fate. She'd fight for him until her last breath.

Chapter 8

The prison cell door opened with a clang, and Tony's cousin sauntered in. The gold braid on his dark clothes caught the dim light, gleaming with incongruous wealth.

Tony looked up from his position on the straw, but took his time swinging his legs around to his front and sitting upright. "My cousin the jailbird," Julius said softly.

"Your doing," Tony snapped. "I would like to know what you're about, Julius."

Julius took a seat on the three-legged stool, the only available seating in this cell. "How's your arm?"

"It'll do."

"Who shot you?"

He grimaced. "I might have known you'd guess what had happened."

"I didn't until just now. So who do you think shot you?"

Tony shrugged, ignoring the resulting twinge of pain. "Dankworth. He probably knows who I am."

"Someone told him, probably his father." Julius got to his feet. "Tony, what the *hell* did you think you were doing?"

Tony jutted out his chin. "That document is here." He glanced to the door, unwilling to articulate, even now, the nature of the document.

Julius nodded. "It is, I'm sure of it. Or one of them is. I think there are more copies, though." He took the two paces, which was all the cell would allow, and spun around, striding back. "I want this one. I want proof of what we suspect, otherwise we can't act with any certainty." He faced Tony. "You, my bully, are going to make amends for your utter stupidity in trying to act on your own."

"As I recall, you were somewhat busy at the time. I deemed it an urgent matter. How did I know how long you would take with Devereux? How is he, by the way?"

Julius waved a hand. "Fine, fine. That isn't at issue here so don't try to change the subject. We both know a few words can get you out of here."

Tony nodded. "But as you see, I waited for you. I've been bitten to death by vermin, and the rats here are bolder than any I've known before, but here I am. Waiting." Impatiently. "If you hadn't looked after Imogen, I'd have ended the farce there and then."

"That wouldn't have done your lady-love any favors."

Tony cast a fulminating glare at Julius. "I shall save a particularly curious rat for you, if you repeat that. A lady's reputation is at stake."

"Don't get pompous with me. If you hadn't taken her to your bed, you wouldn't be in this mess. What got into you?"

"I thought she was the housekeeper."

Julius's eyes sparked fire. "And that made it acceptable, did it?"

"No." Tony shared Julius's belief that servants were not there to be seduced, but this one had proved irresistible. "I decided to marry her."

Julius blinked. "Even while you thought she was a housekeeper?"

Tony nodded. "Even then. I knew what I'd done, and I was prepared to pay the price."

"You still will if your dalliance results in pregnancy."

Tony was surprised to discover how much that prospect appealed to him. Shocked him, as he'd been avoiding just such a fate for years. "I will. But I don't need you to tell me that." The woman he knew as Emmy and Imogen were the same person. She was the housekeeper; she hadn't lied to him about that. He'd let himself believe it in a different way, that was all. "Soldiers have made worse choices."

"You're not a soldier any more. You're an Emperor, and you will conduct yourself like one."

"Or?"

Julius waved a beringed hand. "Don't ask."

Tony could always rejoin the army or find somewhere else to live. Julius was bluffing. Probably. "I heard you arrive. You were devilish quiet."

"Yes. Deliberately. I had to storm the place, because I got wind of Dankworth's plans. He was mustering his men at the inn where I was staying. Not so much of a coincidence, more because it's the only decent inn for miles. I found the authorities, roused the constable in the middle of the night, and gave him my best aristocratic manner. I knew if I didn't get there before Dankworth and his men, they'd most likely kill you. I am still angry with you, by the way. I don't have enough cousins."

Tony grinned. Since they shared a goodly number of cousins, he doubted one less would have mattered to most people. "Good of you to say so."

Julius humphed. "Well, then, if I hadn't had you arrested, he might have done so. And killed you. You could have been killed in the scuffle, or resisting arrest."

"So he knows who I am?"

"I don't know, but you were in bed with a lady he has designs on."

Tony sighed and rubbed his hands over his head. "What happens next?"

Julius shook his head. "I'll send orders that you are to be escorted to Newgate Prison in London. They'll probably put you in chains." He visibly brightened at the prospect, his eyes sparkling and a grin tilting his mouth. "You deserve at least a little more punishment. You'll leave here Tony Shaw, but you'll arrive in London as Antoninus Beaumont. It's more than you deserve. If you can't escape on your own, I'll arrange it for you. But it's best you stay Tony Shaw for the time being. The Dankworths would make hay if your real identity came out."

"I can manage it. Never fear. And I'll leave no trace of Tony Shaw behind me."

Julius strode to the door. "Don't make a mess of this." Turning, he tossed a purse to Tony who caught it deftly. "That should help."

It would help a great deal. He could have managed without, but the money would help his transformation nicely.

"Julius?"

"Yes?"

"Don't tell her who I am. Oh, tell her I'm a relative, but you have a swarm of them. I could be a poor relation. I want to tell her myself."

The time in that little room was precious to him. Never before had a woman offered herself not knowing who he was and what he could do for her. She'd wanted him, Tony, not Antoninus Beaumont, and that memory was sweet.

He didn't want her thinking he'd deceived her to get her into bed and for that to happen he needed to tell her himself.

Julius nodded. "As you wish. You may tell her when you reach London. But if she asks pertinent questions, I will not lie."

She wouldn't. Not if she thought he was a humble soldier.

* * * *

The next day, after charming Imogen's mother out of her skin, Julius requested a short time alone with Imogen. After a sleepless night Imogen couldn't think of anything she wanted less. But at least she'd been in her comfortable bed, in her own room, unlike Tony, who was taken, like to be hanged.

He led her into the morning parlor and closed the door softly behind them.

"Now," he said. "We will have the truth." He took a seat on the long sofa before the unlit fire and indicated the chair with a graceful gesture. "How did you come across Tony?"

Startled, she took the seat. "You know him?"

"He's a relative. I have a large clutch of them on my mother's side. Taking care of their various scrapes takes much of my time." He smiled. "They say that's what families are for."

Tony was related to the great Earl of Winterton? She swallowed her shock and folded her hands in her lap in an attempt at demureness.

"We need to preserve your reputation."

"I think I destroyed that last night." Being caught by nigh on a dozen men *en flagrante* with another would see to that. She met his gaze steadily, not ashamed of what she'd done.

He touched his chin. "Are you aware that you are a considerable heiress?"

Not really. "I have this house, which as you can see is modest by your standards, and a small estate."

"And a legacy that your trustees have invested for you."

"That provides an annuity for my mother." She hadn't concerned herself with that part of her inheritance. Her father had disposed of almost everything else, so she'd consolidated what was left and asked for her trustees to invest it in reliable funds.

"And a dowry for you. By my reckoning it amounts to twenty thousand pounds."

Shock made her rigid. She stared at him. "I don't understand."

"One of your trustees is Sir Thaddeus Beaumont, who happens to be my uncle by marriage. He's a City man, and he has put your funds to good use."

Goodness, the man talked like a dictionary. So beautifully. Had he prepared this speech, or was it extempore? "The money will come in very useful," she said, still trying to come to terms with what he'd told her. "I can buy more land."

"It's your dowry," he reminded her. "Your portion. You won't come into possession of it until you reach five and thirty, or you marry."

Ten years. Not too long. She could make plans for that. "I appreciate your telling me, sir."

"It means you will have fortune hunters beating a path to your door. I believe one already called."

Realization hit her. For the first time in her life, she experienced the bitterness from knowing that someone wanted her for her fortune rather than herself. "Dankworth came because he learned I was worth a lot of money?"

"Not that alone." His voice softened and he leaned forward, resting his elbows on his knees.

She hit back. "What about you, sir? Are you short of funds?"

The shot missed its mark. He laughed. "Hardly. No, my interest in you lies in another direction. You can't stay here in your comfortable backwater any longer." He glanced around at the room with its paneled walls and the heavily carved furniture. "Although it is an intriguing one. I have rarely seen a Tudor house in such perfect condition. Don't change it, will you?"

"I love it as it is."

"We might make it possible for you to return." He smiled, and the expression transformed his face.

This was a friendly smile, one that she responded to. Humanity colored his features, as if he'd doffed a mask.

"But you will have to put up with a little interference first." He paused, watching her steadily. She forced a smile.

"People will forget this."

"No, I'm afraid they won't. Oh, not your indiscretion with Tony. That's a small affair, easily dealt with. I've already taken steps to limit that."

Her relief came in a rush, bringing tears to her eyes. "I can't see how you can do that, sir."

"I can. And my name is Julius, if you care to use it. I wish to be your friend in this matter."

She nodded. "I need a friend. And I'm Imogen."

"You need several friends." But now his smile was a friendly one, and for all the grand clothes, he appeared as approachable as any of her neighbors. "You are an heiress and a suspect person, mainly because of your father's loyalty to the Stuarts. That means the Crown is taking an interest in you. The King and his advisors do not want a rogue heiress running around the country, especially this part of it. You could become a rallying point. A symbol for the Jacobites."

She understood that part. With that kind of money, she couldn't hide away, as she had been doing.

"You are going to court, make no mistake about that. If you behave, you will not have to stay there long. The court will prove a protection against your more persistent suitors."

This was not what she wanted to hear. She didn't care about her fate, although she supposed she should. But she wasn't in danger. The terror that had twisted her stomach since they'd taken him away attacked her anew. "What about Tony? What will they do to him?"

He regarded her in silence, one she dared not break. His gaze roamed over her face, as if making up his mind about something. "He will be well," he said. "They won't hurt him, and he'll be free in a day or two. I swear it."

"Why did you have him arrested?"

"To save his life. The men I brought are representatives of the true authorities. The men Dankworth brought were not. Once Dankworth became aware of Tony's presence, my sorry relative was a marked man. I had no time to muster a force of my own, so using the ones available locally seemed the best thing to do." Julius regarded her closely. Whatever he saw made him say, "Enough for today. You will have to be brave, but we will bring this thing about. In case you're unaware of our history, our family is opposed to the Dankworths for a number of reasons, not all of them political. They oppose us at every turn."

She frowned. "We?"

"In some circles we're known as the Emperors of London. Our parents decided to whimsically name us after emperors and empresses of the past. My father and his five sisters. You may have noticed my real name?"

She recalled the slight jolt when he'd introduced himself. "Julius Caesar?" Despite the weariness taking over now the crisis was past, the notion gave her a smile.

"Indeed." He nodded. He rose to his feet in one fluid movement. "You should prepare for travelling to London."

Politely he waited for her to rise and then ushered her to the door. He told her one more time not to worry.

How could she not?

* * * *

Tony was getting damned sick of people kicking him.

The jailer sitting opposite him in the coach stirred. A thread of drool spilled from one corner of his mouth. This was probably Tony's best chance, if he could overcome the bastard without jolting the vehicle taking him in chains to London.

But when he moved, testing the chains for weight and balance, the man opened one rheumy eye. "Git back, you." He aimed a vicious kick that could have broken a bone if it had landed before Tony moved aside. He yelped in pain anyway, and that seemed to satisfy his torturer. He had a light sleeper on his hands. Damned inconvenient, that.

Night had fallen an hour ago, the sun setting in glowing beauty in a rosy sky, which meant clear skies, which meant a chill in the air. March meant the end of winter frost, though chill winds and rain could make it feel as cold as if the hedges were still touched with hoar.

They pulled into the busy yard of a coaching inn, the carriage taking the corner with barely a check in its pace. Ostlers raced forward to attend to the horses while his guards climbed down, grumbling. The one inside with him scowled and told him to stay where he was.

Tony reconnoitered. They wouldn't leave him alone in a room, so he'd have to overpower whoever slept with him. Unless they put him in a small room. He snorted. They smelled as bad as he did, so nobody would complain about sharing. But that could work to his advantage, especially if they armed his guard.

The inn was bustling. No chance a man in irons would pass unnoticed. These places were busy almost around the clock, but if he didn't get away soon it would be too late.

His jailers dragged him out when the yard had settled down a little, and into the inn. Straight past the tap room, where the smells of beer and stew made Tony's mouth water, to a little windowless room by the kitchen.

The man who'd driven the bone-shaking carriage settled down with him. They brought food, and thank the Lord, Tony's was just about edible, but when he saw the pieces of grit in the bread, he broke most of it up, sprinkling the crumbs for the ever-present rats. He didn't want to lose a tooth on a piece of grit.

Once he got home, he'd order a huge two-course, twelve-remove dinner and eat every crumb.

He didn't relax his attention for a second, waiting for that moment when the man watching him would drop his guard. At the moment, he'd be keen, but the food might make him sleepy. A tankard of beer rested at the man's side—not small beer, as his was, but full-bodied local brew.

They wouldn't reach London for another four or five days, but he didn't want to wait that long. He'd be half-dead if he suffered many more kicks and blows, and he hadn't cleaned his wound for some time or even had the dressing changed. He felt feverish again, though that was probably due to the poor diet and the mistreatment.

Tony waited, ignored the usual taunts, and settled down in a corner of the little room to sleep, setting himself to wake in three hours. Midnight.

When he opened his eyes again, the man opposite was snoring. He gathered his strength and decided on his plan of action. He was chained wrists and ankles, the ankles heavy bands that weighed him down. This man did not have the keys.

The man nodded, his head slowly descending as he slid into deep sleep. Outside, apart from the shifting of horses in the nearby stable, he detected nothing.

He couldn't put this off any longer.

In one lethal move he lunged across the space between them, thankful they'd omitted to chain him to the wall. As he leaped, he lifted his arms and looped the chain, linking his wrists behind the man's neck. As his jailer woke, Tony smashed his head down, smacking the man between the eyes. The man groaned, but before he could call out, Tony had his fingers on his captor's throat, blocking his breathing.

The man slumped heavily and Tony leaned him gently back against the wall behind him. At least he had the key to the door. Swiftly, he skimmed the man's pockets and found what he needed, slipping the penknife into his pocket.

Now for the tricky part. With every step he clanked and clinked. Stealthily he crept to the door, making as little noise as he could manage. Once he'd unlocked the door, he listened, waiting for a full five minutes, as long as he dared, before he opened it and let in what light there was. A thin beam of lamplight shone from a room in the main building, on the ground floor. A kitchen or small parlor, but although other smaller lights flickered here and there, nobody stirred on this side of the inn. Any minute a late-night carouser could come stumbling out to relieve himself in the yard, or a late traveler could arrive, seeking shelter. The sooner he got out of this place, the easier he'd breathe.

Gripping his wrist chains firmly, he took a step. The chains clanked. He held his breath.

Nobody came.

Another step, and then another, the chains dragging against the uneven cobbles of the yard. Using the coach as cover, he moved forward as smoothly as possible. The sound of quiet breathing startled him, but the ostler lying on his bed of straw, covered by a blanket, didn't stir.

There was straw around this side of the yard, so Tony hugged the wall, using the straw to muffle his steps. He took his time, knowing that it wasn't taking as long as his tense mind imagined.

A door. A small door in the side wall, and thank the Lord it was open. It creaked a little when he eased it open, but he didn't have to pull it all the way. He slid through and tugged it closed, careful to hold the latch clear so it wouldn't rattle.

Damn, that was more nerve-wracking than mining enemy lines. He stopped, waiting until his heartbeat got back to normal, listening and getting his breath back.

After five minutes, he willed himself to move. The jailor he'd stifled could wake up at any moment and sound the alarm. Normally a prisoner escaping wouldn't have a hope in hell, but Tony had two things in his favor. His soldiering skills and even more importantly, a purse full of gold.

Only a few houses lay between him and open country at the back of the inn. He hobbled past them and found another useful tool fastening a gate together—a length of stout wire. With these, he reached a nearby copse and took a few moments to get rid of his shackles.

The locks were simple, easily picked. Prisoners retained their chains not because of the difficulty of the locks but because they were simply replaced. It wasn't worth the effort.

Once he'd rid himself of them, Tony found a loose piece of earth and used a stick to dig a hole just deep enough to conceal them. If they set dogs after him, they'd find the chains, but he'd left nothing behind for them to scent. If they caught him, they might kill him. He needed to act quickly.

First, the clothes. If not for the clanking of the chains he'd have stripped his jailor and taken his coat, because his own was filthy and reeked of prison and days of constant wear. He needed decent clothes, but in order to get them, he needed decent clothes. A paradox that made him smile grimly.

No help for it. He'd have to put some distance between the inn and himself before light dawned.

He didn't know this part of the country, so he had little choice but to take to the road.

Loping back to the highway, he continued in the direction the coach was taking. He kept to the other side of the hedge, so the going wasn't as easy, but he couldn't risk any late traveler finding him. So far he'd done nothing wrong, but he was perilously close to breaking the law, stealing clothes or a horse, and horse-stealing was punishable by death. He had no weapon but a piece of wire and a penknife, no food, no water.

What could be easier?

Chapter 9

"I can't walk in this." Imogen immediately disproved her point by stamping to the elaborate sofa in Julius's drawing room.

Julius exchanged a laughing glance with his sister Helena. "You can. And most gracefully, too. Now sit."

She turned around, preparing her skirts. "I feel upholstered." Heavily embroidered brocade in shell pink draped her form, but not in a way she liked. The style was old-fashioned, and she resented the waste of beautiful fabric.

"You look lovely. You'll make everyone at court fall in love with you."

Imogen had made her debut at court the week before, and much to her surprise and shock, nobody had turned their back on her. However, on her backward walk to the door she'd stumbled, and sniggers had rippled through the crowd. She wasn't the only debutante to trip that day, because walking backward in a skirt with a train, even a pinned-up train, wasn't an easy skill to acquire. However Julius had determined that she wouldn't do it again, and he'd made her don the hated mantua every day and practice until she had it right. "Nobody will love me. They'll all laugh."

"They haven't so far."

"That's because of your patronage." Imogen's awe of the magnificent Lord Winterton had lasted less than a week, mainly because he had determined that it would last no longer. While she stayed at their house, she'd seen him romp with his daughter, laugh with his friends, and he'd given her accounts of all the great and good they'd met in the salons of London that she'd been hard put to it not to burst into laughter at the most inappropriate moments.

His sister Helena and his cousin Poppea, or Poppy, had treated her with gentle good humor and stayed with her through the torture of fitting and pinning. What this panoply was costing her, she dreaded to think, but she had enough, she discovered, especially when Madame kindly gave her a discount for buying all her gowns there. Still, the shocking price of lace stunned her into a brief silence. But she'd need the finery for court. She was to be maid of honor to Princess Amelia, whom she'd met, briefly.

Imogen's mama was in alt, so much that Imogen found it hard to remain in her company. Her mother was present now, seated in one of the large blue-upholstered salon chairs, looking as if she'd spent all her life in the drawing rooms of London. "You will be a sensation," she assured her daughter now. "We will never have to return to that house again."

Imogen wanted to. Badly. She felt so out of place here, and she doubted she'd ever become accustomed to it. Missing her home, missing Tony, she wanted nothing so much as a quiet afternoon to regain her equilibrium, but she had none. Ensconced in a bedroom worthy of a princess, with a new superior maid just for her, she didn't know what to do with her time. She would wake and think of the lambing, which must be in full flow now. Her farm manager would handle it, but dammit, she wanted to be there. Home. "What happened to the Prince over the water? Where is your loyalty?" she demanded viciously.

Her mother the Jacobite was thrilled that her daughter had secured a place at court. "You will find a good match at court. We'll see."

"I can hardly breathe in these stays," she muttered.

Abruptly, Julius got to his feet. "I need to speak to Imogen, if you don't mind. Imogen, would you object to a quiet word in private?"

Her mother glared at him, but then her gaze softened. It was far too easy to discern what she was thinking.

Imogen went hot, and then cold, chills chasing each other up her spine. Surely not. She'd come to think of Julius as her friend. Surely he knew she couldn't—he'd caught her, he'd known what she'd done. Did he mean to propose?

Numbly, she watched her mother and Helena leave the room. Forgetting the width of her skirts, she spun around and had to catch the hoops before they tangled her in a twist.

Laughing, Julius held his hands up in surrender. She couldn't imagine him getting in a muddle like this. She had learned early that Julius had the gift of always appearing perfect, even when playing with his daughter. Now, in his full-skirted bronze coat and cream waistcoat he appeared almost otherworldly. "Don't concern yourself. I wasn't intending to do anything precipitate. I merely wanted to give you some news."

No longer interested in disentangling herself, Imogen plopped down in the nearest chair. "Tony?"

Smiling broadly, Julius found himself a seat opposite her. "Tony," he agreed. "He's well. Now."

She'd nearly gone insane when she discovered he'd reached London and they hadn't told her. They'd kept her away. To make it worse, Julius had said he was ill.

Julius went on. "It wasn't jail fever. He'd walked too long in the rain and contracted a fever."

"He could have died!" She'd known men shiver themselves to death, their bodies racked with fever so high they melted away. "I should have gone to him."

"He said no," Julius said. "We couldn't take the risk that you would contract his illness. But he was exhausted, and the fever took him when he was weak. He walked for ten miles before he found somewhere that would take him in."

"Oh God!"

Julius smiled ruefully. "My dear, he's known much worse. But if we'd let you see him, he'd have killed himself with fury. It was for the good of you both. But I admit, mostly for you."

Grabbing handfuls of her skirt, she wrung it hard, uncaring of the costly fabric. "Where is he? May I see him?"

"Soon. He's recovering, and what he needs now is rest. Do you want to undo all the good he did?"

She shook her head. She'd written to him, and Julius had assured her Tony had received her letter, but they hadn't let him reply.

Julius nodded. "He found a place in a stagecoach and got as far as the house of my cousin in Buckinghamshire. They took him in and cared for him. Tony will be in town soon, I swear it. But I want him to rest for a few days more before he travels. I will let you know when he arrives."

She should have gone to him. Nothing was more important. He'd been through so much. "Make sure you do." She tightened her trembling jaw. "I'm sorry, you've done so much but I—I haven't stopped thinking of him."

"A simple soldier?" A smile quirked his mouth.

"Yes. I know I'm mixing with the highest in the land, but Tony means more to me than any other." More than that she couldn't say. Not to another person.

Julius crossed his ankle over his knee, his calf muscles flexing. Although he dressed like an exquisite, Imogen never underestimated the man sitting before her. She had no doubt he spent hours in the boxing saloon and fencing studio. Though she vastly preferred Tony's rugged good looks, Julius's sheer handsomeness had many men beaten.

"Tell me, Imogen, you control the estate completely, don't you?"

"Yes. I administer it. I see every book and every set of accounts."

"Highly commendable." He regarded her in silence, a frown creasing his brows. "Have you ever seen a document you may have thought unusual? Different?"

"No." She'd seen the original grant of lands to her farmer ancestor, the letters patent granting the earldom to her Jacobean forebear, and of course every account book that still existed. It still grieved her that some had been lost in the Civil War. Truthfully she loved reading the history of the estate she now owned, touching the documents people before her had created. But all the papers she'd seen, ancient and modern, were normal, what would be expected. "You mean the document that took my father's title away?"

"Do you regret that?"

She shook her head. "He knew what he was doing when he followed the Pretender abroad. He knew the title was lost, and his lands, except for the ones he'd put in trust for me."

Julius's mouth tightened. "Whereas I believe that family comes before almost everything else."

"Even principle?"

He shrugged, the shoulders of his beautifully cut coat following his movements, giving that hint of muscle. Did he have them cut that way on purpose? To minimize the power of the body beneath? The question intrigued her but didn't interest her as it would have if Tony had been wearing the garment. Not that Tony would own a coat as fine as this. She still didn't understand so many things. Tony was a Jacobite, and Julius had admitted he was a relation, but he didn't seem to treat Tony as a disgraced relation.

"Principle," he said, "only takes a person so far. It has the deadly hydra of corruption and self-interest to fight. However, I temper all that I do with reason. Tony was looking for an unusual document when he came to your house. He undertook the task without my sanction. And nearly got himself killed. That means that somewhere in your house that document still lurks. I have no idea when it came into your family's hands, but following an elaborate trail from Rome, I discovered who had last been in possession of it. Unfortunately someone else followed a similar trail."

Realization came immediately. "Lord Dankworth?"

He inclined his head. "Exactly so. He came, determined to hunt for it. Or to hunt for Tony. He found Tony. I don't know if he found the document."

"What does this document say?"

Julius tapped his finger against his lip. "I don't believe I should tell you at present. It's a dangerous secret, one I do not think you would be better knowing."

Anger simmered in her stomach, churning the excellent breakfast she'd consumed a short while ago. "It is my house. Someone put something there of which I was unaware. I have every right to know."

So used to men treating her as an empty-headed female, all hair and no brains, as she'd heard the squire put it once, she prepared to fight for the knowledge. A document? She was sure she'd been through every document in the office at her house. "I want to know what it holds."

Julius's mouth firmed. "State secrets, my dear. Your father may have come into possession of something that could affect the health of the nation. Will that suffice for now? I don't want you to know, not because I don't trust you, but because I want to verify that the document exists and that it is in your possession. If the document does not exist, if it has been destroyed, there is nothing to discover."

It sounded like utter nonsense to her, but she had enough on her plate at the moment.

"I believe the knowledge is best hidden until we have proof of what it contains." He grimaced. "I'm sorry. That's too enigmatic even for me."

"How do you expect me to search for something when I don't know what it is that I'm looking for?"

Julius sighed. "Give me leave to search. I'll go there alone and sift through every paper in the place." He smiled. "I'll also undertake to release Tony from his prison at Max's house on my way. Though a more luxurious prison you'd find it hard to see anywhere. But he would not come near you while he was the least feverish. He would not even write." He glanced at her. "You do deserve the truth whenever I can give it. But believe me, this truth is a burden, one I would prefer to see buried for all time."

"So when you've found this mysterious paper, you'll destroy it?"

"Yes. If I can possibly do so. It needs burning out of existence."

She thought. Julius had shown her unrestricted kindness. He'd given her good advice, helped her by approving of her.

"I'll write a letter of authorization, giving you leave to go where you will and search where you will. On condition that you tell me if it concerns me or my family. I will not be kept in the dark on this."

Julius nodded. "Very well. I'll see you established with the princess, and then I'll set off for Lancashire. I'll stop at Max's house on the way and inform Tony he can come to London. Max will be starting a major building, or rather, demolition program. I can't imagine it will be at all comfortable then." He lifted his chin.

However much Imogen questioned Julius, he would not tell her what was in the document. But she trusted him to destroy it and leave the rest of her belongings intact. And to tell her what it contained. State secrets she could do without. He was welcome to them. No doubt it concerned the Pretender, father or son. They were always plotting and scheming. She wanted nothing to do with it. She squeezed a bit more of the silk of her gown under her fingers.

Julius got to his feet. "We should join the others, or your mother will have it that we're planning to marry. You know that was what she believed?"

Imogen nodded. "She has a vivid imagination."

"And do stop doing that to your gown," he said, his voice turning lightly plaintive. "I know it's not the height of fashion, but that's hardly the mantua's fault."

She'd been wearing the thing for an hour and was managing the huge hooped petticoat perfectly well. Perhaps she could manage this appearance after all.

* * * *

After Julius left her at St. James's Palace, the Princess's chamberlain showed her to a tiny room and briskly explained her duties. "You are to attend her highness for the next month. She will be staying at the Lodge at Richmond, and you will be assigned a room there. Your maid will sleep next door. You are not required to wear court mantuas except on specific occasions, such as presentations." He studied Imogen carefully, his pale eyes icy. "I understand you are a special case and you may not be required to return after the first month. The princess occasionally gives favors to friends, and this is one. That does not mean that you may shirk your duties."

She dropped a small curtsey. "I wouldn't dream of it, sir."

Filled with trepidation, an hour later she followed the chamberlain to the room where the princess was attending her father, the king. He would leave for his favored palace of Kensington soon, where he spent most of his time. Having seen engravings of the modern smaller establishment, Imogen would prefer it too, to this place of cavernous formal rooms and heavy gilded furniture.

While her ancestors had worked with timber and plaster, the builders here had used stone and mortar. It was not an improvement, in Imogen's opinion. She preferred the warmer smaller rooms of her own house. But if she wanted to keep it, she'd have to stay here for a while. Or, apparently, at Richmond.

The princess was Ranger of the park, and Julius had told her there was controversy about her decision to close the park to all but invited guests. He also warned her not to oppose the princess on her decision. "It's her one blind spot. Princess Amelia enjoys a vigorous discussion on some matters, but not this one."

Julius had proved more useful than the chamberlain, who only sketched out what she was supposed to do. Wait until summoned, and be ready at all times. Dress appropriately. The maid Imogen had acquired would now earn her keep.

Imogen yearned to go home. This place made her feel isolated. At her house in Lancashire, she might only have her mother as a relative, but the staff formed a cohesive unit. She missed the Georges, people she could go and complain to and know her words wouldn't go any further. She could hardly confide anything in the superior being she'd been assigned as a maid. And she didn't keep a journal. Perhaps she should. Develop some kind of code so she could pour out all her dearest secrets. Or just sit in this space, barely big enough for a small bed, dressing table, and washstand, and talk to herself. Her maid probably had a larger room, since she was in charge of her clothes. But this room was larger than the one in which she'd found ecstasy with Tony.

She longed to see him again, even more than she wanted to go home. It ached inside her, that need, as if part of her had left with him.

A knock on her door made her leap half out of her skin. She called out, "Yes?"

"The King awaits, ma'am."

Lord, she hoped not. She'd hate to think he was waiting for her. She fixed a smile on her face and opened the door. "I wouldn't dream of keeping his majesty waiting."

She'd already learned how the king preferred people to address him. At least, people in his or his family's household. Holding her fan at a precise angle, she followed the page sent to find her, her heart thumping hard in her chest. The man in royal livery took her along several corridors and through two huge breathtaking rooms, tapestries, triple chandeliers, and magnificent stately furniture on full display. They didn't look like home, though.

The page knocked at a door and entered without waiting for a command. That surprised her, but not as much as the room. Broad windows opened on to a garden. It contained furniture she could have lived with, red-upholstered chairs and sofas. A porcelain clock ticked away on the mantelpiece, with a few choice china figurines. Porcelain, probably, because they were exquisite. Considering the King's origins, probably German. Meissen, most likely.

The King sat in a comfortable wing chair, one heavily bandaged foot propped on a substantial footstool. Next to him sat the princess, her posture rigid and her fan in her lap, fine lace ruffles cascading over her forearms. Today she wore a leaf green, so Imogen was pleased she'd settled for her new white silk embroidered with daisies and buttercups.

The King's weathered face broke into a smile. "You brought spring with you, Miss Thane." His German accent was barely marked by his long sojourn in England, but he did visit his beloved Hanover as often as he could. Not that he was going anywhere with that gouty foot.

Imogen executed her curtsey faultlessly and waited until he bade her rise, which he did with a wave of his handkerchief.

"Do get up, Miss Thane. If you could pour us some tea, and then you may sit." He indicated another stool close to him.

Her throat catching with tension, Imogen concentrated on her simple task, ensuring she didn't spill a drop. She served the tea in the fragile flower-bedecked porcelain dishes, putting the king's on the table at his elbow before curtseying again, but not so low this time.

"Thank you, Miss Thane."

Considering her background, she should despise him, but she could not. He was old, and obviously not in the best of health, since his face was mottled and his complexion yellowed. But his smile was sweet.

She hadn't realized before that the king was more than a figurehead. He was a man. The princess wasn't just a royal figure, she was his daughter. His feud with his now dead eldest son was well-known, but his relations with the rest of his family were cordial.

Despite the fine clothes and grand drawing room, despite her upbringing, encouraged to regard the king as a figure of hatred or ridicule, Imogen's heart went out to him. She sat on the footstool, but the king waved at her impatiently. "Get up, girl. Get yourself some tea."

She hadn't wanted to risk staining her new gown or revealing her nervousness, but she did as he bade her and found a place to perch the dish and saucer. The king poured his tea into the deep saucer with a shaking hand and slurped, with every sign of satisfaction.

He closed his eyes when he'd finished and put the saucer on the table, so close to the edge Imogen feared for its safety, but she daren't get up to straighten it. However, Princess Amelia had no such scruples and she did so, straightening dish and saucer with precision.

"You will be accompanying me to Richmond tomorrow, Miss Thane, but my father wishes for a word with you before we leave," she said. "You may have wondered at the lack of servants. It is because he wishes the conversation to be private. Do you understand me?"

"Yes, your highness."

"Very well."

That meant she must not repeat whatever they said.

The king reached into his coat pocket and drew out a paper. She blinked, and a surge of excitement leaped inside her. Was this the document everybody was hunting for?

He unfolded the single sheet and glanced at it. "You are a problem, Miss Thane. You are drawing rebels to your house." The king cleared his throat. "You have a good fortune and a tidy estate, so we are decided you are to marry one of our loyal subjects, to keep you safely out of mischief."

Shock reverberated through her, and she fought to retain her polite smile. The king continued, seemingly heedless of her inner turmoil. "My ministers and I have drawn up a list of suitable candidates." His breath came in wheezes, a slight whistle with every inhale. "Select your future husband from this list. We will consider bestowing the title your late disgraced father possessed on your husband. The second creation of the Earl of Hollinhead will be better than the first. More loyal. It will restore your family's good name."

Except her family hadn't had a good name for a long time now. The last time was probably the Restoration, nearly a hundred years ago. Some families had a knack of choosing the right side, or keeping carefully neutral. Her family did the opposite, pressing fervent and noisy patronage on the wrong side and the wrong cause. The losing side.

From a young age, Imogen had determined not to follow that path, had lived in dread that her father would send for her. But he never did, and that, in another way, hurt just as much. On his hurried visits to England, he'd had brief conversations with her. Never touched her.

Pushing her mind away from unwelcome memories, she concentrated on what the king was saying. Married? To someone he chose? She was in deep trouble here. "Sir, may I ask advice of anyone? I'm new to London. I don't know people."

The king nodded. "Yes. Ask Winterton, his father, or another of that family. He will advise you. Nobody else. Not your mother." He pronounced it "Muzzer," and his thickened voice, probably due to some form of ill-health occasionally made his words difficult to interpret. But Imogen didn't make the mistake of assuming that meant he wasn't in control of his faculties.

Julius knew everyone. He was a good choice. Damn, what should she say?

The only thing she could.

She'd received the royal decree, and she must obey. The only thing she could do was pray for time. Perhaps the king would forget. Perhaps he wouldn't enforce his decree. Maybe she could, after all, return home and recommence her life.

Without Tony.

Was his name on the list? Unlikely. He was an obscure relation of Julius, a soldier. Not a man the king would have even heard of, much less listed. When the king held the paper out to her, she stood, curtseyed and took it, careful not to touch him. Royalty was not to be touched unless they wished it, and accidental grazes weren't approved of. Bad manners, Julius had told her. She placed the still folded document on the small table by her side.

She spent the next half hour listening to the princess and the king, serving them tea and giving her modest opinion when asked to.

Too much of this would drive her mad. The inconsequential conversation, the days spent in idleness. At least she only had a month.

She still wanted Tony, but with every day that passed, she realized she wouldn't get him. He was gone from her life now. At least he was well and safe. Would he rejoin the army? Probably, once he'd recovered. He'd—no, she wouldn't even think of it. A lump filled her throat even at the prospect of parting. Too soon. Perhaps that feeling of jagged loss would ease with time, but it was as if a hole had opened up inside her and it wouldn't heal.

Now she smiled and nodded and listened.

At the end of half an hour, when the clock tinkled the passage of time in a series of charming chimes, the king declared himself fatigued. "I will see you again, Miss Thane," he said. "I am pleased with your company."

More time. The princess curtseyed to her father, gave him a kiss on the cheek, and then Imogen got to her feet, curtseyed to the king, and followed the princess from the room.

Imogen had no idea how the princess felt about her father, but at least no friction existed. She kept her head bowed and the paper folded in her hand, exactly as the king had given it to her. Once out of the room she folded the paper over and shoved it in her pocket. The more she held it, the more she longed to see the names.

"We shall leave for Richmond in the morning," the princess told her. "You will like Richmond."

She accompanied the princess to another sitting room and went through the same rigmarole as before, pouring tea, handing the princess refreshments. The royal family drank enough tea to drown a battleship, and they expected her to match them, dish for dish. Of course, she did.

Imogen had no desire to live in a palace all the time. Perhaps the people who did, the ones born to it, were used to it. For one thing, she was bound to lose herself in the endless hallways and rooms. This palace was old, a palace built onto over time, so the building didn't have a regular pattern or a template she could follow. She had to rely on the servants patrolling the place, but since they congregated around the places the royal family lived, she had to find those parts first.

Finally, after a frankly tedious dinner with the princess and some extremely dull ladies of her acquaintance, the princess gave her leave to go to her room. She took twenty minutes to find it, and she only did so because of a particularly ugly engraving of King Charles II, which she'd noticed on her way out earlier that day.

Her maid undressed her and helped her into her nightwear. Imogen was galled that she couldn't get out of her clothes without help. Finally, tucked in the narrow bed, she reached for her pocket and drew out the paper.

She might as well not have bothered. While some of the surnames had significance for her, being of some of the highest families in the land, none of the first names rang any bells in her mind.

She had fifteen men to choose from. Younger sons, most probably, because they had surnames and not titles. That was because the king wanted to revive her father's title, to clean it. She supported that, but did she have to go with it? The bulk of her father's estate had gone, either returned to the crown when the title was withdrawn, or sold off to finance the increasingly desperate efforts of the Stuarts to reclaim the throne they still regarded as theirs.

She held a list of unknown men, one of whom she was expected to make a future with. Perhaps her mother knew them, but she doubted it. Her mother had gone from her parents' house to Rome, where they'd married her to Imogen's father. She'd come back to Lancashire and never gone abroad.

Imogen didn't want that fate, didn't want a husband who'd abandon her and return to another life of which she had no part. Tears slipped past her nose, down her cheeks, and dripped on to the blue coverlet on her bed. She forced them back. She'd never indulged in self-pity, and she didn't intend to start now.

Finding her handkerchief, she mopped her tears and willed herself to lie down and sleep. She'd think about it in the morning and make a copy of the list for when Julius returned. That couldn't come soon enough.

Chapter 10

Richmond was a far more pleasant prospect than St. James's Palace, the house well-appointed and the view over Richmond Park delightful. Imogen found her tasks easier, and as Julius had told her, the princess was more interested in equality of conversation, particularly when nobody else was present.

But protocol was giving her headaches. She understood her own position. Although her mother insisted on people addressing her by the title she'd married into, Imogen wouldn't have liked her odds of retaining it in the presence of the royal family. She was firmly addressed as "Miss Thane."

She missed everything familiar. But she rallied herself and settled into her new life. The princess occasionally attended balls and routs in London, and Imogen soon learned that was the best way to be introduced to society, at least for herself. People were far more willing to accept her once they learned the royal family had taken her under their wing. Clever Julius had been right.

Every night Imogen studied the list. She'd met a few of the men, who were blessedly free of the knowledge that they were under her scrutiny. Either that or their manners were so exquisite that they did not allow themselves the luxury of treating her any differently from the other young ladies in the ballroom.

Imogen found most of them pleasant, easy to talk to, and friendly. But they were not Tony.

She'd put the original carefully away and made a copy to carry around with her, afraid of destroying the document by constantly folding and unfolding it. It read the same every time.

Should she choose Ian Howard, perhaps? Or Gilbert Southworth?

One evening, after night had turned London's fashionable Mayfair into a wonderland of flares and lights, she sat next to Princess Amelia, outrunners and footmen guiding the elaborate carriage to the house of the Duke of Rochfort. Tonight she and one other accompanied the princess. Travelling in state, one might say.

The duke was celebrating the betrothal of his daughter to the second son of the wealthy Marquess of Strenshall. Imogen was beginning to get society's great and good sorted out in her mind, but they still made her head spin, with their different relationships and their alliances. The princess barely explained anything, probably assumed that "Everybody" knew, or everybody who mattered, at any rate. Well, Imogen didn't, and consequently she kept her head down and her remarks on the bland and uninteresting side. Better than causing unintentional offence. She knew from her own life that the threads connecting people were varied and not always obvious.

The duke was a consequential man. When Imogen curtseyed to him, his bow was precisely calculated, and for a provincial with no title, she merited barely a nod. As the princess's maid of honor she deserved a little more, but not much. However he did welcome her to his house and introduce her to his wife, who in turn, with the princess's permission, drew her away to introduce her to other people.

She had the felicity of being asked to dance by the son of the Marquess of Strenshall, the Earl of Malton. Almost she could wish that Lord Malton was on her list, but alas, no titled gentlemen featured.

He had a seductive twinkle to his dark eyes, and as soon as he'd secured her hand, bore her off. "Are you truly anxious to dance, ma'am? I have been busy all day and dinner was a fraught affair. Suffice it to say I ate next to nothing. Consequently, I admit that I'm famished. Would you care for a morsel of supper?"

"I can't think of anything else I'd prefer." She tried to be more fervent, but the food at Richmond wasn't the hearty fare she was used to, often served cold, because of the distance of the dining room from the kitchen. Even if this food was cold, at least it was meant to be that way.

He leaned closer. "*Anything?* Be careful with your reply, Miss Thane, for I'm a man of my word."

She understood his meaning at once and had to suppress her giggle. Most indecorous. "Anything," she said firmly, glancing up at his face. His eyes gleamed with mischief. This man was dangerous to her gravity.

He took her to the next room, where an elegant supper was laid out. Although she wanted to fall on the viands, she had to accept a plate and one or two delicate pastries. A glass of cold white wine completed all she dared let herself accept.

Finding a quiet corner, he sat, placing his well-filled plate at the center of the small table. "We will share this one. Yes, I know, women are supposed to eat like birds, but that's only a myth, you know, and I would wager that after a week in the royal household, you are starving."

"How do you know?" she said, forgetting her resolve to act elegantly. This man drew out the worst in her, invited her to mischief.

A group of people entered the room and one laughed loudly, drawing her attention. They were beautifully dressed, a fact that could not but imprint itself on her first, but they were also lively. Wistfully she wondered what it would be like to belong to such a group. But then, no. Her life led in another direction.

The man with her groaned. "Eat up," he said. "I think we're about to be invaded. But in answer to your question, I spent a month as a page at court, when I was a boy. My mother saw it as punishment for a particularly egregious crime."

While she ate, he chatted. Apparently he'd lied about his hunger, taking it upon himself to feed her. "I had climbed a tree in the garden and knocked down a bird's nest. Mama had been watching that bird rear its young for a month, so she called me to account for my sin. My father fought for me, but my mother persuaded him that I should be taught how to behave in a manner befitting my station."

He laughed, seemingly bearing his mother no lasting grudge. "I never climbed that particular tree again. If truth be told, I should have known better. I was thirteen at the time, and they'd already begun my rigorous training as a future marquess." He gave an elegant shrug, his green velvet coat mirroring his movements. "I don't think they were too concerned. I'd made a wager with my brother, Val, and he usually received the brunt of their disapproval, so I thought I'd collect some of his reputation for myself."

He glanced up. "In case you were wondering, the reprobate approaching us is Val. Allow me to introduce you."

With a soft touch of his finger to her chin, he removed a crumb, showing her before he whisked the offending morsel away. So she was laughing when she stood to greet his brothers. She hadn't enjoyed herself so much for a long time.

Since—she looked up.

Right into a pair of blue, blue eyes she thought she'd never see again. The sight paralyzed her with shock.

Lord Malton said he would introduce her to his brother, someone called Val. She couldn't recall the family name of Lord Malton, but someone called Valentinian was on her list. Surely there weren't many people called Valentinian in London.

But this wasn't Valentinian. This was the man she knew as Tony. He'd lied to her.

Her limbs came back to life. With a cry of pain, she whirled around, uncaring who saw her or what they thought, and stormed off. When she spied the princess at the far end of the room, she headed for her, determined to stay with her for the rest of the evening. Tears blinded her eyes, glazed all the beautiful clothes, furnishings and the people who must be staring at her.

He'd deceived her. Another wager with his brother? Had he promised to steal that document and, finding himself in trouble, used her to escape? Possibilities hammered through her head, turning themselves into probabilities. She'd been taken for the worst kind of fool and spent weeks pining for a man who didn't exist. Weeping over him, worrying for him.

What was Julius thinking, to trick her in such a way? Was it all a plot, to get her to agree to let him search for the document? First thing in the morning she'd write a letter revoking permission and send it by the fastest messenger she could find. Damn the expense. They had fooled her, Julius and his damnable cousin. She'd see them both rot in hell. Tony—Val— had been wearing expensive fashionable attire, the lace at his wrists alone worth a year of Young George's wages. He wasn't a poor soldier. He'd seduced her, God rot him.

How stupid could she be? When she got back to her room, she'd stick a pin in that damned list and take the one it hit. As long as it was no relation of his.

Shoving past someone, ignoring the yelp of anger, she reached the princess's side just as that lady turned around. "Why, Miss Thane, you appear a little disheveled. Is everything well with you?"

Instead of yelling, "No! A man I thought cared for me turned out to be the worst kind of liar!" she forced a smile and bowed her head. "A trifle warm, ma'am, that is all. I came back to see if there was anything you required."

"I don't think so. Why, here is someone I should introduce you to." She leaned closer and murmured, "He is one of the gentlemen on your list. I had hoped to meet some of them tonight. Better than choosing by name alone, eh?"

Just as if he'd given her a great treat. Bracing herself, she turned to face her nemesis, the man she had given her virginity to, the man she would have done anything for—until five minutes ago.

Tony—Valentinian—was wearing blue. Gorgeous, expensive blue, a dark blue heavy ribbed silk, lined in extravagant white. His waistcoat was white, too, embroidered with silver and spangles, fastened with buttons that glittered. Probably crystals, although this magnificence could command diamonds. He wore a formal snowy white wig over his natural dark hair. But he was unmistakably the man she'd kissed, caressed, and removed her clothes for.

His eyes gleamed as brightly as the pin at his throat that fastened the neat folds of his snowy neckcloth. His mouth, currently set in a firm line, was the one she'd kissed so passionately.

Her betrayer and the man she still wanted with far too much need. She should turn her back, but that would lead to gossip. She couldn't afford gossip.

Oblivious to the daggers glares Imogen shot at Tony, the princess introduced them.

"Miss Thane, may I present to you Major Antoninus Beaumont? Major, this is Miss Imogen Thane, lately arrived in London. I believe you may have something in common."

The final arch response brought Imogen back to earth as Tony bowed to her, his gestures far more graceful than she'd imagined him capable of. She frowned. "I thought you were Valentinian Shaw."

"What? No. Oh!" His voice was the same, deep and warm. "He's my cousin. I was with him when Marcus—Lord Malton—offered to introduce us."

Her jaw dropped. "So you really are Tony?"

"I really am." He glanced around. "Miss Thane, would you care to take a turn around the room?" He turned his attention to the princess and bowed. "Your protégée appears a trifle—warm. Perhaps a drink would help, or a short stroll."

"Indeed I was just remarking on her appearance myself. Pray do take her." The princess smiled warmly. "Take your time. Major Beaumont, I have not seen you at Richmond yet. I have some horseflesh I think you'll want to examine. I'd appreciate your opinion."

"Your highness, you are a complete hand, the consummate matchmaker," he said gravely, and the princess went off into a peal of laughter. "I appreciate, however, your kind offer."

Holding out his arm, he appeared the most elegant follower of fashion. Imogen laid her hand on his arm, since he seemed to expect it, and when he walked away, she went with him.

"I thought—" she broke off. He'd said he was a humble soldier. Well, she'd mentally added the "humble" part. But surely he wasn't wealthy enough to afford what he was wearing. "Where did you get your clothes?"

He stifled a laugh. "My tailor has a shop on Bond Street. I fear I don't wear the military get-up since I sold out, although I'm still entitled to use my rank. Compelled, almost."

"But I thought—"

"We will discuss what you thought in a moment, if you please." He led her through to the supper-room, but they didn't stop, other than to collect a glass of wine.

They went through the door at the far end. Here groups of people were sitting and talking. A few looked his way and he smiled and nodded, but didn't stop. The next room contained a state bed. Imogen knew enough to realize nobody ever used the bed, and in any case, some people stood around in here, too, though they were looking at the furnishings.

"The further along the enfilade you go the more privileged you are."

She bit back her response that she didn't give a fig for the enfilade.

He continued smoothly, displaying all the town polish she'd thought him incapable of. "This being a town house, this is where it ends. Except that there's a small cabinet room here." He opened a door and ushered her in, his hand at the small of her back.

He produced a key and locked it. "The best thing about attending a ball in a relative's house, or a soon-to-be one, is that you know your way around. One of the best things about soldiering is that it gives you some skills not usually associated with a gentleman's education." He spoke smoothly, but a slight tremor marred his tones.

Normally she'd consider this a charming little room that contained a small sofa, a table, and an elaborate cabinet. "This is where the duke keeps his special treasures. We will not, if you please, waste our time with them."

He turned her, so she faced him. His hands were warm on her elbows, while he drank her in greedily with his eyes, his gaze roaming over her face, down her body until she flushed with self-awareness. With a groan, he hauled her close and slammed his mouth down on hers.

This was the Tony she knew, the man who'd shown her the path to infinite passion in that little room under the Long Gallery. Taken straight back there, she responded, her mouth opening to admit his thrusting tongue. Their clothes were too elaborate for her to feel much except the power of his body, but she had no doubt that his cock had risen to meet her softening cleft.

Tears sprang to her eyes, even through her passion. She could not allow him to play her like a fiddle. Had to resist. Planting both hands against his chest, she pushed. He didn't go far, but at least her action broke their kiss.

"Now what, sweetheart, was all that about?"

She drew back her hand and, with all the force she could muster, brought it flat across his face.

His yelp of pain and shock went a small way to assuaging her confusion and distress.

"Why didn't you tell me you were a major?" Spinning away from him, she strode to the cabinet and stared a small bird done in carved stones, willing her tears to subside. "'My tailor is in Bond Street?' And why didn't you tell me your real name or how wealthy you obviously are? You fooled me properly, sir, and I should thank you for opening my eyes to the world!"

Driving her hand into her pocket, she dragged out the list and screwed it into a ball, hurling it into his face. He had one hand to his cheek, his eyes shocked, but he automatically caught the paper and glanced at it. He smoothed the paper open.

"I was so worried about you! Were you really ill, or was that a ruse too? Are you a spy, after all? Is it your nature to lie to people?" When tears of anger filled her eyes, she dashed them away. "I'm ten kinds of idiot. You and your relatives have played me for one and I fell right into your trap."

Was Julius really her friend, or manipulating her to do what he wanted?

Tony took his eyes off her to stare at the list.

"You ruined me, so now I have to do something? Marry you? Is that it?" she demanded.

He flicked a glance at her, his gaze cold. "Do you want answers?"

"Answers?" She nearly spat at him. They'd taken her, used her. They probably wanted her married. What was worse, she'd fallen in with everything they said.

Hurt ripping through her, she shoved past him and stormed from the room. After the first chamber, brought to a sharp awareness of the startled looks shot her way, she slowed her pace and rearranged her pose, putting up her chin and adopting the attitude of slight superiority that was *de rigeur* here.

She went through to the supper room. The delicate scent of fresh-baked pastry made her stomach churn. The small group of people including Lord Malton still sat, chatting, where she'd left them. She didn't want to risk Tony joining them again, so she carried on.

In the ballroom she almost collided with Lord William Dankworth. The only sensible thing she could think of saying was, "Oh!"

With a warm smile, he put his hands on her elbows and held her steady, releasing her before she could object.

The last time she'd seen him was in her house, dragging her and her inamorato out of the little room. Would he betray her? Gossip about where he'd seen her last?

His eyes narrowed, and then he relaxed and swept a bow. "Madam, I beg your pardon. My clumsiness is unforgiveable."

She swallowed past the lump in her throat, fighting to regain some semblance of composure. "Not at all. You're forgiven."

When she moved to walk around him, he subtly shifted to make it impossible.

"I cannot believe that you are even more beautiful in town than you were in the country."

She faced the bull head-on. Better to be gored now than walk away and be skewered in the back.

The last time she'd seen him, he was demanding Tony placed into his custody. "We met under less than propitious circumstances."

He placed his hand on his heart. "A matter that has entirely passed from my mind."

What she'd learned tonight, what had rocked the foundations of her thinking, made her question everything that had gone before. Julius and his not-so-humble relative Tony wanted a mysterious document, one they wouldn't even tell her about, and everything Julius and Tony had done was for that. Tony could have seduced her just to get it.

Lord Dankworth could be speaking the truth. He could have her interests at heart after all.

She didn't know what to believe any more. Instead of distressing her, the knowledge made her furious. How dare they dance around her and keep her from the truth?

So she gave Lord Dankworth, who was, after all, a handsome man, a beaming smile. "I'm here as a maid of honor to Princess Amelia. I should get back to her."

"Congratulations." If he was surprised, he didn't betray it. "Allow me to escort you."

When he held out his arm, she had two choices. Snub him or accept. She was affiliated with Julius, Lord Winterton, and his family members were the enemies of the Dankworths. He probably knew that, and this was his way of thumbing his nose at them.

Damn all of them. She'd do as she saw fit. She accepted his offer with a gracious smile.

"Daring of you," he said with a smile. "Do I address you as Lady Imogen?"

She shook her head. "For goodness' sake, no. I'm Miss Thane."

"Thus warning me not to call you 'my lady.'" His smile turned sympathetic and his gray eyes warmed. "You are amongst friends, my lady. Don't worry, I won't call you that in anyone's hearing." His step halted and he turned to face her more fully. "Would you care to dance, Miss Thane?"

* * * *

Tony stormed out of the small room after Imogen, but he was too late to stop her going off with William Dankworth. He ground his teeth, but he could do nothing.

He wanted to talk to her about that damned list. He'd recognized her writing. Fool that he was, he still had the one she'd made of provisions. Now she was making a list of prospective husbands? He'd show her. He'd claimed her first, and he was damned if he'd stand aside and let someone else have her.

Rather than provide an obvious show for the great and the good, he returned to the supper room in search of alcohol. All he found was wine, but it would achieve his purpose if he drank enough of it.

Someone touched his shoulder. "I'd lay off that if I were you. You'll have an appalling headache in the morning. Much better to stick to good French brandy, dear boy."

Slamming the glass down on the table, he spun around, more than ready to do battle. His cousin Valentinian Shaw backed off, holding up both hands in a gesture of peace, grinning, God damn him.

"Steady, my bully. If that's how you feel, you'd better come with me. There's a little hell not too far from here where you can drink all night. The girls are clean, too."

Tony glared at Val. "I just need the drink, and I can get that at home."

Val frowned. "What maggot has got into your head? You're one of the least volatile of the Emperors usually." His face cleared. "Ah! It's a woman, isn't it?"

Tony shrugged and picked up his glass. "In a way."

Val reached for a glass of his own. Someone had poured several glasses of wine, probably intending to fill the trays that servants were carrying. At this rate there wouldn't be any left. "So is she angry with you?"

"Yes. And now she's off flirting with a Dankworth."

"I should take care what you say." Malton, another cousin, spoke from behind him. The one he'd seen earlier with Imogen. He wished he hadn't interrupted now. "Matters are afoot with that family. We should discuss this in private, should we not?"

"Plenty of places here," Malton said. "But since I suspect it will be a long conversation, maybe we should defer it until tomorrow."

Realizing just what he'd have to confess if he decided to let his cousins into the whole plot, Tony decided to defer the whole thing. Indefinitely. "I want to speak to Julius, but he's out of town. When he gets back, we'll talk."

Malton's mouth hardened and small lines bracketed it. "If it involves Dankworths, yes, we certainly will."

Another time Tony would have pursued the reaction. Malton did not customarily exercise himself with the Jacobite question.

"Should I call Nick?" Malton asked.

"No," Tony said. His brother was the last person he wanted involved in this mess. "We should wait until Julius gets back. His discovery could change everything."

When Tony strode through to the ballroom, intent on leaving the gathering, he spied a sight that enraged him. His brother Nick had claimed her, and now she was looking at him as if he were her savior as they danced together.

Almost he would have paced across the dance floor and snatched Imogen from Nick, but that would give rise to the kind of gossip he preferred to avoid. Gossip grew annoying, especially when it couldn't be ignored.

Instead of leaving, he waited until the dance concluded and his brother led Imogen to the edge of the floor. Where he was waiting. Close by a couch full of matrons fanned themselves and watched. Their gossip quietened to a desultory word or two and then stopped altogether.

Nick smiled. Superior bastard. "Have you met Miss Thane, Tony? Miss Thane, this is my reprobate brother, Major Antoninus Beaumont."

She blinked, and her lovely eyes widened. Tony took great pleasure in performing a perfect bow. "I have had the pleasure of making Miss Thane's acquaintance."

Her eyes widened. "Antoninus—Valentinian—"

"And you've danced with Nicephorus," Nick put in. "That's why people call us the Emperors of London. Our parents took the notion to call us after emperors and empresses of the past." He shrugged. "It amused them. It's less amusing to us at times."

"I can imagine," she murmured.

Fury heated Tony's blood when she wouldn't look at him. Her gaze skittered past his face, even though she met Nick's eyes and smiled.

Nick smiled back. "I told you we were better company than the Dankworths." He cast a glance across the floor to where Lord Dankworth stood with his older brother, Alconbury. Dankworth had the temerity to raise his glass to them, shooting them a taunting grin.

"He was kind and he dances well," she said. "I enjoyed my dance with him."

"But he isn't on your list." Tony infused his voice with all the silky menace he could muster.

He'd read the list in mild astonishment. She actually had a list of men? Why had she made it all second sons? None of them were heads of families. Three of his cousins were named, but none of them the eldest.

One answer occurred to him now. If she married an older son, she'd have to live in his house and leave hers behind. He'd seen her devotion to the beautiful oddity.

In his case, he was only the second son of his mother. He and Nick had different fathers. His mouth firmed when he'd seen her with his brother, handsome, debonair Nicephorus, Viscount Westwood.

He tried not to think of him, especially when he had the one thing Tony wanted above everything else.

Chapter 11

The next day, in the relative security of their London residence, Tony bided his time until he had Nick in the breakfast parlor, which was deserted at this time of day, early afternoon. The table was bare but for a tantalus bearing three decanters. Tony resisted the temptation, although he might have need of them later. As soon as Nick closed the door, Tony turned on him. "Leave Imogen Thane alone."

Nick raised a brow in that infuriated supercilious way he had. "I found her quite charming. Unspoiled, you might say. Also quite astonishingly beautiful."

"She doesn't believe it." Why had he said that? As if his brother needed encouraging.

"Why not?"

Tony shrugged. "How should I know? But she's mine. I will claim her, and I don't want you in my way."

Nick's lip curled. "And how do you propose to do that?"

Tony met his gaze, his eyes so much like the ones he saw in the mirror every morning. "Do you want to try my practical swordsmanship against your fencing lessons?"

Nick's face turned stony. "Any time, brother. But I suggest we avoid such measures as our mother—"

Tony rounded on him leaning over the table that was all that separated them. "Don't hide behind her skirts again! This means more to me than a broken toy or a torn waistcoat." Naming those incidents from his youth only served to open wounds barely healed. And what he'd done to get away from them.

Nick turned away, walking to the end of the table, toward the sideboard. He touched the polished mahogany, tracing the grain, not looking at his brother. "Childhood incidents best forgotten."

"Never forgotten." Tony needed to tell the truth. Since he'd returned from the army they'd skated around the issue, been carefully polite to each other, as men should. Now, when Nick threatened to get between him and the thing he wanted most in the world, he couldn't allow the issue to fester any longer. "Or rather, put in the shade by other things. Do you ever see her?"

"Who?" Nick didn't turn around, but his shoulders stiffened.

"Paulina Spencer."

The name dropped between them like a stone in still water. Here, at the back of the house, little stirred, the silence close to absolute.

"I remember her. Did that rankle, then?"

"Shall we start at the beginning?" Tony recalled Paulina's lovely face, her sweetness and her joy. She was the brightest thing in his life when he was eighteen, but his resentment against his brother went much further than that. Forced together by their relationship to each other and their close ages, the brothers had, nevertheless, never formed a bond. Not surprising really, considering their history.

"How about when you nearly killed me? When you sawed through that branch? I had never known anyone so clever at that age."

"I had to be," Nick said. "Papa would have killed me." His mouth tightened. "In any case, nearly killing you wasn't my aim. Destroying your perfect tree house was. Yes, I resented you. What do you expect me to say? Despite being the second child, you were the darling. My mother doted on you. Your father, not surprisingly, preferred you to me and made me call him Papa. Now it's habit, but at the time I hated it. I had a father, and I bore his name. My mother forgot him as soon as the earth was cold on his grave."

"Come, now, you're hardly Hamlet," Tony scorned. "Or are you saying that my father killed yours?"

That was patently foolish. Thaddeus Beaumont would rather cut off his own arm than cause his mother an instant's pain, even if that meant tolerating his predecessor. He'd adored her for years, but kept at a distance until they were wed.

Nick shook his head. Slowly he turned, facing Tony. He folded his arms. The bleak expression on his face shocked Tony. "I only had my resentment to see me through many years. I received training as the holder of the title. Nothing else. Your father brought wealth. My mother brought prestige. They only had eyes for each other. And you."

"You were never given bad treatment."

Tony met his gaze. Nick didn't look away this time. "No, I was not. But in a thousand little ways, it was made clear to me that you were the favored child. So I resented you, set little traps, tried to get you into trouble. Childish behavior for which I am sorry. It wasn't well done of me. All I can say is that I was bitterly and devastatingly alone. That it hurt."

Tony thought back. Seen from his point of view, it was very different. "I knew you resented me." He pressed his fingertips to the table, watching the tips turn white. "I could do nothing about that. I tried to befriend you. You were my only brother, and I very much wanted the same relationship between us as existed between others we knew."

"Our cousins."

"Exactly."

Their preposterous names had brought the cousins together, but most of the families had warm relationships between themselves. "I always wanted that, too. But you wouldn't let me close."

Nick regarded him closely. "That was a mistake. As was Paulina Spencer."

Paulina had drifted through society like a feather in the wind. She was ethereally beautiful and her sunny nature drew every young man to her that season, and the not too young as well. Tony had fallen as hard as his brother. That was when the real trouble between them had burned brightly. And society had watched them fight for her. Tony had no intention of allowing history to repeat itself.

"Not a mistake, but what we did was. Do you see her at all these days?"

Nick shook his head. "She went into the country with her husband. They married shortly after you—left."

"Joined the army, you mean." Better that than face a trial. Except he'd rushed off too early. That was always his way, to run into things without thinking first. The army had taught him discipline and some measure of forethought, particularly when it concerned others, but the impulsive part of him remained.

Never more so than that morning when he'd dueled his brother at dawn and very nearly killed him. "I thought I'd killed you. There was so much blood."

"Papa smoothed matters over. He would have bought you out."

"I know. I didn't want it." He turned his head and stared out the window to the peaceful garden. In the far distance, a gardener was carefully pruning roses, his mother's favorite flower. The garden here was replete with them, as was their home in the country. His father saw to that. He'd even bought her a rare yellow rose. They adored each other, even after all these years.

"I realized what I'd done wasn't easily to repair. I needed to get away, to change what I did and how I did it." That was the nearest he'd come to apologizing for that day. And his brother deserved the apology. Justice demanded it. "There was no excuse for it."

To his shock, his brother laughed. Actually laughed, the peal breaking the quiet like church bells on Sunday morning. "I was as much at fault as you. I adored Paulina, or I thought I did. And you did, too. That only spurred me to act. I provoked you. I wanted the advantage. When I chose swords for the duel, I knew what I was doing. I'd been taking lessons for months. Extra lessons, with sabers and foils and double handed. I chose the sword and dagger because I knew you'd come at me like a madman. I could take you. Faugh!" His exasperated yell echoed around the paneled room. "I was prepared to kill my brother."

Tony went cold. "I challenged you, but only because I wanted to spite you. I could have avoided it."

"No you couldn't have. I was determined you would not. But you would have chosen pistols. You were always the better shot of the two of us. We shouldn't have met." Nick leaned against the sideboard and folded his arms. "It wasn't Paulina, was it? It was years of resentment boiling up in us. It should have ended in an honorable draw, not the fiasco it turned out to be. If I hadn't fainted from lack of blood, you would never have left. As soon as I came to I realized what a fool I'd been. And to cause such a scandal, to grieve our mother so."

"But you stayed to face the scandal and support her." He still felt bitter about that part, and with a jolt of realization, he knew that disgust with himself rather than rivalry with his brother had driven him.

Nick's voice gentled. "You would have done the same thing. There was nothing to gain by having both of us at home. You proved your worth repeatedly in the army. Dare I say it was the making of you?"

Tony couldn't deny that. He'd borne the burden of being the instigator in the duel for years, made any excuse rather than come home when he was on leave. He'd volunteered for tasks, taken on diplomatic commissions, extra duties, anything, until his father had written to him and positively commanded that he came home when he could. He'd faced London and found the scandal an old story, long superseded by others, and society perfectly accepting of him. He hadn't brought ruin to his family after all. "Yes, it was."

Nick was right. Without the army, Tony might still be a resentful younger sibling, trailing in the wake of his brother. Stepping forward, he held out his hand, the first true gesture of friendship he had ever offered his brother. "We will do better this time."

Instead of shaking his hand, Nick used his hold to drag Tony forward into a quick hug. "We certainly will."

Tony returned the hug, but drew away. It still felt awkward. Although he'd long recovered from his childhood sulk, his relationship with his brother had rarely breached the cordial. But perhaps, after all, there was hope for more. He'd welcome it. "What will you do about Imogen?" he asked.

His brother shrugged. "Is she another Paulina?"

The notion repulsed him. Paulina had been an excuse, a way of challenging his brother. He felt entirely differently about Imogen. "Paulina was pretty, but she didn't have a great deal between her ears. She's the perfect biddable wife, and she is much better off where she is." He shook his head. "I'll fight for Imogen with everything I have. It's not you or anyone else. Without her, I'm nothing." Even while he said it, the truth of the statement hit him hard. "I would fight anyone for her. Not just you."

Even that list didn't stop him. He'd thought about it hard and long, and decided he would just have to be the best person on it.

Nick didn't hesitate. "In that case, brother, you have my blessing and any help I can give you. But you know you might have a hard time of it, don't you?"

Tony snorted and finally reached for the brandy decanter and a couple of glasses. This new understanding deserved a toast. "You don't know the half of it, brother mine." He poured two generous brandies and handed one to Nick. Nick accepted it and clinked his glass against Tony's.

"If you want her, you shall have her."

"If she's willing."

Nick's brow rose. "My, you have changed. Indeed. And if she doesn't?"

"I will do everything in my power to give her what she wants. Whatever that is."

For the first time in their lives, the brothers drank in perfect amity, and something inside Tony stilled and settled.

* * * *

"You have a visitor," the footman told her. "He is waiting for you in the green parlor. A lady is with him." He gave her the salver and she snatched up the cards, but thrust them in her pocket. She knew exactly who it must be. Tony had come at last. He would beg her forgiveness, and she would grant it. Perhaps. She wondered who he had brought as chaperone. His mother.

Wasting no time, she headed for the parlor, but when she fumbled for the cards she realized she must have dropped them on the way. No matter.

A footman stood outside the door to open it for her, as if she were too feeble to do so herself. Her heart soaring, she went inside.

Only to come to a complete halt as the recalcitrant vessel sank the bottom of her pretty satin slippers.

"I came to see how you did," he mother said, "and look who offered to accompany me!"

Imogen bowed to Lord William Dankworth. "I am happy to see you, sir." How had the princess not known he was here? Surely such a prominent Jacobite wasn't welcome here. A suspicion crossed her mind, and she wished she'd not been so careless with the visiting cards. He could have used her mother to get in here. Mrs. Thane had an excuse, a legitimate one, so she could have been his Trojan horse.

Imogen's suspicions were confirmed when, after a desultory conversation, Mrs. Thane excused herself on a spurious excuse. "I will return in ten minutes. No less, now!" She shook a finger in a roguish gesture, one Imogen instantly disliked. The motion appeared strange on her normally stately mother.

"Perhaps I should go with you," she said.

"No indeed!" Her mother replied. She bridled, her hand tightening on her fan. "I will ask a servant to show me the way. A female servant."

The necessary was some distance away from this room. Her mother would be fortunate to get there and back in ten minutes. Fifteen and Imogen would leave the room and wait for her. She didn't want to be alone with Lord William.

The moment the door closed behind her mother, he strode across the room to her and took her hands. "Miss Thane."

When she would have curtseyed politely, he held her steady. "No, do not bow to me. I don't deserve it."

Instead, shockingly, he dropped to his knees and gazed up at her. "Miss Thane, you cannot be unaware of the esteem in which I hold you. I have admired you since you first crossed my path in Lancashire, and my devotion has not wavered."

Oh, no. Not that. But it was. This man wanted to ask her to marry him. This wasn't the first marriage proposal Imogen had received, but when Paul had asked, it was with much less pomp and a lot more friendliness.

Lord William had dressed in brocade and gold, the myriad buttons on his coat and waistcoat all gleaming with it. His red coat was exceedingly fine, if not to Imogen's taste. She preferred something simpler than figured velvet. He'd removed his hat, and his white wig gleamed with order and softness.

He gazed into her eyes and drew first one and then the other of her hands to his lips. Imogen stood frozen with shock.

"Miss Thane, I can stand by no longer and vie for the heart that rightfully should be mine. I will cherish you above all others for the rest of my days. Please accept my hand in marriage. Let me call you mine."

Imogen's first response was to snatch her hands away from his grasp. She barely refrained from rubbing her palms together. Lord William was such a handsome man she didn't know why she should dislike his touch so much, but she did. The thought of him stroking her, having the right to take what he wanted, to touch every part of her body, repulsed her so violently that she felt slightly sick.

She recalled the words she should use now, made sure of them. "Lord William, I'm very sensible of the honor you do me. I deeply appreciate your words." Irritation rippled through her. "Please get up."

Gracefully, he did as she asked.

"Sir, I fear I cannot accede to your most flattering offer."

"Why not?" he asked, his voice low. "Are you promised to another?"

If only she were! She would have given anything to be Tony's intended at one point. Considering the haste with which she'd come here, she probably still wanted that in her heart of hearts.

But he was not here. This man was. "No," she confessed. "But I am of a mind to end my days a spinster."

The tight muscle at the corner of his mouth relaxed. "This is not a hopeless cause. I will consider this the first stage in my siege to your heart, for I am determined to have you, and soon. I burn for you, Imogen. May I call you that?"

She was about to tell him no, when with a great rattling of the doorknob, her mother returned. She was pink in the face. Either she'd been listening at the door or she'd run back from the necessary. She looked from one to the other of them. "May I take it…?"

Of course she'd fall in with Lord William's plans. She wanted Imogen for him, had shown him great favor at Thane Hall.

"No, Mother, you may not."

Lord William watched Mrs. Thane whiten, her lips compress. "I will court her," he said, with a teasing glance at her. "The lady is shy, which is her privilege, and like a knight of old, I must court and woo her."

"Would you give us a moment?" her mother asked in a frozen voice.

Lord William acquiesced and quit the room in indecent haste.

"Take him," her mother said. It wasn't a request. "You won't get a better offer."

It depended what she meant by 'better.' But Imogen had no intention of entering into a marriage with him. "Lord William is of a good family, but not with our background. His wife must be beyond reproach, and from a loyal family. Why would he want me?"

Her mother made a sound of disgust, clicking her tongue. "He wants you precisely because of who you are. And because he can keep you safe. He assures me that he loves you with a devotion you will not find anywhere else. I would say that's enough. A title, a fortune, and a handsome man is more than most women find. I'll tell him you have changed your mind and overcome your coyness." She turned to leave.

"No," Imogen said. How could her mother do this to her? "I will merely reject him again."

"No, you will not." She turned back and paused to rearrange her skirts, which were in disarray from all the turning around. "I demand it. I don't wish to live in that old ruin any longer, or to remain separated from society."

"Don't," Imogen said. "I don't need you at Thane Hall. You've never liked it. Find a comfortable house in Lancaster and move there."

Her mother's pale eyes opened wide. "When I could have a house in town? I think not, Imogen. You have enough fortune and looks to snare a prize, and Lord William is that prize. Seize him up before he is gone."

Imogen clasped her hands tightly together. "No, Mama. I will not marry him. I can't stop him courting me, but I can stop him visiting here. The princess will be displeased when she discovers who has called. I said no."

Mrs. Thane's face became a perfect smooth mask, and Imogen sighed in relief. The cold treatment was infinitely better than a tantrum. "You will not reject him again. It is true that he is less than welcome here, but he is more than welcome in other places. Other courts."

Of everything she could have said, that was the one that would firm Imogen's mind the most. "I will not spend the rest of my life chasing after a lost cause for an ungrateful man and his son. I will live in my house and be thankful that at least this remains to me." She swept around and went to the window, pretending to peruse the view outside. "You must be anxious to reach town before nightfall. Don't let me detain you." Just as if she'd been taking lessons in haughtiness from the princess.

Imogen was proud of herself. She'd stood for what she wanted, and at least for today, the fight was over.

* * * *

It rained for the next two days, but the one after proved dry, if cold. Perfect weather as far as Imogen was concerned. It meant the fussier maids stayed indoors when the princess took her brisk morning walk, and when she declared her intention of visiting the stables, Imogen could cry off. Having stayed in for the last two days, brooding over Lord William, worried that Tony wouldn't contact her ever again, she was glad of the potential exercise.

A page dropped a letter on the tray that she had her early morning tea and toast on, and she wanted time to decide what to do.

She read the note twice. It read the same way both times.

"I would appreciate an opportunity to talk to you. Please don't be afraid I will do anything you do not want, but matters are unresolved between us. For both our sakes, please come to the corner of the park, by the great sycamore tree at ten. I will wait. Forever, if I have to."

He'd signed it with his initial. Not the formal A, but the T she knew him by.

What could she do? Of course she'd meet him, and with such different spirits to the way she'd met Lord William! That tree afforded a deal of privacy, especially since the princess had refused admission to the park to the general public. That early in the morning few people would be there. And it was less particular than meeting indoors, in a private room. That was considerate of him.

She extolled the beauty of the park to the princess. "It appears to its advantage in all seasons. I love to walk in it and enjoy nature."

"Enjoy," the princess said magnanimously. "Do not stay outside too long. Return to your duties by eleven, if you please. I wish for your company at breakfast." Princess Amelia followed the custom of having something light when she awoke and eating a substantial breakfast later in the morning, after she had completed her initial tasks.

Imogen had been used to doing something similar in the country, but her companions in Lancashire were often local visitors and members of her household. Sometimes she missed that.

Her stomach churned, making her glad she only had bread and butter and tea in it. What if he didn't come? She'd have a walk, she told herself stoutly. Hunt for daffodils, see if she could spot a rabbit or a deer. And what if he meant a different tree? The rangers had planted new small trees. Did he include them? No, he'd said "great" sycamore. She knew the tree.

Her heart in her mouth, she walked to the edge of the wood, where a hedge obscured the view from the house and the road. Several trees were ranked here, burgeoning green buds, ready for the orgy of summer that would arrive all too soon. And the large sycamore, its gnarled old trunk wide enough to hide a pair of lovers if they stood close together.

The leaves were coming in, fresh green dotting the remnants of the old papery leaves of the previous season. They'd grow, providing a blanket of green cover for summer showers and the wings that would spin down in the autumn.

Where would she be then? Back home, or somewhere new? Would they insist she stayed until the end of the season in June? It seemed so far away. Her estate would be fruitful, hurtling toward harvest time in the autumn. She wanted to be there, to walk between the sheaves of corn, the piles of fruit waiting for the maids to bottle them or turn them into jam. The best blackberries grew on the lea, near the hut where she'd found a wounded Jacobite…

She halted her thoughts right there. Living through that time again made her eyes tear up, and her stomach, already stirring nervously, tighten. At this rate she'd be ill. She'd always shaken off illnesses but this—at the thought of what her nervous stomach could mean, she stopped and lifted her head, staring at the cloud-scattered sky while she took some deep, cooling breaths.

When arms went around her waist she nearly screamed, but her sense of preservation told her she knew that embrace.

Swallowing, she turned around. Into him and his sweet, welcoming kiss. No time to think, or to reject. She sank into him, as she always did when he kissed her.

He opened her mouth with a flick of his tongue, hungrily plunging and caressing. His hands roamed her back, one rising high until he found a gap between her fichu and her neck. He stroked her bare skin with one finger while he kissed her. He might as well have had his hand on her bare breast. Shivers of desire rippled up and down her spine, and she pressed her body close to his.

They kissed like people starved, until she recalled herself. She wasn't pleased with this man. She was supposed to hold herself aloof. With an effort of will, she spread her hands on his chest and pushed away.

At first he ignored her puny efforts, but when she wrenched her mouth away from his, he opened his eyes. Bewildered blue stared into hers, and then he jerked away, releasing her so abruptly that she nearly tumbled over. He rubbed his hand over the back of his neck as he stepped away. "I'm so sorry. That is, I am and I'm not. I truly didn't mean to do that, but you—you overwhelm me. Your exquisite perfume enters my nostrils and I'm lost. Oh hell, I don't know. I'm no poet."

She laughed, more shocked than amused. "I'm not wearing any perfume."

"You don't need any. Your sweet self is intoxicating enough." Now he laughed, awkwardly. "I'm a coxcomb. Tell me to leave. I meant to talk to you, that's all. We do have things to say, do we not?"

"Yes." She took a pace back, putting distance between them. Her heart pounded and her breasts heaved with her effort to pull air into her lungs. "Yes we do."

"You made a list."

"It's not my list." Had he thought she'd compiled it? "How on earth would I know all those people? I haven't even met them all yet, although the princess is determined that I should."

"What do you mean, not your list? It's in your hand."

She paused, her mind working, and then propped her hands on her hips, jutting her chin forward belligerently. "What, did you think I cold-bloodedly made a list of suitable candidates for my hand?" What kind of mercenary woman did he take her for?

He shook his head. "It's not unknown for young ladies to do so. In fact, I think their mothers often do it." He regarded her with a bleak stare. "But I hadn't thought you would do it. I suppose I should be glad you remembered to put my name. But why only younger sons? Do you not wish for a title?"

She didn't know whether to laugh or cry. Did he not realize she'd been prepared to break her lifelong resolve for him? "I didn't compile the list. The King did. I merely made a few copies, so I wouldn't lose it." She swallowed. "I'm to choose one of them by"—a shock made her realize how fast time was passing—"the end of the month." Barely two weeks away. "He is considering reviving my father's title and bestowing it on whomever I marry."

He went completely still, only his breathing moving his dark blue waistcoat, making the cut steel buttons glitter in the cold light of the sun. He blinked. "He is?" He barked a laugh. "Of course. Second sons. I'll have to tell my brother. He won't be amused at being cut out."

"This morning the princess informed me that I might add Lord Westwood to the list if I wished." The news hadn't pleased her, because more people meant more choice. She didn't want more choice. "He has a viscountcy, so my father's title would lift him in rank."

"I doubt he'd be pleased to hear that. His father would not be pleased, either." A smile made his lips twitch. "Especially the fortune that comes with the viscountcy. However, if you chose him, the lesser title would exist in a courtesy title to your oldest child." His chin firmed. "Not that you're going to marry him."

"And why not, pray?"

"Because you're going to marry me."

Breathless, she glared at him, trying to get some air into her lungs. A blackbird sang in the hedge. "What? Do I not get a say?"

"It seems not." His eyes narrowed. "Is that why you thought I was Val?"

"I beg your pardon?"

"My cousin, Valentinian Shaw?"

"Oh." Yes, she had mistaken him. "I thought if you lied about your position in society, you'd do it about your name, too. I thought you'd completely betrayed me. I thought—"

"Oh no!" He took a step forward and then stopped abruptly while air still separated them. He fumbled in his coat pocket and drew out a piece of paper, crumpled and torn in places. The copy of the list that she'd hurled at him that night at the ball. He'd kept it. Warmth spread through her. He read from the list. "Ivan Rowley. Augustus Vernon. Valentinian Shaw. Antoninus Beaumont. Do you see the similarity in the names?"

Staring at him, she thought and thought. They didn't start with the same letter, had different numbers of syllables, the surnames were different. The truth hit her with the force of a brick between her eyes. "Your cousins. They're the Emperors of London. I hadn't realized. I'd thought you were called that because you were powerful."

He smiled at her, gently and dropped the crumpled list back in his pocket. "Yes. That's why people call us that preposterous title. Our names, not our positions. Our parents, specifically in my case, my mother, called her children after emperors of the past. One boy, the Duke of Kirkburton, and his five sisters. The names brought us together. Perhaps that was why they did it, although my own mother always claims it was just foolish fancy, and when one did it, the others followed suit. It's flattering that so many of us are on your list, since the King compiled it."

She glanced away. Their connection was too potent for her to think properly. "He doesn't want the Jacobites in my part of the country, and he wants me to marry a loyalist."

He nodded. "Understandable. Lancashire has caused several problems to him of late." He lowered his voice. "Shall we oblige them, Imogen?"

He was doing it again. Asking her to marry him without actually asking.

Time for her to speak, to tell him what she really wanted. "I never wanted to marry." She met his gaze frankly, watching for his reaction. But she wouldn't shirk telling him. "I have my estate. It's in trust, but the trustees never interfere. I love it. It's the right size for me, and I say what happens there. I don't want to lose that. I worked hard to ensure I didn't create trouble, that I could enjoy what I had without attracting attention."

He reached out and put his hands on her shoulders, his warmth seeping through her shawl, which had slipped when he kissed her. He pulled the folds up in a cherishing way, making her long to go into his arms, to let him hold her and care for her. Just as if she didn't have a mind of her own.

"They were never about to allow that," he said gently. "My sweet, do you not know?"

"Know what?"

He bit his lip. "When do you have to be back with the princess?"

"On the hour."

As if on cue, the nearby church rang the three quarter hour. "We have no time to talk about it now, but you need to know something important." His mouth firmed. "You have a right to know. Believe me, I will tell you, and soon. When may I see you again?"

"I—I don't know." She still didn't entirely trust him. "Why didn't you tell me you were rich and important?"

A wry smile curved his lips. "I'm not. Important, that is. But I couldn't tell you, or my purpose in the district." He carried on. "If any scandal of that kind touches my father, his whole business could be suspect." He paused. "When Julius arrived, we agreed to keep my identity a secret." He paused. "I asked him not to. I wanted to tell you myself. I had no idea that fever would overtake me and delay my arrival in town."

"He told me you were a relative. He said he had a lot of relatives, and until I saw you at the ball I thought you were a distant one, or a poorer one."

His smile turned warm. "I didn't want anyone to know. I had hopes of getting away with my identity as a common soldier. Nobody need know an Emperor had visited and our name would remain unblemished. After Julius arrived, we agreed to keep my identity a secret until I was away from your house. Besides, finding you with me, Antoninus Beaumont, would have forced our marriage. I didn't want to do that."

Her mouth dropped open. "You didn't?" But he'd proposed to her.

He shook his head slightly. The blackbird sang some more. "I wanted you to choose. I still do." He bit his lip, the sharp teeth grazing the soft skin. "The king made a good selection with that list. Every man on it will take care of you. They are all worth your consideration." He tugged her hands, and she took a step closer to him. "I just wish you would not. I want you to choose me. But *choose* is the word. I have no wish to force you into anything you do not wish for. I will not take part in any coercion." He closed his eyes in a slow blink. "I'll call on you and make it clear the purpose is to receive your answer to my proposal. That way we'll have a private interview and I can give you the information you need before you make your decision. You're still free to reject me. I don't want you to."

"Why?"

"Do you need me to tell you?"

His gaze said so much, open and yearning, but she was afraid to take the leap. Her reasons remained the same, that she'd lose herself in him. She didn't know how he'd run her estate or what kind of person he was in public. Her mind ran on a track she'd known before, her dilemma between heart and mind as difficult as ever. "I-I—"

"Just one more kiss," he said. "Please."

How could she resist that plea when she wanted it so much herself? Heedless of her wet shoes and the hem of her gown, which had soaked up enough of the early dew and damp that remained in the shadow of the hedge that it was touching her knees, she stepped forward into his arms.

They folded around her, and his mouth came down on hers. Gently this time, he eased her lips apart, and when he stroked her with his tongue, the caress felt almost reverent. He deepened the kiss slowly, his lips working over hers, his tongue invading her mouth with sweet thoroughness. She slid her arms as far around his waist as he could under his coat, the silk lining warmed by the heat of his body. When he sucked on her tongue, she slid it into his mouth, and his responding groan reverberated deep into her, invading her so thoroughly that she never wanted to separate.

She tasted him, his unique flavor remembered and welcomed. He'd entered her world and he'd never leave. Whatever happened next, this part of him belonged to her.

The way she felt when he held her, when he made love to her, frightened her. She needed to know he felt the same way, but he seemed in control, always. He helped her to make love, to kiss, to accept intimacies she couldn't imagine feeling from anyone else. She was a novice and she didn't like that, not when she'd run her life her way for so long.

He crushed her closer when the kiss deepened, and they became ravenous, eating at each other. But he softened and finished the kiss, smiling down at her. "I will see you tomorrow, sweetheart. Would eleven o'clock be too early?"

She felt obliged to remind him she wasn't in her own household. "The princess doesn't receive anyone before two, so don't come before then. You may come, unless I send you word not to."

"Don't." He dropped kisses on her eyes, her nose, and finally her mouth. "Please don't. Take this with you." He placed a kiss in the center of her palm and folded her fingers around it. "Keep it safe."

Chapter 12

"So you wish to meet this man?" The princess was in a fine mood, her smiles almost as alarming as her frowns. "And you will accept him?"

She didn't have much choice, but she didn't want the answer assumed. "I will listen to him, ma'am, and give him my answer. Should I do it before a chaperone?" The idea had its merits. She imagined the scene—a woman sitting quietly in the corner, perhaps with her embroidery and Tony forced to make a formal proposal. On one knee, barely touching her hand, begging for the privilege of her hand in marriage.

Oh, yes. Perhaps she should do that. Except she had to discuss matters with him that were most definitely not for the ears of anyone else.

Fortunately the princess waved aside her query. "Of course not, girl." She leaned back and lifted her foot to prop it comfortably on the footstool. Imogen sprang forward to help, but the princess shook her head. "I am perfectly capable of lifting my own foot. Do not fuss." Her smile returned. "Considering the scene my footman carefully did not witness this morning, I presume any duenna might find herself witness to scenes she would rather not see." Her grin broadened when Imogen reddened and clapped a hand to her mouth. "Did you think you were entirely alone? Don't worry, he is very discreet." She paused. "Very."

Shocked, Imogen blinked at her mistress. That comment wasn't innocent. Surely it couldn't mean what she thought. But the princess had a reputation. A persistent rumor insisted that she was a mother, but like many in her situation, the child had been fostered out.

Some ladies introduced "wards" into their houses, particularly widows and independent females who didn't wish to marry. Living the independent life Imogen dreamed of wasn't entirely out of the bounds of possibility. Princess Amelia was living proof of that.

"I saw nobody."

"He had orders not to disturb your privacy." The princess regarded her straightly. "My father bade me take especial care of you, and that I intend to do. You are important in some way. I did not ask why, nor do I wish to know, but I suspect it's a political matter. You are not a great heiress, although your portion is first-rate, and beauty does not usually require special care. However, the king has signified his approval of the men on that list, and one other, Mr. Beaumont's brother. That is all. If Mr. Beaumont was not on the list, you would not have seen him."

The Dankworth family was only significant by its absence.

Awed, Imogen nodded. What was so special about her? Rack her brains though she might, she couldn't think of a single reason why the king would single her out to become a maid in waiting and to have her guarded so carefully. To marry her off to a loyal subject, yes, but her neighbor, Sir Paul, would have done in that case and she need never have left home.

She shared her history with several of her neighbors. It had to be the mysterious document Julius had hot-footed to Lancashire to find. Once he discovered it, she would feel much more comfortable. But what it was, she had no idea.

Here, at Richmond, she was safer from attack. Bringing her here hadn't been an accident or a whim of the princess's, and the burly footmen she'd observed were more than servants. They were guards, and not all of them for the princess.

How could she, Imogen Thane, compare with a princess? Royalty must always have guards and beware of sabotage and attack, even one as removed from the succession as Princess Amelia, but a young woman from a northern county with but one modest estate to her name? Imogen could hardly believe it. Only if whoever wanted her believed her in possession of something important.

She clenched her fists and then deliberately loosened them so the princess should not observe her frustration. She would not let them keep her in ignorance, like a child, for much longer. If Tony knew, he would tell her.

* * * *

At two o'clock, Imogen received the stately visit from the footman with the silver salver, via the princess. The liveried servant took the tray to the princess, who glanced at the card and nodded. The footman paced to Imogen's chair, and she did the same thing. Louisa glanced at her and raised a blonde brow. Imogen didn't respond by even a twitch, but she rose and followed the footman from the room.

The only sounds in the quiet corridor were their footsteps, the footman's measured tread and Imogen's firm step. He took her to one of the smaller parlors and opened the door for her.

Tony sat on one of the two sofas. The coral upholstery threw his grass green coat into charming relief, but while the colors caught her attention for a fleeting instant, his eager strained face retained it.

The footman closed the door quietly. Imogen had no doubt he would remain outside it. If he were tactful, he'd give them some space. If inquisitive, he'd stay by the door, but he wouldn't be able to hear much through that thick piece of wood in any case.

Tony came to his feet and halted, his arms by his sides, his fists clenched. He did nothing to hide his stark, open expression, so eager to see her that her heart turned over. "Well?" he demanded.

"What happened to your polished address?" Warmth rose inside her when she saw his obvious keenness. His cheekbones stood out under his skin, what shadows there were in this room casting them into sharp relief. Mouth set in a taut line, creases at the sides emphasized his strain. That wasn't just because he was on the list. He truly wanted her. She could afford a little gentle teasing.

"I never had any."

Recalling him at the ball, in his silks and lace, Imogen knew he was lying. He could hold his head up high in any company. Pride swelled her chest. "I've seen it."

"Do you want a formal address?" He sounded exasperated, but he swept her a low bow and took her hand when she held it out. He bent over it, his lips not quite touching her skin. "Miss Thane, I have watched you from afar, and I have admired you greatly. I know I am not worthy to share the same room with you, but I beg that you at least listen to my humble request. Would you allow me to bestow my name and riches, such as they are, on you? In short, would you do the honor of accepting my hand in marriage?"

By the end of the speech, she was giggling.

He glanced up at her. His lips had relaxed into a smile. "You are not supposed to laugh. You are supposed to say, 'Sir, I am grateful for the honor you do me. I must request that you address my mother and guardians before you speak to me again.' But don't. Please, don't."

Now she laughed aloud, in sheer pleasure. "I don't have to ask anyone. I may marry whomever I choose. As long as he's on the list the king gave to me. Since you are—" She couldn't hold back a moment longer. "Yes, yes I will marry you, Tony."

"Thank God." White-faced but smiling, he rose from his bow, as gracefully as he'd swept into it, and took her into his arms. "I can see I have an armful of trouble here. But never was trouble so welcome." Bending his head, he kissed her.

No gentle courtly kiss this. He opened his mouth over hers and she responded by letting him in. She leaned against his shoulder, knowing she could do this whenever she pleased, her tension melting away as he showed her how much he wanted her. Cupping her cheek, he deepened the kiss, holding her the way he wanted her, his tongue a delicious invasion in her mouth. She moaned, the small sound urging him on. She tasted him, his flavor both familiar and unexplored in a way she couldn't explain, except that this kiss was the start of something, not the end.

When they'd parted in Lancashire, she hadn't known if she'd ever see him again alive. In London, she thought him capable of the most devious behavior. Now, she didn't care. She just wanted him to carry on kissing her.

He lifted his mouth from hers. His lips were reddened, as hers must be, and his eyes slumberous, the lids half-closed. "Sweetheart, you've made me the happiest man alive."

She laughed, happier than she'd been for a long time. "I doubt that."

"I can't imagine anyone happier."

She daren't speculate on what that meant. Because he wanted her, or maybe something else? And she still hadn't told him her news. She didn't know how he'd feel about that. "How do you feel about children?"

"I don't mind children." He laughed down at her. "In our situation they are probably inevitable." Before she could say any more, he kissed her again, and she lost herself in him, gladly giving up sense and reason for this. She could wallow in his kisses all afternoon. But she had to talk to him. Putting her hands on his shoulders, she eased him away.

He gazed down at her, a question in his eyes. "There's something else?"

How did she tell him? She had no experience in conveying news that was so personal to someone of the opposite sex. Before now, men to were either servants or visitors, both to be held at a distance. No father, no brothers to ease her way. She settled for the beginning. "This month—my courses—" She hung her head, rested her forehead against the soft fabric of his coat.

"Sweetheart? Imogen?" His tones grew urgent. "My God!" Carefully, as if she were made of porcelain, he took her to the sofa and eased her down on to it, sitting by her side and slipping his arm around her shoulders. "Are you telling me that you're pregnant?"

Tears misting her vision she lifted her chin. "It's only one month, and so much has happened that it could be something else. It's just that I'm usually so regular—"

"Then we marry sooner rather than later. I was about to suggest that we waited until Julius returned from Lancashire, but in the circumstances, I won't wait."

"I don't want to—"

"I will ask the princess to release you from her service early. We will marry in days." He gazed down at her, his expression inscrutable. "I'll visit Doctor's Commons tomorrow and obtain a special license, and then we may marry. I won't wait, Imogen." His voice grew sterner. "It's my duty and privilege to care for you, never more than at a time like this."

"I-It's not certain," she said. Sometimes women could be mistaken in the first month, or even the second.

"But you said you'd marry me anyway. Do you wish for something grander? Because I will not have people look askance at my child."

"They will anyway."

"They will not dare!" he said so vehemently that he made her laugh. As if he'd take on everyone in London who gave her a speaking glance. From his expression, he might well do that. His blue eyes sparked pure steel.

"If we go into the country they would not." Home. The very notion filled her with happiness. Nothing else mattered, that she could have the man she wanted and the house. "But it will be your house now." Her heart sank. That part of her cherished dream must leave her. Once she married him, her belongings would be his.

"No." He cupped her shoulder, and turned her to face him. "I will take measures to ensure the house is still yours. I'll see a lawyer tomorrow and have that drawn up."

"But I want to live there," she said.

"So do I." He dropped a kiss on her lips. "It's a fascinating place, totally unlike anywhere I've ever visited. To live there would be constant fascination. I can't imagine ever tiring of the place. I have a house, and an estate, somewhat larger than yours, but I've never felt like that about it. It was a convenience. My father bought it for me." His mouth kicked up at the left side. "Will you object to marrying below you?"

She frowned. "What on earth do you mean?" She was gentry, no title, no significant fortune. A daughter of a disgraced peer, nothing more.

"My father is a Cit. Some look down on him, even though he married a viscountess."

"What nonsense!"

He laughed and hugged her. "I agree, particularly since he's richer than Croesus. But he earned his money and continues to work in the City. To some that means he gets his hands dirty."

"I'll wager I get my hands dirtier. It's lambing time now, and I'd be in the thick of it if I were home."

"Do I detect a note of wistfulness? I believe I do." He kissed her forehead. "I'll take you home as soon as I can. Especially with your news. Although the best child care is in London, and I wouldn't have you put in danger for anything."

That consideration made her hesitate, too. Most women who could afford it came to London for their confinement, especially the first, because the best midwives and physicians were here. But enough women had babies in the country for her to be comfortable with that. And she'd be at home. Surely that would ease her concerns. However, she was her mother's only child.

His laughter rang around the room. He didn't seem the least concerned about her news. She'd thought he'd be displeased, especially since he took precautions not to get her pregnant. "You don't mind?"

"Mind? About what? The baby? No, my sweet, my only concern is for your safety at this time. I am ridiculously happy."

* * * *

She was worried. She'd really been concerned that he wouldn't want the baby. If she'd told him before he proposed, he'd probably have abducted her to ensure her compliance. No child of his would be reared by anyone else.

But what they were making here was more than that. Slow warmth kindled in his belly when he recalled that for the next eight months she'd be carrying part of him around with her. Did she know how much that meant to him? How he'd longed for a family of his own, an irrational feeling that he had no way of explaining?

Their trysts in the little secret room had obviously had more results than they'd intended. As he held her, he made plans. They'd marry the day after tomorrow. Today was Tuesday, and ah— "Even the date works in our favor. It's Lent, so we can't marry with ceremony in a church. We must do it quietly and without undue celebration."

"Can we marry at all?" She remembered couples who waited.

"We can and we will," he said firmly. "We'll do it at my house, that is, the house I share with my family when we're in London. We're not allowed to celebrate the occasion with flowers and singing, but we will damned well have flowers and sing if we want to later. In fact, you might get to discover that I have a passable baritone."

He smiled when she did. She had a particularly winsome smile, and she used it far too infrequently. He made a vow to himself to get her to smile more. To make her happier.

But not now. What he had to tell her might mean she lost the happiness from this occasion, but he couldn't keep the secret from her any longer. He had so far respected Julius's request for him to keep the information to himself, but with the wedding brought forward he couldn't in all conscience marry her while she was in ignorance. He had tried to approach the subject a moment ago, but she'd deflected it.

He must steel himself to broach it now. "You are reconciled to this?"

"Yes. I have thought hard and long, and yes."

A pang of sorrow hit him in the solar plexus. He preferred that she accepted him impulsively, because she wanted to, not as the result of long deliberation. However he had her now and he wouldn't let her go. "I promised to tell you something, and it might change your mind. I won't hold you to the acceptance if that is the case. My unpardonable impatience made me demand your answer sooner than I should have done."

Her eyes widened and her mouth dropped open. "What could possibly do that?"

"I'm hoping it will not. But you're not in possession of all the facts."

"What?"

Still holding her, but loosely in case she wanted to draw away, he leaned back on the admittedly comfortable sofa, although the coral color made him feel mildly bilious. He found a cushion and pushed it behind her back. He'd heard pregnant women sometimes had back problems, although he imagined that happened later, when their weight changed. No harm starting now. No, he was putting off telling her. He'd start at the beginning.

She laughed. "Why, can it be that you're flustered?"

He laughed with her, confusion a strange thing to him. "It's you." He trailed his fingers over her shoulder. A shame fabric covered it. Needing to touch her, skin to skin, he took her hand. "Very well. To the meat of the matter." He took a breath and plunged in. "We discovered that the Old Pretender had more children than we had previously supposed."

"What?" Her startled exclamation cut him short. "He—what?"

"You know he married Maria Sobieska in 'nineteen?"

She nodded.

"She left him soon after their second son was born and moved to a convent. She died in thirty-five."

"I know that."

She must have heard that most of her life, but he needed to get the dates sorted out for her. Because she would most certainly not know the next part. "The Old Pretender is a melancholic. He used women to help him with his moods, or so he claimed. So he had other children, legitimate and illegitimate. A monarch has the power to legitimize their children, with the help of Parliament."

"But he isn't a monarch."

"That is a matter of opinion. Of course I agree with you, but others do not. And politics can prove expedient at times. He had one particular mistress, by whom he had a number of children. I say 'a number' because we're not sure exactly how many. His mistress was Maria Rubiero. Have you heard of her?"

Imogen shook her head.

"Not many people have. His counsellors considered it best they didn't. But he was particularly attached to Maria, and it might have been when she discovered this that Maria Sobieska decided to leave him. There were other considerations, of course. They had never particularly liked each other. Maria Rubiero was a beautiful Italian girl who obsessed the Old Pretender. She grew into a clever woman, but she had nobody powerful to work for her. She came from humble origins, but the Old Pretender loved her truly and would have married her had someone not spirited her away until he agreed to the marriage to Maria Sobieska."

She gazed at him in wonder. "Why have I not heard this before?"

"Not many people knew before last year. He had other mistresses, but none as long-lasting as Maria Rubiero. We do not know why he kept her existence secret. Perhaps it was because his wife hated her."

He stroked her hand, caressing her palm with his thumb, as much for his comfort as for hers. "Maria Rubiero kept careful records. She noted the births of her children carefully. She had them as regularly as Barbara Castlemaine did to Charles the Second. She didn't keep the babies because they'd be the center of plotting and intrigue. The Old Pretender never gave her enough money to live in the style she expected. Until he married Maria Sobieska, he didn't have that kind of money. After, he was pouring money into the Cause. Whatever the reason, Maria Rubiero always felt aggrieved and concerned for her babies. There is no evidence that she was a maternally-minded woman, so sending them away may also have been a way of keeping her lover close."

Here it came. He braced himself for her shock. "So she sent her children away with people she could trust, together with copies of their birth certificates and a letter detailing the circumstances of their births. Presumably she intended to use them as pawns. After all the Old Pretender only had two sons by his wife. Daughters are an asset, too, especially to a man as devious as the Pretender."

"Why?" Her voice was thin and quiet.

He squeezed her hand and gave her a reassuring smile. "Because they can be married off to suitable candidates. Allies. And they can strengthen claims, urge causes. Married to a Hanover, they could reinforce the Hanoverian claim to the throne. You see?"

Yes, she saw. Comprehension darkened her eyes. "And the heir to the throne is a boy. An unmarried boy."

"Yes."

Her grip on his hand tightened. Instead of yelping with pain when his bones ground together, he bore it stoically and kept his voice quiet and unthreatening. "So it's good for these children, wherever they are, to be married to other people?"

He hadn't thought of it that way. Too bound up with his own ambitions, he hadn't even considered it, fool that he was. "Yes, I suppose so. Maria Rubiero died in a fire in 1740. As far as we know, all her records perished with her, but she might have kept copies somewhere. Nobody has found them. So the number of her children and where she sent them is lost." He caught a breath.

"I was born in 1730." She had realized the significance of the story and what it had to do with her, then.

Her grip slackened, and she released his hand. He forced himself to lean back and let her go. Never had she appeared more beautiful than she did now, her expression bleak, her eyes sparkling with intelligence and understanding, but her lips still reddened from his kisses. He ached when he realized he might never taste those lips again.

"Yes you were. Imogen, we believe you might be one of those daughters."

"And my parents?"

"Foster parents."

She nodded, her face a picture of regal impassivity. "That explains why my mother has never behaved particularly fondly toward me but insisted on remaining in this country and ensuring I received a proper education. She rarely touches me, you know."

His heart went out to her. His mother had never withheld her affection from either of her sons. Whatever problems the siblings had, they never lacked parental love.

He wanted to reach out to her and hold her with all the possessiveness he had, and he wanted to do it badly, but she might push him away. He would become another problem for her and not the help he wanted to be. "You could be a Stuart. You have some of the characteristics. Your dark hair and eyes and your creamy skin. Maria Rubiero was an accredited beauty, and you are beautiful."

She shook her head, her dark curls bouncing against her neck. Most of her hair was drawn up into a knot at the back, but a few curls were left to tease and hint. He wanted to wind the silky softness around his fingers, use them to pull her to him. He could not. A barrier had sprung up between them, one of his own making. But she was bound to discover it sometime, and he couldn't let her marry him not knowing.

"So the documents Julius went to discover?" Her voice shook at the end.

"Your birth certificate, or the copy of it. And the letter, if it exists. We have only found one illegitimate daughter of the Old Pretender so far, and she had a different mother to yours. But the circumstances of her birth led us to this discovery. And the fact that the Dankworths want it as much as we do, but for different reasons."

"What reasons?"

She'd completely cut herself off from him and it hurt worse than he'd imagined. And he'd imagined pain. Cutting off his arm would hurt less. "They want power. They want control over the children. They are important political pawns that we knew nothing about until very recently. The Dankworths stand less for the Cause than for themselves. If they could marry one of the daughters to a son, or discover a son who could challenge the succession, they would retain their importance. Or gain control over a Stuart woman who would marry young Prince George. And there are other factions. Rome, for instance, and France. And the Stuarts themselves. This could threaten the position of the Young Pretender and his brother. It could rock the foundations of the Stuart dynasty."

"But they need one of these so-called pawns."

"Yes, they do."

"I see. And does Princess Amelia know this?"

He shook his head. "I don't think so. But the king surely does. He wants you safely married to someone who will not be a threat. So do his ministers."

Alarm widened her eyes. "Do they know about me?"

"I don't know. Some of them must have an inkling. But there is no proof, and while there is no proof it's hard to do anything."

"Let the marriage go forward. Ours."

Oh now his heart broke. Now he wanted to go back to when she kissed him so sweetly, went into his arms because she wanted to, not because of duty. He had no doubt it was duty made her say that, duty that pushed her to it. "We can wait until Julius returns."

"No. We must do this quickly. Especially with my—other—news."

"Very well. I'll make the arrangements."

"I'll talk to the princess and see if she will release me early, but we must marry anyway."

He got to his feet when she did and met her gaze. "I'll always do my best for you, Imogen. Please believe that."

"I do."

* * * *

Imogen didn't cry. What would be the point? It wouldn't change anything. She was a political pawn, someone who mattered more for *what* she was than *who* she was. Even the man she had imagined loved her was working for his family. He'd come to her house in search of the certificate, and he'd found her instead. Was it all a plan? Recalling the way he kissed her, made love to her, she didn't know, couldn't tell. But when he learned of her possible pregnancy, he'd wanted to even more.

He'd told her. That was an honorable thing to do. All that interminable afternoon while she sewed and listened to the others gossip she went over the events over and over again.

At the end of the afternoon, the princess formally dismissed her and gave her a present to thank her for her time. "If you wish to return, my chamberlain will be happy to speak to you," she said.

But for fate and the decisions of a man who was now, astoundingly, her ancestor, the scene could have happened the other way about. Imogen was fervently thankful that it was not. She had no desire to become a woman argued over, who had to take her personal pleasures in secret, whose actions were discussed and watched all the time.

Princess Amelia was welcome to it. Imogen would take her modest estate and her life—and her handsome husband-to-be.

He didn't appear at all when she left Richmond, but a carriage waited for her with an abundance of outriders in Julius's livery colors of blue-and-silver. Her now generous wardrobe would be packed, supervised by her maid. She felt like a fraud when she sat on the soft leather upholstery and let them drive her to Julius's house, where she'd be married. She'd move to Tony's house.

It didn't seem possible. But she was someone who mattered now, although in herself she felt like exactly the same person she'd been before. Even if she wasn't. Even if she was royalty. This new knowledge wouldn't turn her against the Hanovers. They had worked hard and helped to create stability and prosperity out of the turmoil and near bankruptcy of 1688.

Tony sent his apologies to the house, explaining he was busy drawing up an equitable contract and waiting for the license. But he asked her to be ready the next morning at ten.

Ten. That was it, then. Married for life to a man she didn't really know, but a man who was the father of her unborn child—if there was an unborn child. She still wasn't sure. She had none of the much-vaunted sickness that pregnant women were supposed to suffer. No other symptoms associated with pregnancy. Anxiety seemed a more reasonable cause of her missed courses. But Tony had seized on her stammered explanation and not allowed her to discuss it. Not that she'd have known how. Her experiences of intimacies with men were limited. Tony and—a few snatched experimental kisses with neighbors, glimpses of forbidden passion in meadows and copses. That was all. And the books in her library, which had formed the greater part of her education.

Claiming exhaustion, when she arrived at Julius's she took to her room and refused to see anyone. She sent her maid to tell them she had a headache and she wanted to be fresh and fit in the morning for her wedding.

A maid brought dinner on a tray. She sent it back untouched. Her maid found a gown for her. She approved it without paying it too much attention. Tony didn't come. Neither did her mother. The latter was more telling, because at least Tony had sent his excuses. She didn't know if her mother was avoiding her or if she just didn't care, but either way, the absence hurt her, and she'd never felt so alone. She would demand a reckoning after she'd attended to business tomorrow. Her mother would answer for her silence all these years. Determination added strength, and she no longer felt like weeping. She spent the rest of the day attending to business, reading the letters from her man of business. Everything was well.

She blinked awake when light filtered through the drapes at her window. She could have sworn she hadn't slept all night, but the candle that had guttered its way down to a stump and extinguished itself stood as the lie to that.

Her maid knocked and entered, bearing a tray of food. She surprised Imogen by imploring her to eat. "You must have some sustenance, ma'am, otherwise you'll faint dead away."

That was the first sign that her maid was even human. So Imogen thanked her, sat up, and did her best while Digby supervised the filling of a bath tub in front of the fire. March was in its last half now, and the weather was considerably warmer than when she'd first arrived in London, but she still appreciated the fire.

Digby bathed her and dressed her. Imogen held out her arm for the sleeves, stood still while her maid arranged the skirts over her hoops, sat and tipped back her head for the more than usually elaborate hairstyle. But she refused the powder. "I don't like hair powder unless it's absolutely necessary."

Her maid gave her a scandalized look, but said nothing.

Imogen was wearing an ivory-colored gown, and her hair would form an effective contrast. But more than that, she wanted to retain something of herself, to marry as Imogen Thane, not a princess. Her hair, being dark and lustrous, was one of her glories. The rest took care of itself. She permitted Digby to apply rice powder to her face and a little Spanish rouge to her cheeks.

After clasping her pearls around her neck and adding the matching bracelet to her wrists, she shook back the double lace at her elbows, picked up her fan and declared herself ready.

Her mother had still not asked to see her.

Imogen went downstairs to see her intended waiting for her in the drawing room. Not a muscle twitched as he bowed over her hand. He'd brought others to witness his wedding including his older brother, who he seemed in vastly more cordial terms with than before. They even smiled at each other. And she met his parents, who she had only met briefly at a ball before her service to the princess, and two of his cousins, one with his wife, a serenely lovely blonde lady who her husband, Alexander, Baron Ripley, treated with blatant adoration.

Imogen had once dreamed of such treatment, of a man who would gaze her with love and cherish her next to his heart. Childhood dreams all of them, but Alex and Connie made her glad that at least their dreams had come true.

First she must sign the marriage contract, which she read through twice, although it was a concise document compared to some of the labyrinthine property agreements she'd read before. But he'd done exactly as he'd promised. Her house was hers. He'd accomplished it by retaining her trustees and setting up a new trust, so that although the property passed to him when they married, it was placed immediately back into trust, for her and her heirs.

Her heirs.

Pushing her mind away from that unwelcome thought, at least unwelcome this morning, she declared herself content and signed.

At one point in her life she'd dreamed of marrying in the local church, which had been endowed by one of her ancestors with magnificent brasses and marble statuary, some of which had survived the Civil War more or less intact. She knew every chip, every dent, because she'd taken her turn polishing the place and adorning it with flowers for festivals. Today the flowers in the drawing room were gone in deference to the season. Lent did not allow for celebration.

The gravity of the ceremony reflected her mood. As she repeated the words after the vicar engaged for the purpose, she tried to think about the promises she was making, but the language escaped her, apart from the "with my body I thee worship" part, which seemed embarrassingly personal to repeat in a room full of guests. About twenty people had gathered to watch this momentous occasion. For her, at any rate. For Tony, his life need not change to any significant extent if he did not wish it. But after what he'd done with the contract, neither need hers. She could go home, have her child, and recommence her life. Except that perhaps she'd add a few more stout footmen and gardeners, in case her secret became known.

If Julius found that certificate, she'd burn it. Nobody need know.

Tony touched her when asked to, slid a plain gold band onto her finger when requested, and repeated the words as expressionlessly as she had.

However, they said the words and they were married.

A patter of gloved hands followed the vicar's announcement that they were man and wife, but when the official frowned, the sound desisted.

Her mother did not applaud.

Tony treated her with punctilious care, but no fondness. He helped her to sit, but as soon as he'd done so, he didn't touch her again. He ensured she had what she needed to eat, which was next to nothing. Since it was Lent, they kept the modest celebration to the family, for which she could only be grateful. She smiled by rote, tried to appear happy, and that satisfied most people.

Life was running away from her, taking her in directions she'd never imagined, much less ever wanted. Why couldn't she go back and start again? Where had it gone wrong?

When she'd discovered a wounded man in a run-down hut on her estate. She should have demolished that ruin years ago, boundary dispute or not.

He might have died, left out in the open in February, bleeding. She shuddered at the thought.

"Are you well?" he murmured. "Would you like to retire?"

Yes, more than anything else, but she refused to allow people to see her weakness. Or seeing her leave early with her husband, coming to what would be a false conclusion.

So she sat, and talked, and laughed, as if this were the happiest day in her life. She even managed to eat something and moved her food around her plate to make it appear that she'd eaten more.

Tony's father, Thaddeus Beaumont, was a tall, imposing figure, his natural gray hair tied back in a simple queue, but he was possessed of the kind of presence that drew attention wherever he went. His resemblance to his sons—son—was remarkable. If Tony looked like that when he was sixty, Imogen wouldn't be complaining. If she and Tony were still together at that age. Although divorce was difficult, separation was not so hard, and while the couple couldn't marry again, other possibilities existed.

God, if he took a lover she'd die. Or want to.

Imogen's helplessness infuriated her. She had no seductive wiles; no techniques she could use to ensure Tony wouldn't stray, or would even want her, something she was beginning to consider. He would remain separate, and they would drift apart, never to see each other except when they were compelled to be together. Even in her small part of the world, that happened. The couple—existed.

He had agreed with Julius to take one of the dangerous political pawns out of play. That was Imogen. His demeanor toward her proved it. He barely touched her, treated her with punctilious politeness. He had achieved his mission and need not seduce her or show her anything but courtesy.

After a gathering in the drawing room, the guests began to drift away. They took kind leave, wished the newlyweds well, and left. Sand through a sieve. Even her mother, after kissing her on both cheeks, left, pleading exhaustion. She left before the last few people so Imogen couldn't ask her to stay. She had so much to ask her, maybe she should save her questions for another time, when she could gather her thoughts and think of the right things to ask. Not the ones her heart demanded, such as why her mother had never told her, but the ones she needed to know about the circumstances of her birth. And those damned certificates.

Her mother. Her real mother, the unknown Maria Rubiero. Her father, not the man she barely knew but one she didn't know at all. A man who was *still alive.*

Chapter 13

Tony took her home. Not to her home, but to the London house he shared with his family. Nick traveled in the carriage with them, although he'd initially demurred and said he would walk. To give the newlyweds privacy, no doubt.

Imogen smiled and made polite conversation, her endurance close to breaking point. But the last thing she wanted was any of Tony's exalted family to believe she was a provincial and didn't mind her manners. Anything but that. Her mouth turned up in self-derision, she stared out of the window to a London thronged with people, all going about their business. How many more weddings happened in London today? Even in Lent? How many people had been hanged, suffered a bereavement, undergone an event that changed their lives completely? Or ended them?

Living in a city of this size emphasized the fact that nobody lived his life completely alone. Many people existed here who were better off or worse off or in the same case. That should make her feel better, that she wasn't alone. But it didn't.

Tony lived in a house very much like the one she had left, but in Cavendish Square. Perhaps a little larger than the one Julius leased, but the same shallow steps leading to the front door under a similar portico of Doric columns and the same shiny black paint and gleaming brass doorknocker. The door opened before they reached it, revealing a set of servants, all bowing to receive her. She wouldn't be the mistress here, something she was glad of. That was Tony's mother, Lady Beaumont, for although her husband didn't have a title, she retained the style of her first marriage. She had already retired, leaving the newlyweds to do the same. A tactful retreat.

A maid showed Imogen to a room where her own maid waited. Digby helped Imogen to undress and ready herself for bed almost in silence, and once she'd wrapped a robe around her, she left.

The door opened and her husband entered, also in undress. He sported a magnificent robe and for the first time that day her smile was unforced. "I ordered some supper served," he said. "Come."

She rose and followed him. The last thing she wanted was food. At least she thought so until she smelled the delicacies set before them. Shocked into impulsive behavior she spun around to face him. "How did you know?"

"That you liked lamb cutlets and green peas? I asked."

"Who?"

He smiled. "Your mother."

Her mother had noticed? She'd never have guessed.

Tony held back her chair for her and she sat, but he didn't touch her more than he needed to. He took his seat opposite her and without asking placed a generous helping of food on her plate. It was good, plain food, the kind she preferred, the sauces kept to a minimum. "I know my tastes aren't sophisticated, but this is what I like."

"That's something we share, then. I learned early to eat what there was. I've caught food myself and cooked it over an open fire. Rabbit, trout, whatever I could find. And it always tasted magnificent, because I was hungry and the meal was fresh. No sauces there." At least his polite cordiality had changed to friendliness.

They laughed together, and something inside her unwound, leaving her even hungrier. She hadn't eaten properly all day, and she'd been up early so she could make the journey from Richmond in time. He sounded more like the man she'd met in Lancashire, minus the gunshot wound, of course. Had the wound settled? How did it look now?

"How is your shoulder?" She forked up a mouthful of fragrant peas.

"Much better. A little stiff, but that will pass." He proved it by flexing his arm. "See?"

She did. The reminder of the muscles that lay under the smooth silk of his robe made her mouth go dry. She still wanted him, a reaction she didn't seem to be able to control.

She took a healthy gulp of the white wine in her glass, relishing the cool slide down her throat. He smiled, as if he knew what she was reacting to. "I'm glad it's healing. I was worried, especially during the fever."

"The first or the second?"

He was trying to make light of it, but she couldn't do it. She'd nursed him through the first, agonized through the second. "You nearly died. Twice. And the second time I wasn't there."

His gaze met hers, his blue eyes wide. "I didn't want you there."

She tried to conceal her pang of hurt. If he'd wanted her like she'd foolishly thought, he'd have desired her presence.

He moved his hand, but drew back before he touched her. "The first time was a chill. I thought I'd contracted the second. Jail fever, smallpox, it's hard to tell in the early stages."

"I know." The pain struck her with immeasurable force when she heard that from his lips. "So why would I not be there? I wanted to come, but Julius wouldn't let me. He said you didn't want me."

"Not quite true." His smile turned wry and he put down his fork, laying it precisely at right angles to his plate. "I didn't want to put you into danger. No more. It stopped at that point, and while I lay there I swore that if I recovered, I would do everything I could to shield you."

She should be happy. She had a protector. But one thing concerned her. "I want the choice, Tony. I want to know what's going on. Everyone is doing things, and it concerns me, but nobody will tell me." Tears threatened to fall, her throat swelling with them. She picked up her glass again and swallowed it away.

He lifted his hand, then dropped it, taking hold of his table knife in a death grip. "From now on they will. You know what I do."

"I want to know everything. I want to know it all." Now she sounded childish." Glancing down, she realized she'd almost finished her meal. "I'm sorry. But if a matter concerns me, I don't want to be shielded from it. I want to know."

"I take it we're not talking about the fever anymore?"

"Yes." She paused, gathering her thoughts. "My mother avoided me all day. I want to know why. She has never been demonstrative, but today she was positively frozen. She knows something, and she doesn't want me to ask her. I want to go and ask her."

"Not without me."

She glanced back up at him, in control of her emotions once more. "She's my mother."

"I want to know too. It's part of my life now."

That seemed reasonable. "Very well. Tomorrow."

"Not tomorrow. The day after." He pushed back his chair and got to his feet. "Have you finished, or do you want more?"

The food had fortified her, and renewed strength pulsated through her limbs. The events of the day had not yet resonated completely. If they ever would. She followed suit before he could help her up like an invalid and turned around, heading for the room she had been given.

He followed her in and closed the door, leaning against it. "Will this suit?"

The bed was canopied in dark blue silk, the chairs and the daybed in the same fabric. White muslin draped her dressing table, which contained a collection of crystal bottles and silver-backed brushes. The windows bore elaborate drapery, currently closed against the night and prying eyes. Oriental carpets softened the polished parquet floor.

It was luxurious in the extreme. Standing by the daybed, she gave a choked laugh. "Will it suit? You mean, will this slum suffice?"

"Some might think of it as such. Eventually I'd like us to have our own establishment in London, but we need to wait until Julius returns to town."

"Yes, with the paper that both makes me a bastard and the child of a king."

"A pretender," he corrected her gently.

"Yes." Not that she cared at the moment, except a bastard of a ruling monarch would probably have fewer problems. "I think the king can rest easy in his bed tonight."

"You'll be comfortable here?"

"Perfectly."

He kicked away from the door. "I'll bid you goodnight. You must be tired, and we have to take care of the child, don't we?" His face was expressionless as he turned his back to her.

Frozen, she stood still, rooted to the ground. Their wedding night and he wanted to leave her alone? "Can't you even hold me?"

His shoulders slumped as he lowered his head. Leaning forward, he butted his forehead against the paneled door. The *thump* echoed around the room. Imogen winced as if it was her pain. "I can't do that."

"Why not?"

He didn't answer immediately. When they came, her words were low, barely audible. "Because I can't. Because I daren't touch you." He turned around and his face was no longer devoid of expression. His eyes were wide, his mouth hard. Bleakness threw his features into sharp relief. "If I touch you I will never stop."

"You touched me at dinner, and when you put the ring on my finger." She held up her hand. "This finger."

All his attention went to the ring. He took a step forward, as if pulled by an invisible chord, jerkily, reluctantly. "You know what I mean. That was social, impersonal."

It hurt to hear that he'd found the act of marriage impersonal. "Why did you do it?"

"Because I'm responsible, at least in part, and I never walk away from my responsibilities."

At least he didn't suspect her of infidelity. Some men would, just to find an excuse. "I don't doubt your honor. I could have coped. I could have gone away for a month or two, had the child and adopted it later as my ward. I could have visited a physician. For a small fee they—"

"No!" His next step forward gave her a small victory. "They can cause untold damage."

"I don't know that I am pregnant. I'm only two weeks late. I have no other symptoms. Are you sure you didn't marry me for other reasons?"

His mouth twisted, half smile, half sneer. "I never wanted to marry anyone. Not until I met you. That was all I wanted. But now—things are different, aren't they?"

"Why are they different?" She wanted to hear him say it. "Because of who I am? Who I truly am?"

"I'm less a husband, more a protector. I will keep you from harm to the best of my ability, but you're valuable to certain people. I've taken you out of the path of our enemies."

"In what way?" She wanted it spelled out. Hear it now and then do her best to cauterize the pain. Clean it out, like she'd cleaned his festering wound.

"Lord William Dankworth. Maybe even his older brother, Lord Alconbury. They would have married you and then used you."

There, he'd said it. He'd married her to take her out of the political game. Not because he wanted her or felt anything for her. She hadn't believed she could hurt any more, but with every part of her body aching, she discovered her potential for infinite pain.

He spread his hands, his dressing gown loosening, the tie slipping undone. Beneath he had on shirt and breeches, but that was all. His head was bare, revealing the dark hair she had once caressed. Her mouth dried, her body's response to him instinctive. "They would have abducted you. They've tried it with others before."

"So I'm on my own in this marriage?"

Vigorously he shook his head. "I am here. With you."

"It feels as if I'm on my own."

He took a step back, and part of her heart died. But she would not plead, wouldn't beg.

"I won't ever leave you to face this on your own. Whatever happens, I'm here now."

"That's good to know." She folded her arms under her breasts and watched as his attention went to them when they plumped up. So he wasn't immune to her. "But I want you, Tony." This was the nearest she'd ever get to telling him. Any more and she'd break. "I can't manage this alone. I want more than you by my side. I want you in my bed."

He swallowed, the motion moving his Adam's apple. "I wanted to give you some time to think. You've learned so much about yourself recently. And you think I married you for this?" He laughed harshly. "I would have married you if I'd been a humble soldier and you were a housekeeper. That was what I wanted. Not this—this mess." He waved his hand, indicating the luxury, the wealth that surrounded her in stifling abundance. "I don't know what to do, how to deal with this."

Slowly, she absorbed what he'd just said. Did he mean it? He'd given her no idea. "You wanted to marry me when you thought I was a housekeeper?"

Blinking, he nodded. "I decided after our second night together. Our first, really. I'd ask you and tell you who I was. I had no idea you were Imogen. Nothing else need have affected us."

"You're dreaming." He had his head in the clouds. "Even in my part of Lancashire people would have shunned us. I would have been neither housekeeper nor a member of society. I wanted you, too, but I didn't think I'd have you."

"And here we are."

Now she took a step forward in her turn. "Here we are." His confession made her bold, and she closed the distance between them in two short steps and then did what she longed to do. She touched him, put her hands on his chest. His muscles flexed under her palms, and his heart pounded. "Why should we not try for what we want?"

His hands came up and he covered hers. Warmth engulfed her.

"Are you sure?"

"I want you so much I can hardly breathe for it."

With a groan, he bent his head and touched his lips to hers. She was lost. So well-remembered and so missed!

Sliding her hands around his body, she held as much of him as she could, dragging him against her aching breasts. The muscled wall of his chest warmed and soothed them like nothing else could. His remembered heat welcomed her home.

He broke the kiss to gaze down at her face. Cupping her chin, he stared into her eyes. "You mean this? I won't go away, not again. I can't make this effort twice."

Her kind, honorable husband saw everything in terms of right and wrong. He'd transgressed by taking her before she knew the truth about herself. She understood that, and he'd only married her for the possibility of a child, before it was too late to say they'd conceived the child out of wedlock.

But what she saw in his eyes now, she dared believe that at least part of his purpose was for her. That he wanted her for himself. "Is it for me or for you that you do this?"

Frowning, he studied her. "I don't understand."

"Men want women in bed. It's their nature. Is that all you want?"

His face cleared. "No." He hold tightened on her chin. "Not that. Never that. I need you, Imogen. God, you've been driving me insane! Since I got to London all I could think of was having you again. When we're close, my skin yearns for your touch, my arms feel empty. I married you because I wanted to own you, to make you mine. It was unforgivably selfish. I'm ashamed."

"But I wanted you too. I still do. Is it selfish of me, too, then?"

A bitter smile curved his lips. "Two selfish people? We need to do something about that, don't we?" He shook his head. "I tried to do the honorable thing. God knows I tried. But no more. Now you're mine, and what I have, I keep."

He allowed her no more words, but brought his mouth down hard over hers, ravenous and devouring. She moaned just as he did, their lips melding, their tongues tangling. He ate at her mouth, working it rhythmically, his movements reminding her of what they'd done before and what she longed to do again.

Her cleft dampened and became wetter, the tops of her thighs growing slick with the evidence of her desire for him. She rubbed them together to give herself a measure of relief.

He lifted his mouth from hers, but only just. The heat of his breath warmed her lips. "I could kiss you all night, but I want something else more. Feel me, Imogen."

When he ground his lower body against hers, the ridge of his erection branded heat from his breeches through her robe to her belly. All too well she remembered what that hard rod felt like against her bare skin, the tip shiny and wet, the shaft hot, the skin delicate.

Guiding her across the room until the solid softness of the bed hit her buttocks and waist, he moved away far enough to unfasten the sash to her robe and the frogged fastenings at the top that were all that held it together. With a smile, he glanced down. "That shade of yellow is magnificent on you, but I prefer the creamy pink that lies beneath."

Lifting her arms, she allowed him to drag off the brocade robe and the white linen night rail she wore underneath. Her slippers were easily kicked away. She was naked, unashamed. She wanted to flaunt herself before him, make him want her in a primitive feminine urge she didn't know existed before.

He took her hands and stepped back, perusing her body with a hot need that tightened her nipples and tensed her muscles. Dark eyes became even darker; he released her and stripped, letting the robe fall to the floor, and then he dragged his shirt out of his breeches and over his head. She loved his chest with the sprinkling of dark hair that softened the slabs of muscle, but left his brown nipples bare. They were beaded, as if imitating her larger ones. To ease her ache a little, she cupped her breasts and squeezed her nipples.

A low groan punctuated her actions. "Little tease. You shall pay for that, my lady."

Swooping down, he dragged her close until his chest hair abraded her nipples, and then bent to suck one of the tender morsels into his mouth, drawing on it hard enough to bring her some relief, but when he flicked his tongue on the tip, he only exacerbated her need. Jagged shards of longing arced from her breasts to her groin, and she cried his name, wanting more and not knowing how to ask.

With a rough laugh he lifted her, and as her breast left his mouth, he pushed her on to the bed, none too gently. He stripped off the remainder of his clothes and came to her, climbing up and over her where she lay on her back on the elaborately embroidered cover, the threads scratching her skin.

He pushed one hand under her and used it to lift her, dragging the cover away in a careless show of strength, and then laid her on the crisp linen sheets. "That silver thread will scratch you, and I don't want you hurt, unless I'm the one doing it. For every sting I give you I will bring you ten times as much pleasure. Talk to me, Imogen, tell me what you need."

"How, when I don't know what I want?" Tentatively she touched his shaft, the hard rod earning its nickname of cock, the word crisp and descriptive.

He groaned. "Not too much, sweetheart. I'll go off too early." Placing a hand by her head, he lifted up and met her wondering gaze. "No more withdrawal. I want to come deep inside you, to feel that wet, sweet heat engulf me and take me to paradise." As he waited for her answer, his disparaging half smile told her what he thought of his own poesy.

"Yes, I want that too. Very much. Am I ready?"

"Find out. Touch yourself. Let me watch you do it."

Imogen caught her breath on a gasp. He meant it, but could she? She'd discovered that knot of flesh at the apex of her cleft that brought her temporary relief. Could she do this with him watching?

Yes, yes she could, because he wanted her to. Slowly she cupped her breast, pushed it up so it thrust out at him, and then slid her hand down her body, over her still flat stomach, the indentation of her navel. Spiking her fingers, she combed through the thatch of curls at her groin, taking her wetness on to her fingertip. She had never felt herself so wet before. Although sure she was ready, she continued, stroking the nub, gasping at the intensity of sensation before exploring further. The lips that protected her most secret places were hot and swollen, sensitive to her gentle touch, and her opening filled with her juices. She dipped a finger inside, exploring.

Tony slid to one side of her, lying next to her, watching what she was doing, tension of a different kind tautening the skin on his face. Greatly daring, she lifted the leg farthest from him and propped her heel on the bed sheets, opening her body for his avid perusal.

She tried another finger. It felt good, the walls of her inner channel opening slowly, soft and wet, trickling out to slide between her buttocks with shocking sensitivity.

When she moaned, he murmured her name. "Imogen, you are perfect. An angel of sensuality. Watching you explore yourself like that makes me wild. I want to take you, thrust hard inside you until you scream for mercy, and then fill you to the brim. You are so beautiful. Everywhere. That delicate pink skin, the scent of you—I cannot have done anything in my life to deserve this. You're mine, do you hear?"

His fierceness shocked and excited her. She'd always sensed this possessiveness about him, and now he was giving it free rein. She loved it.

Climbing over her, he dragged her hand away, even though she whimpered, wanting more. Wanting to drive him crazy with it.

"Another time," he said, as if he knew what she was thinking, then he was on her, kneeing her thighs apart, urging her to lift her legs, and making a place for his body between her thighs.

His cock probed her, pushed, and he was in her, driving in to his balls. He drew out and thrust in again, meeting little resistance, her body accepting and enclosing him. Claiming him as he was conquering her.

This close she saw every flaw and every perfection. A scar ran from his ear down his neck. Not a deep one, just a thin white line. He had another tiny one above his eyebrow. Fascinated, she wanted to draw along the lines with her finger, claim him for her own, every part of him. All sense of time and place disappeared when he thrust again, and again.

"Tony!"

"I'm here. Always here." Bending his head, he kissed her, thrusting his tongue deep, ravenously taking her as she arched her body up and into his, needing as much of his shaft inside her as possible.

They were back. Tony and Emmy, two people living in each other, with each other. Nothing else mattered.

His balls drummed against her lower buttocks when she lifted her legs and wrapped them securely around his waist, dragging him into her. Imogen determined not to let him go until she'd found that distant goal he'd helped her to discover before. It lay there, just out of reach. Each thrust brought her closer. Ripples of sensation rose higher, encompassed her, until she cried into his mouth and he pulled away. He bared his teeth as he growled her name, exhorting her to higher levels. "Come, damn you!"

Even now he could make her laugh, but he jarred it out of her when he drove her up, to oblivion. Delight crested over her, froze her muscles, and struck directly to the very heart of her. Her channel pulsed against him, clenching as if determined never to let him go, and with a sharp, wordless cry, his cock throbbed and he came.

The concluding flutters of her orgasm left her weak, helpless to do anything but clutch him. With a series of kisses to her mouth, her cheeks, and her throat, he reached his hand down to loosen her legs' grip on his waist, persuading her to lower them so he could withdraw from her. He nipped her throat, and then back to her mouth, his kisses more soothing than arousing.

They hadn't even got as far as the pillows, but lay sideways on the big bed. She sighed and threaded her fingers through his hair as he kissed and licked her skin. "That was better than before."

He came up on one elbow, smiling, as relaxed and happy as she'd ever seen him. "We have more room. Wait until I get my breath back."

Laughing weakly, she pulled him down for a kiss. "How could you not want this?"

"It wasn't a matter of not wanting. It was a matter of wanting too much." He rolled to one side and moved to the top of the bed, urging her to join him. She went gladly into his arms, and he reached down to pull the covers over them. The maid had left the fire, though banked down, but the night was chilly. His body warmed her as she flicked out her tongue to claim a taste of his salty skin.

"I backed away from you because I told myself I couldn't retain control." He kissed her nose, her mouth, small fairy kisses that teased. "I hate to lose control. Hated. You just taught me to trust myself with you. I never would have done that if you hadn't called me back, and for that I'm truly sorry."

"I don't understand. I taught you nothing."

He came back up and met her gaze so frankly it took her breath away. "I watched you as you came. You gave yourself up to me, trusted me to care for you. Only then can we achieve what we need. I had to do the same when it was my turn, otherwise something would always remain between us. So I trusted you."

"Oh."

He kissed her, and tiring of discussions, she hooked her arm around his neck and deepened the kiss. That she had the courage to touch him and demand things from him, inexperienced though she was, spoke to how far they'd come since they'd entered this room.

He drew away, smiling. "One thing. There are two dressing rooms attached to this room and a boudoir, but only one bedroom. Until we find an establishment of our own, I'm afraid we have to share a bed." He didn't seem concerned.

She wasn't in the least perturbed. She clicked her tongue. "Such a shame!"

Laughing softly, he dropped a kiss on her forehead. He was making up for the dearth of kisses in one go. "We must endeavor to make the most of it. I was planning to sleep elsewhere. Not now. You have me here, and I do not intend to go anywhere. What should you like to do now?"

Reaching down, she touched his shaft, expecting to find it sleeping. She knew enough about males to know they could not perform endlessly. But to her surprise it was far from quiescent, in a half-hard state already. It twitched when she touched it, seemingly leaping into her hand. Although that was fanciful, the idea appealed to her. Perhaps she could make it leap in less convenient circumstances, tease him a little. Her heart lighter, she felt more able to cope with the trials that lay ahead for them.

"Can we just go into the country and forget everything else?"

"Is that what you truly want?"

She nodded. "To be what I was. Perhaps a little more. With you."

He cradled her breast, returning her caresses in his own way. She relaxed into his hold, letting warmth seep through her. "I confess, that sounds tempting. I've traveled enough, seen enough to relish a quiet life in the country. Not entirely, though. I want some opportunities to show off my beautiful wife." He stopped her protests with a kiss. "Whoever told you that you weren't beautiful was lying. Whether you realize it or not, you're an accredited beauty. The caricaturists are going into a frenzy, but I wouldn't recommend you seek out the results. The gossip sheets are speculating about you, who you'll marry and so on."

"They'll know now."

He paused, his hand stilling in its actions. "Yes, they will, and I can't be sorry for it. We might not have announced our intentions or married with a fanfare, but we are sharing the same room and we haven't appeared outside it for two days."

"I'm glad."

Smiling, he kissed her again. "So am I. We'll just wait here until Julius returns to town, shall we?"

She snuggled closer. "If he finds that document, I want it burned. I don't care. I don't want to be a political pawn and I'm not interested in power brokering. As far as I'm concerned it brings nothing."

Silence followed, and then a long sigh. "Are you sure?"

"Why? Do you want me to become the center of intrigue?"

He cinched her tighter. Even his cock grew limper. "No! It leads to broken dreams and promises, a lifetime's obsession with something impossible or near unobtainable."

"And hurt to everyone concerned." That was her main concern. If stepping up and claiming her parentage would do any good at all, she'd do it, but she couldn't see how that would benefit anyone.

"Indeed." He relaxed his hold. "We will burn it and anything that comes with it. You are now Mrs. Beaumont."

She grimaced. "Soon to be the Countess of Hollinhead, if the king makes good on his promise."

"You object to that?"

Not having considered the issue before, she did so now. "I'd thought my father's title gone forever, tainted. But I had forgotten the people before him. I would like to try remaking it, giving it the honor back that it used to hold. No, I don't mind. The decision must be yours."

"Then I'll accept." A slow smile crept over his face and his eyes glowed. "Lord, what this will do to my brother, I don't know. I'll outrank him!"

"Will it create trouble?" She didn't want that. She wanted no more trouble, ever again.

"I don't know, but I think not. My brother may be a mere viscount, but his wealth is considerable." The smile faded. "We have not acted in accord, but recently we cleared the air. I'm not saying it will be smooth from now on, but our new understanding is growing easier for both of us."

He gazed down at her, a question in his eyes, but she couldn't tell what he wanted to do or ask.

He released his breath in a sigh. "I trust you, of course I do. Nick's parents' marriage was dynastic, arranged by our mother's parents, the Duke and Duchess of Kirkburton. There was never any love between them. His father died just after Nick was born, and just over a year later, my mother married my father, Thaddeus Beaumont. As soon as it was decently possible. That was, and continues to be, a love match. My father loved my mother for a long time, but he was a mere Cit and she was the daughter of a duke. She earned her right to marry as she wished the second time by marrying Nick's father. I was less than a year after their marriage, so but two years exist between my brother and I. Indecent haste, Hamlet called it. Not quite. My mother gave her late husband a year. Thaddeus tried to be a good father to us both, but Nick always resented him, and me."

She touched his hand. "May I ask, do you—that is, are you full brothers?"

He gazed at her, sincerity in his eyes. "I'm not sure. Knowing my mother, I doubt it. The viscount was a sickly man when she married him, earlier bouts of illness weakening him. My mother was his last chance of getting an heir. My father stayed away during her marriage, or so I understand." He smiled and touched her nose. "I was the favored child. I admit it freely now. Nick played tricks on me and forced me to take the blame for his wrongdoing. I received many a beating that should have been his, but I wanted my brother to love me. He never did. Or he didn't want to. I—I'm not proud of the next part." He bit his lip.

She touched his chest and traced her finger around his nipple. It hardened under her touch. "If you don't wish to tell me, I'll understand."

He shook his head. "You should know everything about me. I want you to. You will understand why relations between my brother and me are not precisely sunny. When I was eighteen, he pushed me too far. We both fell in love, or thought we did, with the same woman. We fought a duel, and I pierced him in his shoulder, low down. By then I resented him bitterly, all the small hurts he'd inflicted on me over the years coalescing at that part. But that was no excuse to contemplate fratricide. When I delivered the killing blow and thrust my sword through his heart, I thought him dead. I panicked and ran off to join the army. I joined as a private, took the King's shilling, and went where they sent me. I had served six months before my father tracked me down and bought me a commission."

Brothers fighting over a woman? No wonder Nicephorus had flirted with her. He'd wanted to get his revenge. "But your brother isn't married, is he?"

"The lady in question married someone else. She rarely comes to London, but when she does, I wonder if it was she or if our rivalry had to come out somehow and that was it."

He stroked her from breast to waist, gazed at her nipple as it crinkled. "Knowing what I do now, I don't think either of us were ever in love. She was beautiful, but she had very little between her ears. As a wife she'd have bored either of us within the space of a year. She was also helpless. She can't hold a candle to your resourcefulness, my love. Or your beauty."

Chapter 14

Imogen tried not to show her reaction to Tony's casual endearment. How did he mean that? Did he love her as she loved him? Courageous though he claimed her, she didn't have that final piece she needed to ask him. His tones were matter-of-fact, as if it stood to reason that he would say that.

He'd fought a duel? "Were you in disgrace after the duel?"

"No. We never named the lady, and our seconds swore that the injury was the result of an accident." He smiled ruefully. "She didn't deserve the notoriety she received anyway, but it was a nine days' wonder, soon over. Nevertheless, she accepted an offer from a much older man. She seems very happy with him."

"Does she know what she did?"

He traced a line around her navel. "No. And she did nothing to deserve society's opprobrium. Nick and I did it all. Now, with our new rapprochement, if I'm to become an earl, I would prefer to tell him before the matter becomes public. If he dislikes it—"

She lifted her hand from his cock and put it over his. "You must refuse."

"If you don't put your hand back where it was I will request that the earldom is changed to a marquisate or a dukedom."

For a second, she missed the import of what he was saying. With a throaty chuckle, she did as he requested. He placed his hand over hers. "Like that. Firmer."

She loved that he showed her, and she easily assimilated what he asked for. Gripping him harder and using a pumping motion had its desired effect, and he grew, hardened under her touch.

He rolled on to his back. "Would you do me the greatest honor of repeating what you did when we first made love?" The gleam in his eyes belied his formal tone.

Smiling in sheer delight, she sat up, enjoyed the caress of his eyes on her as she lifted her leg and straddled his powerful body. His cock jutted out, hard, the tip red and wet.

She recalled what he'd done for her once. Could she do that to him? The answer came as a resounding *yes*, if his moan when she licked that liquid from his cock head were anything to go by. Intrigued, she rolled the flavor around her mouth. Musky and intensely male with an aftertaste of salt. And an accompanying sound and hard jerk of his body. He hadn't expected that.

Chuckling, she explored some more. She got the head into her mouth, but he was far too large for her to encompass completely. His fingers touched her shoulder and she glanced up. His blue eyes had turned to pure fire.

"God, Imogen, I don't think I'll survive this."

He was forced to cut his breath short when she sucked, and then licked around the flange that separated the tip from the rest of his shaft. She cupped his balls, felt their texture, the soft bag with the two hard ovals inside. When workers on her estate had referred to them as "balls," she'd thought they were round, but they weren't. They were longer, like an egg. Although she took the greatest care, he still squirmed, and she discerned what he liked from the way his body leaped and jerked, as if in shock. He watched her, caressed her, so softly, but with trembling fingers.

And she did this to him. She was doing it, bringing him the pleasure he'd given her. Reciprocation was as delightful as receiving. Almost as good, but that feeling of soaring when he—ah yes, more liquid. She sucked, claiming it for her own. Everything, his taste, his abandon, it belonged to her and would to nobody else. Between them lay that unspoken pact, that this experience was for them alone, and in order to be so, in order to retain the perfect trust and sharing, it had to remain so.

This man had given himself to her today, and she had returned the favor. They had a lifetime to learn. She would probably need it if his several reactions were typical of him. His moans edged on to pain, but his touch remained gentle, until she tried that pumping motion he'd taught her. He writhed, almost pulling out of her mouth, and covered his eyes with one hand.

"I've unleashed a monster!"

She growled in mock response and gave him another playful lick. When she made a sound, it vibrated against him, making him extremely vocal in his response. He muttered imprecations and encouragement, one moment cursing her and the other pleading for her not to stop. Ever.

But when his balls tightened, he moved quickly, pulling her away with a cry. "No, no, I want to come inside you. You have me addicted to that, sweetheart. Ride me. Like your most fractious horse. Take me and ride me hard."

Panting, she laughed up at him, eyeing his wet cock with fondness and delight that she had made him so hard, so needy. Such a big man, and she had reduced him to a pleading mess.

Pushing herself up, she slid up his body and dared to touch herself, sliding her fingers along her crease as he had done to ensure she was wet. Of course she was. Growling, he shoved her hand out of the way and did it himself, tweaking her clitoris, and then down to her opening, pushing two digits inside her with little effort. He moved them, wriggled them, and then withdrew. He touched something and she started with a jolt of sensation. "My goodness, what was that?"

"That, my sweet, was this." Bringing his thumb into play, he grazed her clitoris with it, and at the same time did whatever he did inside her.

With a strangled groan, she closed her eyes as a sharp bolt of sheer pleasure shot through her.

"Now let's see if we can do it with my cock instead of my fingers, shall we?"

So saying, he withdrew his hand and helped her to move so she hovered over his straining shaft. He steadied the thick column of flesh while she brought her body down onto him. When he breached her, she made a small involuntary sound deep in her throat.

"That feels wonderful." He filled her up, completed her, although she hadn't been aware of being half a person before.

Placing her hands on his chest, she gazed down at him. He met her eyes, his own open and aware. "My love," he said, and this time there was no mistaking his words or putting them aside as a vague fondness. "I love you, Imogen. You are my one true love, and you always will be."

"I love you, too." It seemed a paltry thing next to his fervent declaration, but none the less true.

He accepted her words with a short nod. "Never hide from me. Never shirk from telling me what I need to know." He put his hand over hers, the one covering his heart. "I need you, my truth, my beloved."

"Yes. Don't let me run away or do what isn't right. My strength, my heart lies with you."

"I will never give you cause to regret your decision, my love."

"I know you won't." And she did. She could depend on this man, her rock, the center of her existence.

She lifted up almost quietly, easing his body out of hers, and then came back down, leaning on her hands to keep her balance. He watched, his attention going to the place where they were joined, but he did nothing other than keep his body braced for her explorations. This was for her, she understood that.

"Can you feel that place I touched inside you?" he said.

She shook her head, her hair, now completely unraveled from its night time braids, the unruly curls tumbling around her shoulders. "But it feels so good."

Placing his hands on her hips, he adjusted her, moved her back a fraction, and rotated his hips until she gasped and froze. He smiled broadly. "Aha!"

Squirming down, he moved again and hit the same spot, his erection grazing past the extra-sensitive place until she tried to move, the sensations shooting through her far too much for her to take.

Firmly he moved her back. "No. Wait. Melt into it. Let the feeling take you over, don't be afraid of it. I'll take care of you, Imogen. Always."

She trusted him to take her wherever he wanted to and keep her safe, so she did as he bade, even though the feelings were intensifying all the time, growing more insistent. She opened her mouth, moaned his name, and responded every time he moved inside her.

With one hand on her hip, he guided her movements, so she could still move up and down, riding him as he said, the movements becoming part of her. They flowed past her, her body moving easily and fluidly, the feelings of cresting excitement pushing past all her safeguards, every warning her body might give her that it couldn't stand much more of this. She held on, kept moving, his words of encouragement bathing her in warmth.

Warmth became heat. Imogen threw her head back, gasping for air, cries emitting from her with every hard thrust into her body. They entered a world of their own, where only this action was important, where nothing else mattered a damn. If she didn't find her culmination, she'd die. She was sure of it.

Internal lightning tore through her, taking her with it to a place where nothing existed except this, except them. The vicious slash took her again, the double shock rendering her helpless in the midst of the storm. She had to remember to breathe, to draw air into her racked body. But it came with such joy, a freeing of her soul that she would want this all her life.

Pressure on the nub told her he was touching her, and as she came down, he pressed, driving her to a new place, even more than before.

When she thought intensity was done, it grew more concentrated, the white light so blinding she opened her eyes, staring at the elaborately embroidered and padded bedhead. It meant nothing to her.

Lowering her head slowly, her hair tickling her skin, every part of her ultrasensitive, she saw that starkness, the open honesty he showed her without stint. Her body clenched around his, and finally he let go.

Heat gushed into her. Wetness touched her thighs, such was the generosity of his libation. Glorying in the sheer physicality of their loving, she laughed aloud, her body still not completely under her control. She shuddered with the aftershock of another smaller peak, and then another, a thrill shivering through her.

He slid his hands over her hips, urging her down to spread her body over his. With their bodies still joined, he held her close, murmured to her. He pushed back her hair, tucking it behind her ears, and he kissed her, gently at first, and then deeper, licking into her mouth in long, lavish caresses.

Imogen flung her arm around his neck and held on, slowly coming down from the heights, held securely, her head resting on his broad shoulder, her body supported by his. He finished the kiss and smiled at her.

"I love you," she said.

"A feeling that is more than reciprocated. I love you very much. Adore you. I can't imagine my life without you as the center, as the heart of it." He kissed her again, lingering over her mouth.

Overwhelmed, she responded, hearing his words with wonder and a deep sense of recognition.

"Do you think you're pregnant?" he asked.

She no longer feared pregnancy, she anticipated it eagerly. "If I'm not, I will be soon enough."

He chuckled. "My love, we shall have to make sure of it."

She couldn't imagine a more worthwhile occupation.

Chapter 15

Tony kept his wife in bed all the next day, telling her she needed to rest.

"If I needed to rest," she told him, with much laughter, "I'd get up."

That was fair enough. Now she'd let him in he couldn't get enough of her. Couldn't imagine a time when he'd ever tire of exploring her heat, her curves, and her sweet flavors. He was already addicted to her.

Trusting her had been the best decision he'd ever made. When they weren't making love, they were talking, and not just about their problems. They shared their hopes for the future and their desires to make themselves anew. When she revealed her sorrow about her mother's coldness, he didn't remind her that Mrs. Thane, or Lady Hollinhead, as she preferred to style herself, was not her mother in any sense of the word, but he comforted her, and held her while she shed a few tears. After all, the lady had taken care of Imogen, and brought her home when she could have remained in Rome.

Or could she? Was she, perhaps, ordered to do it, and so resented the baby that wasn't hers, who she'd have to sacrifice all her personal ambitions for?

As he held his sleeping wife, happiness simmering inside him, Tony let his thoughts wander. The most important thing in the world to him now was keeping her safe and happy. He would do anything to achieve that.

The dowager was a problem, privy to who knew how many secrets? Outside the Emperors, she was the only person who knew the secret of Imogen's birth. He no longer doubted the veracity of her origins. She even had the Stuart hair and eyes, soft velvet brown eyes, the kind that had beguiled a nation into civil war and persuaded the same nation to restore the status quo. Almost. Because these days the monarch ruled by the will of the people.

If the Stuarts returned, they'd make an attempt at absolute monarchy again. The only Stuart in the direct line with a modicum of good sense had been King Charles the Second. The current members of the family consisted of a privately promiscuous melancholic, a dim drunk, and a pious fussbudget. That was their main problem. If anyone had seen any worth in the family, they might have had a chance to return in '15. As it was, the Old Pretender had refused to convert to Protestantism and lost his chance. His son had converted more recently, but he was lapsing into his Catholic ways, once it became obvious his ploy had no effect.

And here lay he, Tony, holding a royal princess. A princess born on the wrong side of the blanket, that was. Her breath puffed against his shoulder, and he smiled. His princess, always that. He would give his life to ensure she kept hers. And now he knew what she wanted, they could work toward that. Once Julius returned to town, Tony would have that document off him and thrown in the fire—if Julius didn't have the sense to deal with it already. His cousin had fingers in several political pies, but he wouldn't use this particular bit of information to help him do anything but set Imogen free from her concerns.

She stirred and he watched her eyes flutter open.

"What time is it?"

"Time to make love." It was always time to make love with her.

Gently, he rolled her onto her back and relished her slumberous smile welcoming him. His cock was already hard and leaking, its perpetual state over the last day. If he wasn't recovering from making love to her, he was preparing for a new bout. Or holding her, or snatching sleep before something woke him—her soft breath on his chest, a sinuous wriggle as she adjusted her position next to him or a murmur as she awoke.

She opened her legs as he sank between them. She wasn't ready yet, her folds turned in, as if she closed like a flower when she slept. The idea of her feminine beauty as a flower appealed to him. An orchid, perhaps, with the fleshly soft petals opening for a very special bee.

No. Thoughts of stamens and pollen turned the whimsical into the unbelievable. Besides, he wasn't a poet. He expressed himself much better physically, or perhaps when he was making plans for a campaign, planning strategies.

His cock nestled between her legs as if born for that purpose alone. He kissed her, relishing the press of his body against hers, although he took care to keep his weight off her by using his knees and elbows to support himself. She ran her hands down his body, smoothing him like a cat, until she reached his buttocks. She cupped them and urged him in.

It only took a few nudges for her intimate wetness to flow. He lodged his cock against the opening to her body, content to wait until she was ready to accept him. Finishing the kiss, he tipped his head back, watching her as he slowly entered her, letting their bodies dictate the pace and not forcing anything.

The feel of their bodies slowly melding and joining struck Tony as miraculous. She absorbed him, taking his hardness into her lush, wet heat, bathing him in her essence and undoing him completely. For this alone he was hers, but her humor, her intelligence and her fierce spirit ravished him just as much. With her by his side he could achieve anything. No, *they* could achieve anything, together. Acting as one, as they were now.

Lifting her legs, she put her feet flat on the crumpled sheet beneath them as he moved in her, finding the right angle to rub against the sweet nub of her clitoris as he thrust inside her and withdrew. Arching her back, she aided his endeavors, and when she flinched, that tiny movement told him he'd reached the right spot.

The familiar heat engulfed him, their joining a physical expression of their togetherness, of the partnership they would forge that would become stronger every day, every year. No other notion had reverberated in him with such certainty before—that they belonged together and they would create something wonderful together.

Her remark earlier about being pregnant had only filled him with a sense of wonder. She'd come through the ordeal safely—there was no other alternative, nothing, though he would find a way to prevent her getting with child year after year and wearing herself out. When he took a woman, which was rarer than most people thought, he took his responsibilities seriously. Withdrawal didn't work, and now, he was so addicted to coming inside Imogen that he doubted he could even do it anymore.

She stiffened, and her channel softened and widened, her heat washing over him in great waves. He let go, let sensation take him and push him over the edge, knowing she would be with him this time.

Her cries of completion hastened his peak of ecstasy. Her channel tightened around him, milking him, taking everything he had to give her and demanding more.

A gentle, gradual loving, none the less intense for all that.

He slowly withdrew from her body, careful not to jar her sensitive flesh, and rolled onto his back, taking her with him. Before he spoke again, he kissed her, the flavor that was so uniquely hers infusing him with strength and purpose.

Her smile bathed him in warmth. "I love you." They had told each other that simple truth over and over, as if holding it back another day was impossible. It was certainly pointless. Even if he hadn't told her, he'd have revealed it by now by the intensity of his lovemaking.

"You are my heart." He caressed her cheek and with regret pointed out the light. "We've been here a day and two nights now. We should at least make enquiries to see if the world is still there. I'll order them to bring breakfast to the sitting room." Their own room. He'd ordered simple meals, but they'd eaten them together, without servants.

They hadn't ventured farther than that yesterday, and their powder-rooms to wash and freshen up. Even that necessary time apart had given him a bleak, lonely feeling.

She lifted her head and looked around. "What's the time?"

He eased her back and rolled over, reaching for the watch he kept on the nightstand. He flicked it open, the lid springing open with a touch of his thumb. "Nearly ten o'clock." He glanced back at her. "And all's well."

After their kisses, she asked him, "Why don't you have a clock on the mantel?"

He grinned. "I don't like the ticking. I got them to take it out. I can have one brought in if you like."

"No." She nodded at his watch. "I'll get a stand and find a watch that doesn't tick very loudly."

His barely made any noise at all once he'd closed the lid. That was why he liked it here. "I'll get you the best I can find." He replaced the watch and turned to her. "One more kiss."

As it happened, it was half an hour before they left the bed, but Tony didn't feel the need to rush. He'd been afraid she'd be too sore, unaccustomed to making love so often. As it happened, so was he, and he was feeling the effects a little.

They'd taken time to wash, and after they'd eaten, they'd found the bed remade with fresh sheets. Even that discreet evidence that the household knew what they were about drew her blushes. He loved her blushes and couldn't resist teasing her a little more but only gently. This kind of intimacy was new to them both, but they had all the time in the world to develop it and learn to savor it in all its delightful moods.

In the sitting-room, someone had left their post. A plethora of invitations told them they were not forgotten. On the contrary, society, now beginning to gather for the beginning of the season after Easter, was agog to see them. No doubt partly to examine the state of the bride's belly. Tony's lip twisted in a wry smile. Maybe they had reason after the last two days, although even if their previous encounter had had a fruitful result, it would not show for a while.

He laid the gilt-edged embossed pieces of pasteboard aside to peruse after he'd read the other correspondence. A slew of advertising matter lay in another stack under the invitations. He didn't bother to give them a glance. A few letters. Three, to be precise. One came from his mother, a fond note with a little gossip that he read once and laid aside to read in detail later. They might share the same house, but during his service in the army, she had become used to writing to him, and he enjoyed her letters, so they had continued the practice when he got home.

Another from a cousin, Claudia, a lively young woman, one of the two sets of twins born to his aunt Wilhelmina. A baggage. Only a baggage would write to a newly married man, but an amusing one. He had a simple, uncomplicated friendship with Claudia, something that was rare in his life. And one from Julius.

He examined the outer part before he slit open the seal. Hand-delivered, the outside clean, which probably meant his cousin was back in London. At last. He skimmed the contents and told his wife the gist of it.

"It's brief enough. He has returned to London, he has news, and he requests an interview with us as soon as possible. He sends his best wishes, of course."

She looked up from her own correspondence. He understood her much better now. Whether it was because she was no longer trying to hide her emotions from him or whether he had just grown to understand her better, he wasn't sure.

In any case, the starkness of her cheekbones and the fire in her eyes told him she wasn't pleased about something, probably in the letter she held in her hand. "My mother says she will leave London tomorrow. She has had enough, she says, of fine living. That isn't true, Tony. She's ached to visit London and give me my season. Something is sending her running."

He reached out over the table, and without hesitation, she put her hand in his. "How do you feel?" he said. "Could you bear an interview today?"

"I think we must. Or my mother will bolt. I can't help but suspect that the two events are linked. Julius's return and my mother's departure." She sighed, and he squeezed her hand in sympathy.

"I'll make the arrangements. How quickly can you dress?"

"Ten minutes." She grinned. He loved that she felt so natural with him now. "But for town, probably half an hour to an hour. I won't powder."

"Why hide that glorious hair?"

She grimaced. "I never thought it so when it tangled around me in the wind and rain. I cut it myself once and my mother didn't speak to me for a week."

His laugh surprised him, bursting out, pure joy filling him. This woman was his, and he loved her. Anything else they would cope with.

Chapter 16

Julius had a very elegant drawing room, but he made good use of it. He used it for family gatherings and ordinary everyday use, despite the fashionable furniture and Meissen figurines. His daughter, Caroline, was allowed to play there, but she wasn't there today. Only Julius, resplendent as always, immaculately turned out. He was sitting on a sofa, an open file by his side, containing a number of papers.

Leisurely he got to his feet in a smooth movement and met them, hands outstretched. He took Imogen's hands first. Disdaining the formal greeting, he drew her closer and kissed her on each cheek, and he shook Tony's hand. "Congratulations. I'm very pleased for you both." He drew back. "But not as pleased as you two are, from the look of you. Come and have some tea."

Tea. Tony would have preferred brandy, considering the news Julius might have to impart. But he took Imogen to the sofa and seated her as if she were too fragile to do it herself. While she could ride around her estate, deliver a lamb, or help with harvest, he'd learned that treatment amused her. He was understanding the woman he was in love with, and with understanding would come a deeper connection. As there was with his parents. Without that example, he didn't know how people had the courage to go ahead, but Imogen had. His respect for her increased every day, and his wonder that she'd agreed to take him.

Not that he would dream of explaining any of that to Julius. The owner of a hundred fancy waistcoats and lavender-and-pink breeches was every inch a man. He didn't share his emotions, nor did he ask anyone to do that with him.

Tony gave a swift account of what had happened in Julius's absence. "Basically fairly quiet except for the last few days. I will take care of Imogen from now on."

"As it should be." Gently, Julius swung his leg, which he'd crossed over the other. The facets of his cut-steel buckles flashed when they caught the beam of sunlight coming through the wide windows. Muffled sounds of passing traffic filtered through from the street below—horses clopping, the wheels of carriages trundling, street sellers shouting their wares. Everything normal, in fact. "I will gladly relinquish my care of her person. If you wish, I can send you some likely men."

Imogen tapped her tea dish with her spoon. "Excuse me, I am here."

He'd wondered when she'd say something. He exchanged a smile with her. "I know. And you shall have control of it. Except you must give me an opportunity to care for you, for if I don't, I'll likely run mad."

He made the statement light, but he wasn't joking. The imperative to take care of her, to ensure she came to no harm, thrummed powerfully in his blood. He needed to do it.

She nodded. "But I'm tired of people doing things and knowing things about me that I don't. That they're not thinking to tell me or share their knowledge with me. I want to know." She turned to Julius. "Tony has told me that I could be a daughter of the Old Pretender and a woman called Maria Rubiero. Is this true?"

Julius nodded. "Did he explain the circumstances?"

"Yes." She took a sip of tea, but the dish quivered with a sharp *chink* when she returned it to the saucer. She wasn't as calm as she appeared.

Julius would have noticed her nervousness, but he wouldn't say anything. Julius never missed a thing. "I didn't know how to tell you. I didn't know if it was true, even though you have a resemblance to the Old Pretender and his sons. The full lips, the dark hair and eyes, they are present in you as they were in your ancestors. Maria Rubiero, now, I have found a picture of her. I employed someone to sketch the likeness." From his side he picked up a paper and handed it to them.

Tony leaned over to see when Imogen took the copy. Maria had been a beautiful woman, with perfect oval face and sparkling eyes. The sketch wasn't in color, so only the tone was visible. Dark. And her hair, richly curly, but lighter than he'd expected. Imogen must get that rich dark brown from her father's side. But the resemblance was there in the shape of the face, the sharp little nose, and the lush mouth. "How tall was she?"

Julius laughed. "How should I know? I'm still trying to discover details about her. Her family, her origins, those details. What do you wish to know?"

Imogen had gone pale. "Everything. Is this certain? I mean that I'm their daughter?"

"Nothing is certain until we find material proof and preferably someone who knows more. Who was there." He waited, and while Tony realized his meaning at once, he waited for Imogen.

"My mother." She shook her head. "The woman I believed to be my mother for all these years." Clasping the arm of the sofa, she moved forward. "She said she was leaving today."

"She is not. I ensured she couldn't and threw petty details in her way. A horse threw a shoe, her maid didn't pack properly. She's out shopping at the moment, as I suggested she might like to go out one more time."

"She's leaving to avoid me, and because you have returned." Imogen's voice sounded so tight Tony wanted nothing more than to take her in his arms. But he would not, because such intimacy before others was new to her.

Instead, he stretched out his hand, relieved when she took it and gave him a tiny smile before turning back to Julius.

"At our wedding, she hardly approached me. She only said what she had to, and that grudgingly. She sent me a note saying she would take her leave."

"I see." Julius saw a great deal, and he would know what her statement meant. Her mother was avoiding her.

"She was never fond, never demonstrative," Imogen continued. "But recently she's withdrawn even more. She was pleased to come to London, always hated the country and our quiet life there. If she loved the city and fashion so much, why not stay in Rome with my father? She gave up her chance of an heir. My father visited infrequently, so that I hardly knew him at all. When he came, I was usually set extra lessons." She shook her head, her mouth flat, not a trace of tears. How much had she gone through before she reached that state of resigned acceptance? The people she considered her parents didn't want to see her at all, so they virtually ignored her presence. That would never happen again, not to her, and not to their children, if they were fortunate enough to have any.

"I believe your real mother thought a lot of you, so much that she sent you out of danger. It must have been a wrench for her to do it, but she did it not only to you, but your siblings. You have realized that you have brothers and sisters, haven't you?"

Biting her lips, Imogen nodded. "I still can't believe it. They seem shadowy, of no substance."

"I can introduce you to one," he said gently. "You have already met her. She's the daughter of the Pretender, but not of Maria Rubiero, so she is only a half-sister."

Imogen gasped. Uncaring now of appearances, Tony hauled her close and dragged her into his arms. She came unresisting. He kissed her forehead and held her close while they listened to Julius.

He showed no reaction to Tony's action, apart from a slight relaxation of his lips. "It's by no means certain that any of this is true. It's all speculation. I've taken the liberty of requesting your mother's presence here when she returns. You may go or leave. Whichever you choose, be sure I will keep you informed of everything that takes place."

"Do you think you will get the truth out of her easier with me here, or do you think she'll be more resistant?" Imogen asked. She still hadn't shed a tear. She'd probably shed them all before.

"It makes little difference," Julius said. "I will have the truth. I warn you, that if I have to, I will not hesitate to use all the methods at my command, barring actual physical violence. I won't be easy with her, with or without you present. I also want to lead this. If you think you can get the truth from her, you are welcome to try, but once I take over, I want a free hand."

He gave no quarter, but Imogen nodded. "I want the truth, too, however we have to get it. I take it you discovered nothing definite at Thane Hall?"

"Nothing. Except that the estate is excellently managed. Your managers, by the way, are utterly loyal to you. It took me a day to persuade them that I was acting on your instructions, and I had to talk with them until I was blue in the face."

"I'd like to have seen that," Tony said appreciatively.

"I daresay," Julius responded dryly. "The Georges, old and young, were particularly recalcitrant. I'm not sure how they will react to the news of your marriage and the transfer of the property."

"There is no transfer," Tony told him. "I have set up a new trust for Thane Hall on the same conditions as the original."

"That was well done." Julius smiled, the first he'd given for some time. "You have your own property. You should become the Earl of Hollinhead in due course. If you wish it?"

Tony shrugged. "It's immaterial to me. The rank I earned in the army means more, but my wife would appreciate the opportunity to redeem her family name."

Imogen nodded, her curls already bouncing free from the artful knot her maid had pinned them into. Today she wore the frivolous scrap of lace society deemed a cap, not the heavy linen one she'd worn as the housekeeper of Thane Hall. No barrier to her delightful curls, which seemed to have wills of their own. He loved winding them around her fingers, using them to pull her to him for a kiss.

He wanted to kiss her now. Her soft body, warm against his, reminded him forcibly of their condition only a few hours ago. He'd never tire of sharing a bed with her, of making love with her. He knew that now.

In deference to Julius, who might not appreciate witnessing the intimacy, he forced himself to wait. When the front door slammed below them, he eased her away, in preparation for her mother's entrance.

In fact, the fresh tea Julius rang for arrived before Mrs. Thane, who came in fifteen minutes later. In the interim, they'd talked of other things, all appreciating the break from the intensity of emotion to come.

Mrs. Thane greeted the woman she'd acknowledged as her daughter with heartbreaking coolness, touching her hand before serving the tea and sitting down in a chair that Julius drew up for her. She gave him a gracious smile. Julius returned it, although frostily, and took his seat on the sofa, lifting the file that had lain under the portrait of Maria Rubiero.

"I trust this will not take too long?" Mrs. Thane said. "I have ordered my luggage stowed on the carriage, and I would appreciate taking my leave before the day is advanced too much further." She nodded at Imogen. "You do not need me any further, and I am tired of town. I want to go home."

Julius glanced at Imogen, tacitly asking her permission to begin. Imogen hesitated, and then nodded. A wise decision. Julius had interrogated others in the past, although Tony wished Imogen didn't have to be here for this part. He would have offered to take her home if he'd thought she'd accept it.

"Mrs. Thane, I believe you are about to become Lady Hollinhead again," he said. "The King is willing to offer the title to Tony as the Earl of Hollinhead of the second creation. Of course you are still not legally entitled to call yourself such, but that will not concern you, I am sure."

Mrs. Thane inclined her head. "Since I married the Earl of Hollinhead, I never thought of myself as anything else. I take it I am to live at Thane Hall?"

Every cell in Tony's body repelled that notion. The last thing he wanted was his putative mother-in-law on the premises. She had the power to stir all manner of trouble, and if she'd spent the last twenty and more years complaining, he had no doubt she'd continue the way she started. "I believe you were not entirely happy there. I have other properties that you are welcome to occupy, if you find them more to your taste." Perhaps she'd like a villa by the Thames. He'd buy one tomorrow if that would keep her away from his beloved wife.

She seemed surprised, her brows rising and her eyes opening wider. She had pale blue eyes, as unlike Imogen's as they were possible to be. Her face was narrower and her complexion deathly pale, instead of Imogen's creamy lushness. "I had thought you would live in one of your grander houses."

"Thane Hall suits me well. If you want grand houses, refer to my cousin Maximilian, or Julius."

"Or my father," Julius said with a wry twist to his mouth. As a duke, Julius's father owned some of the grandest estates and houses in the land. Tony had no desire to find himself in that situation, and wished him joy of it.

"You must please yourself, madam." He wished he could cross his fingers for luck as he said that.

Mrs. Thane inclined her head as graciously as any duchess.

"You were born in England, ma'am?" Julius asked her, approaching the subject gently.

"I was, sir. But my parents went abroad to Rome, to be with the—" she broke off. "The Pretender," she finished, but no sign of discomfort crossed her face when she said the name.

"You supported the Cause?"

"My parents did."

"How do you feel about the Stuarts?"

She paused, stared at him, her eyes watchful and alert. "What do you mean? I was a dutiful daughter. Then I was married to Lord Hollinhead." She had avoided the question.

"Pray continue. You intrigue me, ma'am."

"When Imogen was born, my husband took steps to safeguard her. So the house was put aside for her, and I brought her home."

"Even though you had made no heir to the title?"

"He lost that soon enough." Now she sounded bitter. That came as no surprise, since she had always demonstrated her reluctance to give up using the title. "But we still saw each other. He visited."

"Clandestinely."

She nodded. She hadn't touched her tea, but kept her hands tightly folded in her lap. "He's dead now, so what does it matter? And we didn't conceive an heir."

"Except for Imogen."

She jerked a nod. "As you say."

"Except Imogen isn't yours, is she?"

The sound of the carriages outside increased as dead silence fell in the room. Everyone sat completely still, not even the rustle of silk disturbing the fraught atmosphere. "Whatever do you mean?" Mrs. Thane's voice lifted in pitch. She cleared her throat.

Tony watched, Julius questioned. They'd played this game before, but never with such intensity. The result of this conversation meant the difference between Imogen's knowing the facts of her birth or remaining forever in limbo—not knowing.

"Of course she's mine! How could you think such a thing?"

"She was given to you, for sure. But she is not of your get. You have never borne a child, have you?" Julius was relentless, but he knew the power of silence and waiting for an answer as much as any army interrogator.

"She is mine. I gave birth to her. She is my daughter." She lifted her chin, glaring at Julius defiantly.

Julius swung his foot and smiled. "I think not," he said. "Before I left town on my errand to Thane Hall, I set a few other enquiries into motion, and one of them bore fruit." He stirred the papers in the file, leafed through them, and came up with another. "I traced one of your maids, one who has since left your service. Do you recall Susan Prentice?"

Mrs. Thane went very still. "No."

"Come now, I feel sure that you do." He flicked a piece of paper.

"You would trust the word of a servant girl against mine?" she said, disdain dripping in every syllable.

"Yes."

She glared at Julius and then got to her feet, clearly intending to leave the room.

"I must insist that you stay, madam, else face the consequences."

"Better men than you have tried to best me."

Imogen's mother's face was reddened, her eyes glittering with pure fury.

Julius remained calm, his foot still swinging gently. "Please sit down. I believe there may be more tea in the pot. Imogen, would you be so kind?"

As she moved to fulfil his request, Tony exchanged a glance with Julius and froze. He knew that look. Julius had more to say, and a sudden realization made him deny the understanding that sprang into his mind.

"If you will excuse me for a moment, I'll ensure the horses are attended to. This discussion is obviously going to take more time than we imagined," Tony said, getting to his feet and groping for the first reasonable excuse he could think of. A quick exchange assured him Julius would care for Imogen in the short time he meant to be away. He would find this out for her, even if he lost her in the process.

* * * *

Imogen sat perfectly still, as she had so often in her childhood. Facing this woman had proved so hard, even though she'd had Tony with her through the ordeal. If she sat like this, people sometimes forgot she was there, or took no notice of her. If she was lucky, that would happen now.

No such luck.

Her mother shot a venomous glare at her. "What have you been telling them?"

"Only what I know, which is precious little," she said bitterly. "That you deceived me all my life. That you've been living in my house under false pretenses. I am not your get, and I am not the daughter of the Earl of Hollinhead. No wonder the man I thought of as my father showed little interest in me, save ensuring I was safe."

"He was told to keep away," she said bitterly. "Not to draw attention to you."

"Yes," said Julius. "That makes sense. So you had little time to make an heir for your husband."

Mrs. Thane took the documents Julius handed her, retook her seat, and leafed through the papers.

She clicked her tongue, a sound Imogen had familiarized herself with years ago. She still hated that little sound of exasperation.

"Why should I concern myself with providing an heir to a bankrupt estate? Imogen had the part of it that was worth anything at all, and nobody could remove it from her. My husband had donated the house and estate to the Cause. I had nothing. A child of my own would not have helped that." She tossed the papers down on the sofa next to her. "How did you get all these?"

"A long arm and a deep purse," he said. Julius leaned forward, pushing into her mother's—Mrs. Thane's—area of the room. As if he'd shoved her, she flinched back.

"So you know it all."

Julius regarded her closely, his blue eyes a deep intent sapphire. "What else do you think I know?"

Mrs. Thane shrugged. She had so often sent Imogen with a flea in her ear when Imogen had asked her about her babyhood that Imogen had stopped asking. Just so, with a careless shrug and an, "I don't want to talk about it."

She couldn't get away with that now.

"Do you know the Duke of Northwich?" Julius demanded.

"Of course. I've met him since we came to London."

"Did you know him before?"

She laughed shakily. "I don't know what you mean. No, of course not. I knew *of* him."

"Of course," Julius said. "Everyone has. He's a noted Jacobite, but he's never been caught in traitorous activities. He lets other people do that. Tony married Imogen in such haste because the duke has been showing a particular interest in her."

She shot Imogen an irritated glance. "She should have waited. Lord William is a considerable catch, and he was very interested in Imogen. His affiliations are such that women are vying for his hand. A younger son with a modest estate could not compare to that."

Imogen clenched her fists in her lap. "I was not interested in him."

"Really, Imogen, a female in your position can't be too fussy!"

Yes she could. She really could, since she cared little for social standing and political fussing. She had found the one man she wanted, and already he was an essential part of her life. She couldn't imagine life without him.

A report sounded outside, so loud it made her start in alarm. "What was that?"

Julius was already on his feet and heading for the window. Shouts and running feet sounded from outside. "Stay here," he rapped out. "Don't go near the windows."

He raced across the room and left.

Shocked, the two women stared at each other. No, she couldn't wait to discover. What was she, a weak vessel? Men so often underestimated women like her. Imogen got to her feet and approached the window from an angle, so if there were any danger, nobody would have a clear view of her. Mrs. Thane protested, but Imogen ignored her. Something she should have done years ago, but now she had better reason.

"Come back, you stupid girl!"

Easy to ignore the insults once she realized they meant absolutely nothing to her. Using the drapery to cover her, she peered out of the window.

Across the street, a carriage had halted, and only the coachman remained with it. She'd have to move closer to see the cause of the commotion. People were running toward the house, converging on something in front of it.

The portico obscured much of her vision, but a travelling coach was drawn up before the house. The one meant to carry Mrs. Thane home, she supposed. Now redundant, as she didn't want to let her go just yet, sure she knew something she wasn't telling them.

Trunks and bags lay on the pavement, and a footman was busy recovering them and handing them to the servants who were carrying them indoors. Where was Tony? She couldn't see him from her vantage point.

The horses, put to fresh, were stamping and shaking their heads. The coachman was fortunate that the bang, whatever it was, hadn't made them bolt. Perhaps someone dropped one of the trunks. That would make a resounding sound. But why were people gathering around? A smashed trunk wouldn't bring so many, surely?

The sound of voices raised in alarm, or anger, or both, reached her ears, but the window wasn't open so she couldn't make out any words. But the ring that had formed around the door and coach contained excited, agitated people from all walks of life, and none of them appeared too anxious to approach any further.

When heavy footsteps came from the stairs, Imogen spun around, careful to keep out of sight, as Julius had bade her—well, almost—and faced the big double doors as they burst open to admit a clearly perturbed Julius.

His wig was awry, and she'd never seen that before, never imagined it happening, revealing a glimmer of his fair hair, and his coat bore stains. Dark stains.

Oh, God—bloodstains.

"Come at once," he said. "He's been hurt. Your husband is shot."

Chapter 17

Imogen's first foolish, irritated thought was, "Not again!" but that was replaced immediately by alarm. Her heart swelled, seeming to occupy all her chest, pounding as if it wanted to escape the cage of ribs containing it. Her breath shortened and spots appeared before her eyes.

No fainting, none. Not now. She reached out blindly, and Julius took her hand, gripping it hard enough for her to regain her senses, at least partly. "It's bad," he said. "Come at once." He tugged and she followed.

Ignoring Mrs. Thane's shrieks and lamentations, Imogen ran out of the room with Julius and up the stairs to the bedroom. Servants milled around, the house a place of chaos and confusion rather than the order she was used to.

He'd taken Tony to the bedroom she occupied when she stayed here, so recently vacated in much happier circumstances. A widow so soon? It would not happen. Could not. She had found such happiness and it would not be taken away from her.

A man stood outside the door, one of the burly footmen Julius employed. Helena stood outside, hands on hips, visibly annoyed. "This fool man won't let me in. For God's sake, I can help!"

Julius took her hand. "I fear you cannot, my dear. Please, go and care for Mrs. Thane. She is deeply overcome. Let me take Imogen in."

Helena stared at him in silence for a second, her eyes widening, and her mouth dropping open. "No."

Julius sighed. "Come in, then."

He opened the door. Imogen put her head up, her habit when facing adversity, set her chin, and went inside, Helena close behind.

Julius closed the door quickly.

Instantly warm arms closed about her, and Tony's lips were on hers. Heedless of anyone watching, she returned his kiss. Relief and thankfulness surged through her in a wave so strong she thought she might die. Tears rolled down her face, relief achieving what tragedy could not.

He kissed her fiercely, and held her close, then released her. "Sweetheart, my love, I'm so sorry. I refused to do this unless Julius found you and brought you here immediately."

"What?"

"I was shot at, again." He set her a distance holding her upper arms, and gazed down at her face. "He grazed me, a mere scrape, but it created enough blood to make it believable. I went down with the impact, and by then Julius was on me."

She sighed in relief and closed her eyes, concentrating on drawing breath. She would not give in now.

Julius took over. "This is the second time someone shot at my cousin. It is clear that whoever it is will not stop until they have him. Unless we strike first. I've let out that he's gravely injured, close to death."

She gazed up at him, assimilating what was happening. "Will you tell your family?"

"Yes." No equivocation there. Everyone who cared about him would know. She could agree with this outrageous scheme if he did that. But what next? "What do you plan to do?"

"Draw him out," Tony said. He had a bandage roughly wound around his upper arm, bloodstained, but the blood was no longer flowing. "We know who this is, don't we?"

Her head whirled with possibilities. Who could she trust? The people she'd known all these years weren't who they thought. Were these people telling the truth? This man, holding her so securely?

Could she even trust herself? Because whatever he was, she still loved him with all her heart.

She made her decision. If she was foolish, so be it. But her mother had never shown the care Tony had. She'd never noticed when Imogen was out of sorts, or busy, or too tired to sit through a dinner with their neighbors.

Horrified, she searched her mind. Yes, they knew. "One of two people. Lord William Dankworth. And my mother, or the woman posing as my mother." Lord William wanted her, and Tony was standing in the way. Mrs. Thane might want to cover her mistake, and given the order earlier, before she knew the game was up.

Tony clasped her close. His heart beat strongly against her cheek, and he cupped her head with one big hand. "I love you, Imogen. I'm never giving you up. I won't have this trouble hanging over us. I decided to stay down when I heard the report. They brought me here, but by then I realized the wound was not serious and sent them away until Julius came."

"They have played into our hands." Julius took a turn around the room, the skirts of his green town coat flying behind him. "If we say the wound is serious, we will bring the assassin out into the open, like a partridge flushed out of the wood."

"And we have the advantage." Helena's honeyed voice poured over them, the richness of her tones not concealing her pleasure in the notion. "Why would you say it was one of those? Mrs. Thane was with you in the drawing room."

"You don't have to hold the pistol to be responsible," Tony said. "In this instance, whoever did it shot damned close to the first one. I suspect either that's their poor aim or they used the same weapon, and it pulls to the left. I was standing completely still this time."

"What were you doing?" She stayed close, held against his warmth, counting every miraculous beat of his heart.

"I was supervising unpacking your mother's luggage. I beg your pardon—Mrs. Thane's. It occurred to me that women often have secret drawers in their jewelry chests or their stationery boxes. Something of that nature could hide a document, or secrets. Julius wouldn't have missed them if they were at your house. He'd have searched most thoroughly."

"A lot of papers are lodged at the lawyer's, but mostly they're duplicates, or they have the originals and we have the duplicates. I don't know of any documents unique to either site."

"I assumed that was so," Julius said, "but I visited your man of business with your letter of authorization, just in case. I claimed we'd mislaid your birth certificate. He produced one, patently false, and I asked to look through your other papers, since you gave me permission. He refused, as a good lawyer should, but I judged him a man of honesty and sense. He deals with too many clients to want any of them to accuse him of dishonesty."

She smiled against Tony's chest and eased away to look up at him. He met her gaze and returned her smile. "I want to do this because I want you to be safe. Completely secure. This last push and we're done. Then we'll go home."

"Yes."

He kissed her, but soft and sweetly. A sigh behind them told them Helena was watching, but Imogen didn't care.

"The hell of it is that I have to stay here while you and Julius do the work."

"I get to stay with you."

"I wouldn't have it any other way."

"So," Julius said, walking around to where she could see him, "how do we go about this? We've seized the advantage. Now we have to use it."

* * * *

The next day, a sad procession prepared to depart from the London residence of the Earl of Winterton. The whole of the town had heard of the shocking attack on the earl's cousin, Mr. Beaumont. Julius had ensured that everyone knew it by the simple expedient of discussing the matter in the servants' hearing. Nobody could spread gossip as fast as a good domestic servant.

Consequently, a small crowd had gathered to watch the sad departure of the gravely injured Mr. Beaumont for his cousin's country home. Imogen had dressed in a suitably somber gown, and although she didn't look to right or left when she left the house, she had ogled the crowd from the window upstairs before they left.

"Come back to bed," Tony had suggested. "Let's do what Julius suggested and send substitutes."

"No." Regretfully she turned from the window. "I'd like nothing more, but whoever is watching will know me."

"If it's not a hired man."

"Even then, Lord William won't have made the mistake of sending someone who didn't know his target. He brought servants to Thane Hall. Maybe one of them is waiting for us. Or nobody at all."

Tony threw back the bedclothes. For a gravely injured man, he'd been remarkably active last night. He winked, and she laughed, immediately clapping her hand over her mouth. The footman outside had orders to keep everyone away, but she should not risk a laugh. Sighs, groans, and the occasional cry of "Oh, yes!" had her concerned, as well, but he'd wrung all those out of her too.

He had no preparation to make, as he was travelling in his night clothes. Not that he was wearing any at the moment.

When Imogen let the curtain fall, he got out of bed and crossed the room to the washstand. She'd carried the pail of hot water inside herself, laughing at his consternation that she should carry anything that heavy. "Baby calves weigh more," she assured him, as she poured the water into the basin for her morning ablutions. She couldn't believe how happy she was for someone facing yet another dangerous trial. But very soon she would put all this behind her. She felt as if she were leaving everything behind, including her unhappy childhood, and setting out for a new world, a new happiness with the man she loved with all her heart. And who loved her.

His muscles flexed as he raised his arm to pick up a clean washcloth and rinse it out. They'd agreed he wouldn't shave, to aid the deception, but he swabbed his body with the soapy cloth. She watched his unconscious movements greedily. The smoothness of his actions belied the presence of the bandage on his upper arm, and the injury under it was, as he'd claimed, negligible, but he'd had the presence of mind to stay down when the initial impact had spun him around and knocked him off balance. He was tall and lean, his firm buttocks adding sensual curves to a back that was only the more powerful because of it. His arms bulged with muscle—arms that had held her through the night, arms she'd woken up with wrapped around her. His hair had grown a little since she first met him. She liked it—long enough for her to run her fingers through when he had her under him and he was driving deep inside her.

He turned around, catching her watching him. "Come here."

She was getting to know that throaty tone well, but she couldn't resist it any more than she could the first time she'd heard it. She went forward and felt, yet again, his arms close around her. Resting her head against his chest, she murmured, "I love you. I don't know what I would have done if you'd died."

He kissed the top of her head. "Which is why I have no intention of doing anything of the kind in the near future. Do you think I'll make a good country gentleman?"

"Country earl." For the most astonishing thing was the speed with which the king had prosecuted the creation of the title. Fearing for Tony's death, he'd had the papers rushed through, and now, but for the formal ratification, they were the Earl and Countess of Hollinhead.

"Indeed. Passing strange, that. A few years ago that might have created division between my brother and me. Now he just laughed and congratulated me. I wonder if he'll find his own princess?"

Her face troubled, she lifted her head. "Don't say that. I'm not a princess. I'm the daughter of a disgraced member of the royal family and his mistress. That's all."

"You're my princess. You always will be." He bent his head and kissed her, his mouth moving over hers in a familiar way, the way she loved best. He licked her lips, and then her tongue when she touched him with it. His cock rose to press against her stomach insistently, and they were in strong danger of missing their appointment with the carriage upstairs.

Tony lifted his head when someone knocked on the door, a gentle rap but a powerful reminder of what they must do. "Come, my love. Tonight we will at least be one step further on in our attempt to put this behind us."

That sounded good. "Perhaps in a few days we can be at home, at Thane Hall." If their plan worked.

He eased away from her and picked up a towel, scrubbing his body vigorously. "If I'm to be confined to a bedroom while we smoke out whoever is trying to kill me, I will need a deal of exercise. I'm not used to being in one place for too long." He winked at her. "After all, it's how we got into this to start with." His gaze softened. "I'd do everything again, just for that."

"Without the bullet."

Laughing, he turned to pick up the clean nightshirt that she'd laid out ready for him. "Without that we wouldn't have anything."

She studied the scar from the bullet hole, where it had left his body, still red and puckered, but he never gave any indication of it bothering him. The hole was smaller the other side, where it had entered. "It will be a clean scar." She had seen far worse in accidents with farm implements, but although she told herself that often, it didn't do much good. She still quailed when she thought how close she'd come to losing the most precious thing in her life, before she even knew she had it.

He had other scars, too, even another bullet wound, this one on his thigh, high up, too close to a major blood vessel for her to laugh when he'd joked about it.

"I didn't even know I had it until I dismounted. The damn horse fell under me. The bullet had hit us both, but we made a speedy recovery, man and horse both. I don't know which the army was more pleased about, because we were undergoing a shortage of horses at the time."

She hadn't joined in his laughter, but traced the puckered white scar with one finger and sworn to live the quietest life imaginable. No more scars, no more bullet wounds.

He covered his body, the white linen falling over his powerful muscles, shrouding them. Shuddering at the thought, Imogen turned away and found his robe, handing it to him silently. He'd chosen a dark blue one after she'd rejected the scarlet one Julius had offered. Too much like blood, too powerful a target. If they were right, someone was waiting outside somewhere with a weapon.

A knock sounded on the door. "Are you ready, my lady?" One of the servants.

"In a moment!"

Tony crossed the room and leaped back into bed, dragging the covers up to tuck under his chin.

"Come!"

The men came in, followed by Julius. "You can trust these two," he said. "They'll be acting as outriders. But they won't be carrying a lump like you around unless they have to. One will carry you downstairs, the other will make sure the first doesn't drop you. The servants will be watching." Which meant after their departure, the domestics would gleefully carry the news to the next house, and the next, and so on.

Tony cracked an eye open and grinned. Flinging back the covers, he approached the servant, arms wide. "Take me to my fate."

The servant grinned back, but swept Tony off his feet like a groom lifting his wife on their wedding night. He carried Tony downstairs with tender care, and Tony did his part, lying limply in the man's arms, occasionally groaning, but not overdoing it.

In the hall, he climbed on to the litter, which was nothing more than a piece of canvas strung between two rods. Julius shook out the blanket and tenderly tucked Tony in while Imogen stood by, handkerchief in hand. She'd had the foresight to sprinkle it with water, just enough to dampen it. She didn't take her eyes off her husband, which was hardly a trial.

Out of sight of the servants, he winked at her. She could have killed him. Couldn't he take this seriously? Since they'd made their plans last night he'd been in high spirits. She had to admit she felt a little lighter, and now, going out of the front door to the carriage, she knew why. At last, they were doing something, taking the initiative and moving forward. Planning their own fate instead of haplessly following in another's wake.

They loaded him into the carriage, and Julius handed Imogen up.

Inside there wasn't a great deal of room. The blinds were lowered over the windows in the half of the coach nearest the driver, in deference to the patient, but also to conceal the presence of two of Tony's cousins, Lord Valentinian Shaw, son of the Marquess of Strenshall, and Ivan Rowley, son of the Earl of Leverton.

Ivan's dark good looks reflected the emperor, or tsar, he was named after. Valentinian had chestnut hair and hazel eyes. Val flashed a smile, from his uncomfortable position squatting on the seat, and made room for Imogen to perch on the edge opposite Tony. He had a gun under the blankets of the stretcher. Four unsheathed swords lay on the floor, one an army saber. Tony let one arm fall over the side of the seat his stretcher laid on and seized the sword hilt.

Ivan handed Imogen a pistol. "Welcome to the family."

Imogen returned his friendly smile without looking at him directly, somewhat bemused by the rank of their bodyguard. She'd met them briefly at society gatherings, but neither had appeared so dangerous. If she tasted the air, the flavor would be reckless. She didn't have much room, which was why she'd chosen not to wear a hoop but a riding habit, a garment women frequently used for travelling. This one was much grander than her old one at home, but it had the same familiar feel, the jacket hugging her body and the skirt draped over her legs, rather than the cage she wore in town.

The coachman called out and the vehicle jolted into movement. Val and Ivan could see rather more than people might suppose, even if they knew the men were there, because small mirrors were mounted outside the coach, hidden as part of the trappings. They could see behind them and in front. Imogen watched the houses they passed, and the coachmen and outriders were monitoring the rest.

Yet Tony was still in clear view. He stirred, moving so he could see, too, but kept his eyes half-closed. This was the part Imogen was dreading.

Would they strike here, or would they, as Julius had posited, wait until the coach reached Hampstead Heath, where highwaymen and footpads lurked, waiting for the unwary? Or would they strike at all?

Ivan owned a small house just outside London, and they were ostensibly heading for that. "I sent word," Ivan murmured, "but I haven't used it for years. If they don't attack, we'll have to spend at least one night there."

"Imogen and I only need one bed," Tony murmured without moving his lips.

Imogen had no idea how he did that, but she'd get that secret out of him. Despite the tension gripping her, turning her breakfast over in her stomach, the skill intrigued her.

Tony and she had come the closest to a serious argument when she'd insisted on travelling with him. But as she'd pointed out, whoever wanted him also wanted her alive. She was the pawn, and dead, she was useless. When Julius agreed with her, Tony was forced to concede, but he hadn't done it happily.

"Alex will be livid to miss this," Ivan, the brother of Alex, Lord Ripley, said with a grin.

"Ah yes, he owes the Dankworths a favor," Val murmured, his gaze speculatively surveying the view. As usual, people thronged the streets, people of all classes, but now they'd left the street, nobody took special notice of them. Not yet, at any rate.

Imogen had heard how Alex's wife, the lovely Connie who'd spoken to her so kindly on her wedding day, had spent time in one of the most notorious brothels in London, courtesy of a Dankworth. Not the same one, but as a clan they were a menace. At least now they knew why. That damned woman, Maria Rubiero. Imogen's birth mother.

Now dead, with all her secrets, except the ones turning London into a battleground.

Next to her, Ivan slowly eased into a seat, lowering his legs by fractions until he gave a deep sigh. "I couldn't hold it any longer. But we're not about to open the doors until we have to, are we?"

On the other side of her, Val did the same. "I never realized how painful that position could be." They took care to keep their bodies well back against the seats, and they'd drawn the blinds on their side, so they were still hidden. The coach took another corner. They were nearly into the City now, and they'd turn on to the Great North Road to give the attackers a chance. The outriders would drop back on some excuse, to tempt them into the open.

"I am growing distinctly bored," Val said. "Is anything about to happen?"

Tony gave a short laugh. "Try being a soldier. You can spend hours sitting around, waiting for something to happen. It does, and you pray for the boredom to return."

"Humph."

Ivan studied the mirrors. "Sharp corner ahead."

Tony glanced at her, reminding her tacitly of her promise. If matters came to a head, she was to drop to the floor of the coach and cover her head. Julius's travel coach had metal-covered lower doors, for protection against ordinary footpads. It would help to protect her if she needed it now.

A sharp sound rang out, and then another. Recently Imogen had heard enough shots to know one from the crack of a whip or someone dropping something heavy. That was a shot. It zinged off the side of the coach, and another shot followed on the heels of the first.

Tony rolled on to his stomach, his gun at the ready. Val and Ivan jumped to the floor, covering Imogen, protecting her. Imogen cocked her weapon and pointed it high, above the head of Ivan, sure the shot had come from that direction.

Hooves thundered outside as the outriders went into action, fulfilling their true purpose.

They were still in a busy part of London, approaching Covent Garden, on the fringes of the notorious rookery of Seven Dials. As the coachmen dragged the horses to a halt, commotion reigned. People didn't usually fire shots in this area. Too dangerous, too uncertain.

Shouts from outside maddened Imogen. Here she was, surrounded by men more intent on caring for her. "You shouldn't have shown yourself so soon! Let them come!"

"I saw him," Ivan said grimly. "So did the outriders. He won't get away."

He didn't. The clopping of hooves on cobbles announced the return of the outriders, slower than they'd left. Ivan stepped back as the door to the coach opened and Tony kicked the stretcher to the floor and moved over.

They'd already secured the assailant's arms, tied behind his back at elbows and wrists. He kicked out as he sat, catching Ivan who swore and kicked back. The man yelped.

He wore a dark green cloth coat and plain waistcoat, with a cocked hat that he'd pulled over his eyes. He scowled at Imogen when she peered at him, and then his face cleared and astonishment took its place. "Your highness!" He'd have dropped to his knees if Tony had allowed him, but Tony had busied himself with a length of rope, securing the man's ankles.

"Back to my house," he ordered the outrider who waited outside the open door. "We'll continue matters there."

The man kept his mouth clamped shut during the twenty minute journey to the house in the uncomfortably cramped coach. Imogen changed places with their prisoner so she was sitting next to Tony, who held her hand, because they both needed it.

He was right. That period of inaction followed by five minutes of action had exhausted her. Not that she'd admit that to anyone. She wanted to see that right to the end. She was at the center of this mess, and she would remain there until they'd concluded it.

Oh, but she longed for home! She wanted so much to walk along the creaking corridors with the curved walls and twisted timbers. She missed them, the marks she'd made on the walls, the places she'd hidden to cry or to read or just to sit and look out over the rose garden.

It was home, and it was hers. Thanks to the man at her side, it was still hers. Her kingdom. The only one she wanted.

Chapter 18

Fury simmered low in Tony, and it had since someone had dared shoot at him again. He'd let some of his frustration loose when he'd made love to his wife the night before, but he had kept his lovemaking as restrained and gentlemanly as he could. She needed soothing and reassuring; she didn't need him to fall on her like a madman.

Now he could let go. He would discover who was doing this. He'd kill him. A rage suffused him like he'd never experienced before because it concerned the person who meant more to him than anyone else in the world.

Ivan and Val took the man into the small parlor at the front. It had one window that overlooked the street, but had a fall that could well kill a man. If he jumped and fell straight, he'd fall into the area below, in front of the kitchen, where the staff would take him back. With any luck he'd break a leg. If he jumped out, he'd fall on to the spiked railing meant to protect passersby from the plunge.

Either would suit him. When he'd finished with the bastard.

Val and Ivan were the more reckless of his cousins, Val with a sense of humor his parents were trying to allay by betrothing him to one of the most staid women in London, and Ivan by reining him in when he went too wild. His father was none too steady, and until recently his older brother Alex was a reprobate of some magnitude.

Tony could trust his two cousins to back him up and not force caution on him. He had until the restraining force that was Julius got there.

They tied the prisoner to a chair, and Tony got to work. Much as he wanted to, he couldn't kill the man. Not until he discovered what he needed to know.

Forcing calm on himself, he considered the situation, assessing it swiftly and decisively. Later he'd let his anger loose, but for now he caged it.

"Who?" he demanded.

Predictably, the man said nothing.

Tony backhanded him, careful not to damage his mouth too much. He wanted the man to talk. "Who sent you?"

The man's upper lip twitched, as if he were trying to sneer. A trickle of blood slid out of the corner of his mouth.

Tony tried a little reason. "We can hand you over to the authorities, in which case you'll hang, you can let us beat you to a pulp, or you can take a hundred guineas for the information. It's your choice."

The man stared. So Tony broke his fingers, one by one. At least by the end, the man who would have killed his wife was screaming. And eventually, they had a name. More for personal satisfaction than because he doubted in any way who'd done it.

"Northwich! Long live the true King!"

"Lock him up." Tony spun on his heel and left his friends to patch up the man. He was no longer interested in him. He had more important things to do.

* * * *

An hour later Tony had tracked down his quarry. In the middle of the day, Lord William Dankworth was still abed, or rather, as the superior being at his house informed him, preparing for the day ahead. "Tell him I'm here." Tony took a seat on the maroon leather chair by the window, crossing his legs and showing no inclination to leave. "I would appreciate a prompt appearance, but I understand why not. His early morning exertions have probably exhausted him."

The room was comfortable enough, certainly not a den of iniquity. Still, he held himself together with effort, tension snapping in his gut. On edge, ready for battle, he waited.

But not for long. The Duke of Northwich entered the drawing-room, his long face glibly welcoming and his eyes snapping with curiosity. They exchanged courteous bows.

"I must admit seeing you here is somewhat a surprise, your lordship." He pronounced Tony's new title without a sneer, but he didn't need to, really.

Tony ignored the veiled insult and forbore to use any title. "Why? Did you expect to find me dead?"

The duke turned around and addressed the servant who'd slipped in behind them. "Please ensure we're not interrupted."

The man bowed, murmured, "Your grace," and left.

It was far too civilized for Tony's liking. He retook his seat and watched the duke. Not a twitch marked his reaction. The duke settled himself on the sofa opposite, taking his time to flick the skirts of his brown coat into place and arrange them to his satisfaction. Although the duke was older than his cousin, both men exuded urbane sophistication, something he had little patience with or wished to aspire to. Impatience filled him with annoyance because a dance lay ahead where he wanted plain speaking. "I expected to see Lord William."

"My son is unfortunately from home."

"Your man said he was still abed."

"He's mistaken. I will speak with him."

Tony smiled. "Send him to me. I'll find a post for him. Perhaps pig man on one of my farms would suffice."

The duke returned the smile, though thinly. He swung his foot, the brilliants on his shoe buckles catching the light. "I do not envy the pigs. My son generally performs his role adequately." He paused, watching Tony, his eyes sharp.

Tony waited.

The duke shrugged. "We may as well get to the point. My son made an error. It will not be repeated."

"What error?"

"Twice." That was no answer but Tony understood. The duke hadn't known Tony's intentions. He could have had Lord William taken up for attempted murder. Since he'd captured the man who'd attacked him the second time, and perhaps the first, too, he could put him in court as proof. The duke must get his son out of the way, and sending him abroad was an expedient way of doing so.

"The holes in my chest and arms?"

The duke nodded, his eyes closing. He pinched the bridge of his nose. "Indeed. You will accept my apology." It wasn't a request. "And his, naturally. I believe he will not return to town this season."

"He won't appreciate that." Not that Tony cared. But he did want to know where the man was, so he could keep an eye on him. But he felt a profound sense of relief that the man had left London.

"Indeed, but he will find some solace in Rome."

If that was where he had really gone. Northwich was so devious he would beat a corkscrew for twists and turns. Unlike Tony. Straightforward honesty. "I don't want a repetition. I don't care what you or my cousin or anyone else is up to, my wife is not to be put in danger."

The duke's foot stopped swinging. "Your wife?" He sighed. "When did that happen? I should really keep an eye on the newspapers, but chasing after my family took all my time this last week."

Tony didn't believe that for a minute. The duke wanted to appear as if he'd taken his eye off the target. Tony knew better. He'd wager the duke knew everything his son had done and had probably sent him to Lancashire in the first place. But he humored the duke and told him what he already knew. "We married recently. Did you send your son to court my wife?" He did not expect a straight answer now. He doubted the duke was capable of one.

"She wasn't your wife then."

Not an answer. Tony cocked a brow in query.

The duke sighed as if he had the weight of the world on his shoulders. "I found it reprehensible in the extreme that my son put the lady who is now your wife into any kind of peril. She is a precious commodity, not to be harmed in any way."

He, on the other hand, was expendable. Even more so now he'd married the woman the duke wanted for his son. "I have no intention of doing so. Do you?"

"No. You must keep her safe. I depend on you to do so."

So the duke knew what Imogen was, who her parents were. That came as no surprise to Tony, but he appreciated the confirmation. "On that we agree. I wish her safe because I care for her. Why do *you* wish her kept safe?"

The duke dug a hand in the large outer pocket of his coat and drew out a bundle of papers. Old but not grimy, although the edges had become somewhat tattered, they seemed innocuous enough. But then, general's orders often had that deceptive appearance too and frequently carried explosive information.

Tony got to his feet to take the papers and strolled over to the window. He opened the first and froze. "Where did you get these?"

"Lady Hollinhead brought them to me yesterday. Oh, not your wife. Her mother. You may retain them if you wish, but I would prefer to keep the letter. I have copies."

The official documents weren't originals, but they were certified copies, which froze his blood to the marrow. "Presumably the originals were destroyed in the fire," the duke said.

He was holding his wife's birth certificate. The true one. Another document, a copy of marriage lines. And a letter, the spidery writing difficult to interpret, even more so because it was in Italian.

Something clicked in Tony's mind. "And Lord William has gone to Rome to try to find it?"

A smile insinuated itself across the duke's features. "Indeed. Into the lion's den, so to speak." He shrugged. "I assure you that while my family's sympathies may be with the Pretender, we intend to do nothing treasonable. If my son encounters the court at the Palazzo Muti, he will not offer them a royal bow and he will remind them where his loyalties lie. Personally, I doubt the original exists. I believe Maria had it with her when her house caught fire. However, there will be an official copy somewhere. Knowing the propensity of the papacy to collect useful documents, it's probably resting in the Vatican. In that case, we may have a more difficult task."

Tony regarded the duke through narrowed eyes. "You will let me leave the house today without a fight?"

The duke shrugged. "You are a member of a family that could cause me endless trouble. Why should I murder a much-loved member of it? However, accidents happen, and I cannot prevent them."

His heavy-lidded gaze swept over Tony with a contemptuousness only the wealthy aristocrat could manage. It sent a shiver over Tony's body. He ignored it. "If they do, I'll leave instructions. I have people who will carry them out without compunction. Suffice it to say that they don't involve the law or wrangling in court. My wife will be left in peace, and because she cares for me, so will I." He meant that. As an ex-soldier, he had access to people who would count their loyalty to him. Several owed him favors that he had no intention of collecting, except in this case. Nobody knew, least of all his family. That way they could genuinely claim they knew nothing.

"You understand that while you are married to her, she is of little use to me."

Of course. The duke wanted Imogen married to a member of his own clan. Hence sending his son to court her. "I'm glad to hear it. She is out of the game. There are others where she came from, we both know that. Look for them."

"I fully intend to."

Tony folded the documents, careful to keep to their original creases, and tucked them in his pocket. "These belong to my wife, not my mother."

The duke gave him a considering stare, his eyes unblinking. But Tony had met snakes before and knew better than to break the connection. He met the duke's dark eyes.

Eventually the duke shrugged. "No matter. I will find more. The important thing is that I know."

Cold swept over Tony at the realization. He had to get out of this poisonous place.

* * * *

Imogen was enjoying the luxury of a lazy and late breakfast in her room when Tony found her. He tossed a bundle of worn papers down by her plate. "I retrieved these from the Duke of Northwich this morning. I'll send copies to Julius for his information, but as far as I'm concerned, this closes the matter. He won't bother us again."

She saw her birth certificate, the real one. Then another document, a letter. "I don't read Italian," she confessed.

Gently, he took the document for her and read it, translating it as he went.

"I, Maria Rubiero, on the tenth of March, 1730, do declare that seven days ago I gave birth to a baby daughter. She is the child of James Stuart, James the Third of Great Britain, and my husband. James Francis Stuart and I were married on the 20th September, 1717, at the Chapel of the Virgin, in Fontaine Square, Rome. This letter is to accompany a copy of her birth certificate and my marriage certificate. I am sending her away with a person I can trust, for her own safety, Lady Hollinhead, who has sworn to bring her up as her own, and keep her from danger. I swear this by the Virgin Mary and all the Saints. May God give me mercy."

"So these are my birth certificate and her marriage lines."

She perused the other two documents. They were easier to follow. Dazed, she stared at them, absorbing the information before lifting her troubled gaze to his face. Once she'd seen the papers, she'd understood at once why her husband had put himself in danger. "Northwich wanted me married to his son. He wanted a pawn."

Tony took her hand. "He wanted a legitimate daughter of the Old Pretender to challenge the authorities. That would give him the power he's lusted after for years."

"I don't want it, Tony." She shivered.

He kissed her wrist. "You think I don't know that?"

Imogen shivered, arousal still working its magic. But shock added to her reaction. "The Old Pretender won't acknowledge me, will he?"

"He might. His two sons are disappointments to him. His oldest is rash, and these days he drinks too much. His younger is a cardinal and never like to bear heirs for the Cause. Women can inherit the throne just as well as men."

"But I don't want it," she repeated.

"You need not have it. We will never be completely out of danger, but you aren't Maria's only child." He flicked a contemptuous glance at the papers. "We'll lock these up and never think on them again. We will claim the certificate you've had all your life is the true one. The one that says you're a daughter of the Earl of Hollinhead and his wife."

"Why would my mother—the dowager—do such a thing?" She was still finding acceptance difficult, that the woman she'd called "Mother" all her life was in reality no such thing.

"She was working under orders from the Pretender's court. The Old Pretender." He grimaced. "Factions on all sides. The younger brother, Cardinal Henry, wants nothing to do with the throne. You and your unknown siblings are threats to the Young Pretender, for obvious reasons, but matters between him and his father are strained. The Old Pretender is a wily old fox who knows his claims to the throne are weakening, but he has one last throw, while Prince George is still a minor and his father ageing."

The way he put it seemed so straightforward, but she knew there were as many factions as there were people. And she wanted nothing to do with it. Her appetite gone, she put her napkin next to her plate. Its crumpled folds taunted her, reminding her of innocence destroyed. She had been an innocent when she lived quietly in the country, and more than anything else she wanted that back. Even though she couldn't have it, couldn't un-know what she had learned.

Now she wasn't eating, he took her other hand. "Let me hold you, sweetheart."

"Yes." With a sigh, she rose when he did and went into his arms.

"My love, you are mine, and as long as I live, you'll have a place in my heart."

More than anything else she needed to assure herself that was true. "My home is here, with you." Before her courage could fail her, she stood on tiptoe and pressed a kiss to his mouth.

He curved a hand around her neck and held her close, responding with all the fervor she could ever wish for. He thrust his tongue into her mouth with blatant hunger, and she responded in kind.

Already his hand was at the silk bows holding her gown together, and the soft tugs punctuated their need for each other. They broke apart, panting, for him to strip off his coat and unfasten his waistcoat, by the simple expedient of grasping one side and pulling. The horn buttons slipped through the silk buttonholes for the most part, although a few clattered to the floor. Neither of them looked to find out.

He let his clothes drop. By now familiar with male clothing, she set to work on the fall of his breeches, unfastening them in feverish haste, wanting nothing between them.

He had her robe off her, and the stays that fastened down the front, blessedly easy to get rid of. Shift and slippers disposed of, she was naked, and he didn't take long joining her. Leaving their clothes scattered over the floor, they made their way to the bed in stages, pausing to kiss and caress. He cupped her breasts; she slid her hands down his chest, her palms skimming over the slabs of muscle and then the strong, long muscles of his thighs.

With a half-chuckle, half-groan, he lifted her and tossed her on to the bed. She landed on her back, the metal embroidery of the elaborate coverlet scratching her back like tiny pins set in cloth. Before he could join her, she wriggled and tugged it away, careless of the delicate fabric, her only aim a need to have him inside her.

He gazed down at her, eyes glittering with intent. "A banquet, just for me." His wry smile showed what he thought of his own whimsy, but she liked it, and her mouth curved in a smile. "It's difficult to know where to start."

But start he did, kissing and nibbling the side of her neck until she decided it was her turn to explore. Catching him off-balance, she swung her body over his, pinning him to the soft blanket. He looked glorious, lying there for her perusal.

"Do as you wish," he said. "I'm all yours. The only subject you're ever likely to have, so go to it, my lady." He lifted his hand, cupped her chin. "Your highness."

When he said it, the word became a caress, a declaration of intent rather than a meaningless title. From him she could accept it, and the acceptance became sweeter when she tasted his skin, licked along the line of the upper muscle of his chest, and touched the tip of her tongue to his nipple, which, intriguingly, hardened, as hers did when he touched and squeezed.

Just—like—that.

Nearly overwhelmed by his caresses, she continued, kissing around his navel and following the line of dark hair down toward forbidden territory—forbidden to everyone but her. His cock stood proud, flushed with arousal, the tip damp. She claimed the bead of clear liquid, sweeping her tongue over it, making him groan her name in what sounded like surrender. The smooth, shiny skin felt heavenly under her tongue, and she lingered to taste and savor. That salty muskiness of him surrounded her, seduced her as she immersed herself in him.

"No," he said in what sounded suspiciously like a choke. "Come here. I want us to make love, and I want to see you as we're doing it."

Reluctantly, because she'd planned to do a lot more down there, she came back to him, and he lifted her over him, before swinging around so she was underneath. His smile was tender but desirous. "That's where I want you. Where I can care for you and protect you. Forgive me, my darling, but I'm feeling particularly possessive today."

She could understand that. After their ordeal, it was time to claim their mutual reward.

He eased her legs apart with his knees, his hairier skin abrading her softer, more tender places, stimulating her. Slipping a hand between their bodies and down, he took the time to open her folds and slide his finger briefly inside her. "You're ready for me."

As she wrapped her arms around him and lifted her knees to hug his waist, she gave him the smile that generations of women had bestowed on their men. "I could have told you that, but I liked what you did."

"You'll like this better." He guided his shaft to her opening and breached her, pushing inside with an insistent urgency that found its echo deep in her soul.

She closed her eyes, the better to enjoy the sensation, then opened them again, and smiled up at him. His broad shoulders blocked out most of the light from the spring sun. If they went home soon, they'd catch the end of lambing and the beginning of the planting season. Maybe they'd find a quiet hedgerow somewhere and emulate the local rustics, making love in the open air. She laughed from pure joy.

Tony didn't ask her why she laughed, but joined in, the vibrations jostling where they joined, making the sensation even more exquisite. Laughter gone, she arched her back, pressing her lower body against his, urging him without words to harder, more definite thrusts. Still smiling, he obliged. A low grunt of exertion and pleasure came from low in his throat, and she responded, her body at one with his, attuned to their mutual arousal.

The waves of pleasure came closer together, heightened. Imogen knew what to do now, and she had the utmost faith in him. She had no compunction in letting go, releasing her safety to him, opening herself up to anything he wanted to do.

He wanted to thrust, and once he'd found the right spot, which she informed him was, "Yes, there!" he set up an insistent rhythm, pounding into her sure and hard, making her cry his name and cling while she rode out her orgasm. Still shuddering, her channel rippling around his cock, she felt his balls throb as he jetted his essence into her.

He caught his breath, the gasp loud in her ear, and then held on as if for his very life. He slumped over her, surrounding her entirely with his heat, skin to skin from head to toe, and she loved it.

Would have wanted him there forever, except that after a few minutes she had difficulty drawing breath. Even then she didn't complain, because the sensation of him lying over her so helplessly was too delicious to give up.

Laughing weakly, he heaved himself up, gazed down at her, and then took her in a luscious kiss. They explored each other as if they were starting all over again, but he drew out of her gently as they embraced and rolled to one side, holding her close, their heated bodies fitting together perfectly.

"I love you." He touched her chin, smiling, his face relaxed, his eyes full of adoration.

"I love you too."

"Mmm." He kissed her again, gently brushing his lips against hers. "That's what counts. We'll go from here. What would you like to do, my love? Name it and I'll make it so."

"I want to go home." She spoke simply, directly from the heart. Once she said it, it sounded so easy.

"That's what we'll do. Tomorrow, if you like, because I have plans for today. They don't involve clothes."

She snuggled against him, easing the tenderness in her breasts. "That sounds good to me."

Meet the Author

Lynne Connolly lives in England with her family and her mews, Jack the cat. She comes to the USA every year to visit her publishers and readers. She was born in Leicester, England and was brought up in a haunted house. She is part Romany, and in her spare time she loves reading the Tarot as her grandmother taught her, and making and filling dollhouses.

Turn the page for a special excerpt of Lynne Connolly

Rogue In Red Velvet

If Connie loses her standing in society, she risks losing everything...

except Alex.

When country widow Constance Rattigan finds herself in a notorious London brothel instead of at the altar, only one person can save her from the auction block. Alex Vernon walked away from Connie once before, when he discovered her engagement. Now that her fiancé has betrayed her, Lord Ripley doesn't intend to leave her again. But Connie has other ideas… She won't marry him until her name is cleared.

Alex decides to make Connie's wishes come true, but it's not that easy, even with the help of his powerful relatives known as the Emperors of London.

On sale now!

Chapter 1

March, 1754

The library door crashed open, shattering Connie's peace and admitting the last man she wanted to be alone with. Pretending unperturbed tranquility, Connie put her pen in the standish. She clasped her hands on top of the book she'd been working on to still the trembling his presence caused.

Wide-eyed, chest heaving, the normally elegant, cool Lord Ripley, slammed the door and put his back to it.

She met his blank, dark stare and cursed her fluttering pulse. Whatever had put him in this state, it couldn't be trivial.

He blinked, straightened and assumed the town bronze most of his sort used like a cloak, covering whatever he felt beneath. He gave the perfectly tied strip of linen at his neck a twitch, arranged his sleeve ruffles, then straightened his wig. As poise and elegance returned, he transformed from a hunted fugitive to a gentleman and pushed away from the door. He strolled to the old, scarred table at which she sat. "Here you are."

What a ridiculous statement. "I believe I am." She read a line in the journal before her, more to look away than because she needed to, and took a steadying breath before she met his eyes once more. "May I help you, Lord Ripley?"

"I merely wondered why you lock yourself away here every day, Mrs. Rattigan. And I came to see if I may assist you in any way."

"I'm perfectly fine, sir. I doubt you could help me, or have any interest in doing so." She'd avoided him for three days and wanted none of his games. She didn't care why he'd shot in here, only she wished he'd shoot out again, just as fast.

"Is it something too difficult for my paltry brain? Are you a bluestocking, ma'am, that you labor here day after day without joining the revelry?" In full control, his society manners polished as ever, he walked to her side of the table and loomed over her.

Her heart beat faster and her breath quickened. She worked to hide his effect on her and castigated herself for a fool. He wasn't interested in her in that way, much less when she had her hair scraped back in a knot, wore no cosmetics at all and had donned her old clothes in preparation for the dusty work. She was just an excuse, an escape from something. Or someone. She was no empty-headed miss. She was a respectable widow, but it didn't stop her becoming tongue-tied. "I—I—"

"You find yourself bored by our antics. You'd rather study Plautus, or is it Marcus Aurelius?" Chuckling, he leaned over her shoulder, flipped the book closed. With one long finger, he traced the name on the cover. "Saucy stories perhaps?"

The door opened and admitted Miss Louisa Stobart, one of the young ladies invited here to meet Lord Ripley. Connie's godfather had confided to her that he might choose a bride from among them.

Now she understood why he'd shot into this room like a pursued fox. Miss Stobart had been the most assiduous of Lord Ripley's pursuers, indefatigable in her chase. He'd been escaping her.

For a change, Connie was in charge. How delicious.

Lord Ripley straightened and gave Connie such a look of pleading that she almost laughed. "Help me," he mouthed, before assuming his easy smile and facing his tormentor.

She would have preferred that he said that in different circumstances, but what she dreamed at night remained between her and her pillow. This would do. A little gentle revenge was called for. She slid the book over to his lordship and pointed at random. "Here is a word I cannot read, sir. Do you see?"

"No, ma'am." Bending over her shoulder, he peered then looked at her.

Far too close, his breath heated her cheek and her heart quickened. This close, he'd see her reaction for sure. Inwardly, she groaned. She hadn't bargained on him doing that. She should have shoved the book away from her.

His eyes widened slightly. He turned his attention to the book. "I think it says wormwood. An old spell book?"

She laughed. "An inventory, sir. As you well know."

His shoulders relaxed under his country-coat. In an ordinary man that slight movement might remain unnoticed, but Connie had spent the last few days watching him surreptitiously. He was the most handsome man she'd ever seen and while she could tell herself that she was merely observing, it did no good. For the first time in her life, she longed to be younger, wealthier and socially higher ranking. Then she could compete. Instead, she'd dressed in a practical country gown that would survive hedgerows and house dust, and hidden away here. "Yes, of course. Wormwood."

Thank goodness he straightened.

Miss Stobart stood on the other side of the table, her delicately draped pink silk gown mocking Connie's sturdy dark green garment. Miss Stobart's was a fashionable ideal of a gown to be worn in the country, sprinkled with exquisitely embroidered spring flowers. Miss Stobart's gaze skimmed over Connie and to his lordship. Her ruby lips pursed in a winsome pout. "Sir, I had hoped we could take a turn in the gardens. I quite thought you had promised me at breakfast."

"I had no idea." He glanced down at Connie. It was her cue to say something.

"I'm so sorry to interrupt your"—*Courtship? Pursuit?* —"walk. Of course you must go."

Miss Stobart drummed her foot against the wood floor, maddening in the quiet library. "Indeed sir, I quite thought you'd forgotten me, so I came to find you." Her voice was sweet; her foot was not.

"I beg your pardon, but I had promised today to Connie for some time now." He gave her an easy smile.

Connie stared at him in astonishment. He'd used her first name. She wasn't aware he even knew it. When he put his hand on her shoulder, she nearly leaped up. His skin wasn't in contact with hers, due to her modest gown and fichu, but it might as well have been. She felt it like a shock of recognition. Of what she didn't want to consider.

"Connie and I are old friends." The familiarity of her first name implied he was much friendlier with her than anyone had imagined. "When she mentioned her task, I immediately volunteered to help. Her—er—errand is something I am particularly interested in."

Not to mention, he didn't have the faintest idea what she was doing. She'd never discussed her project in company and nobody had expressed an interest except for her godfather, whose commission this was.

He was casting her as his rescuer when he hadn't asked her first.

"It is a special project I've been meaning to undertake for some time." Should she lie, draw out the moment? She wasn't used to being the center of attention.

Miss Stobart fixed her cold, blue eyes on Connie, probably for the first time since she'd arrived.

Connie gave the young woman her sweetest smile. "My visit here provided the perfect opportunity."

"A bluestocking?" That was the second time in ten minutes she'd been accused of that. Did everyone in society who opened a book get accused of that?

Miss Stobart's lips curved in a superior smile. She clearly considered herself the victor in this encounter. After all, who would not? Connie was below the notice of a young lady of marriageable age and considerable fortune.

"Not exactly." She glanced at the book.

Leaning over her once more, Lord Ripley flipped the volume over, revealing the faded label on the front. "It's an inventory of the house from the sixteenth century. Family history is important."

Damn, she couldn't torment him anymore. He'd guessed right. "Lord Downholland has particularly wished to gather all the documents pertaining to the house in one place. I merely offered to assist him."

"And I offered to assist Connie," he said smoothly, back in control. "I'm sorry, Miss Stobart, but her claims had precedence."

Wonderful. He was fast making an enemy on her behalf. Miss Stobart would resent her intensely if she came between the chase and ensnarement of her quarry. "I'm only doing this until my fiancé arrives."

Miss Stobart relaxed, nodded regally. "I see. But Lord Ripley has other commitments."

"I'll be down directly, ma'am." He walked to the door and held it open. "If you would not mind waiting for a few moments, I would greatly appreciate the time."

Miss Stobart swept through and he closed the door behind her.

Breathing deeply, he slumped against it. He met Connie's gaze and smiled. "Thank you."

So that was what she was good for. A distraction. "I'm not prepared to act as your chaperone, sir."

Laughing, he waved a hand in one of the most elegant movements she'd ever seen. "I would be eternally grateful to you if you did so." He sauntered toward her. "I never thought I'd be in need of one, to be truthful."

Connie resisted the temptation to move away. She was not afraid of this man, or intimidated by him, even though he had just gone from being the object of her fantasies to a real live human being. His panic, his silent appeal for help had transformed him in her eyes. Although, sadly, his appeal remained.

Seizing her hand, he dropped a kiss on the back, and immediately restored it to her. "I can't thank you enough, ma'am." He grinned wickedly. "Connie."

"I wasn't even aware you knew my first name."

"I do."

How did he know her name when she wasn't even aware that he'd noticed her? Had he made a point of learning it?

"Connie, I truly appreciate your help. Is there anything I can do for you in return?"

"You can answer this. Why is it so important to avoid Miss Stobart?" She dared to turn around and look at his face, bracing herself for the visual contact, as she always did when she looked at him. "You raced in here as if the hounds of hell were after you. Surely you have enough address to avoid her?"

He perched on the table by her side. Too close.

Anger was taking the place of curiosity. She no longer cared about the social gulf between them, or her dowdy appearance, or anything else other than the consideration that he had treated her badly. "Sir, I'm a widow, from the country, but I'm not prepared to be treated as if I don't exist."

His eyes darkened as he gazed steadily at her. "I owe you an apology. I am truly sorry if I implied anything of the kind. I meant it. I owe you a favor. Anything."

The devil take him. What she could do with was an extra pair of hands, and someone who knew how to read the spidery old writing she was fighting every day. She folded her arms. "Very well, since you ask. I want an assistant in this task. I agreed to help my godfather gather the books he'll need to compile a family history. It's proving more difficult than I imagined. Some of the books are heavy and stored in virtually inaccessible places."

His broad shoulders eased. "I would be honored to help."

"Even if it meant getting a speck of dirt on your clothes?"

"Even then." His lips curved in a disconcertingly attractive smile.

Meeting his eyes became more difficult and she fought the urge to fidget. She'd have to change her chair, it was becoming most uncomfortable. "I'm working at this task most of the day. Until my fiancé arrives."

"Dankworth, yes." He snapped the name as if Jasper had done something to annoy him. "I should wish you happy, I suppose."

"Content will do. Thank you."

He quirked a brow. That irritating smile returned. "Contentment only? You don't wish for wedded bliss?"

"Not in the least. A rational partnership is my dearest wish." It was the truth. Love had done nothing for her. She wished for a comfortable marriage that would improve the lot of both parties, nothing else. She'd decided that years ago, and now her ambition was within her grasp, she'd do nothing to change it. "The marriage will suit my godparents, who have been kind to me and have no child of their own to inherit their estate."

"They know about Dankworth, then?"

Did he? Eyeing her pen, she wished she could take it up again and lose herself in the old inventories. She didn't want her decision questioned in this way. What good would it do? "They know he can be foolish on occasion. Marriage will settle him and ensure heirs for the estate." She tired of this game. This man was only baiting her. "I understand you're here seeking a bride, sir. You won't find one in this room."

"Will I not?" He leaned forward, pressing home his advantage. His citrus and spice scent was altogether too seductive. His low voice hinted at unforgiveable sins. "You're not formally betrothed yet, ma'am."

"I will be very soon." She wasn't very good at flirting, never had been. She scraped back her chair, got to her feet, and made a business of shaking out the skirts of her drab green gown. "You cannot show the guests such discourtesy. They are here for you, at least a good many are."

He grinned wryly. "It would be more discourteous to run away screaming. If I don't have this escape, I might very well do that." He stood, took a few paces toward the door, and turned back, the skirts of his country coat swinging around thighs that filled out his breeches creditably. "I see I must confide my predicament and throw myself on your mercy. Miss Stobart is determined to trap me into a connection I have no desire to acquire."

Miss Stobart had either ignored Connie or treated her with barely concealed contempt since her arrival. Connie had heard rumors as well as witnessed Miss Stobart's relentless pursuit of his lordship.

He sighed and scrutinized the silver buckle on his shiny black shoe. "I suspect my father put her and her mother in the way of finding me here. The old man wants me married and as soon as possible. The truth is, I was caught in a compromising position with Miss Stobart at a ball and I decided to leave London for a while until the affair blew over." He lifted his hand as if to run it through his hair, but he was wearing a fashionable wig.

From the color of his brows, she'd say his hair was dark underneath and she had an irrational but powerful desire to see it for herself. To touch it, in a way entirely forbidden to her. Annoying that this unwanted desire wouldn't leave her. His confession didn't endear him to her. *Compromising position* could mean anything from a private conversation to full-blown seduction.

"The incident happened at a ball," he continued. "Miss Stobart said she'd torn her gown and asked me to help her pin it. So there I was kneeling at her feet in an anteroom when her aunt dramatically flung open the door. She'd been clever enough to bring witnesses."

That wasn't so bad. "Didn't you explain your task?"

"They chose not to believe me. Miss Stobart swore it was a declaration of marriage. It was not, but my absence from town was advisable. She chased me here." He closed his eyes, and when he opened them they were filled with surprising bleakness. "I must sound like the veriest coxcomb, imagining every woman in the house after my hand."

"No indeed, sir. You are from one of the foremost families in the land, accepted everywhere, and in possession of a large fortune. Why should you not think that?." Since he was being so honest, why should she not do the same?

He arched a brow. "If I said I wanted to be desired for myself, I'd sound foolish. But it's true. Connie, I have few friends, people I can be honest with. It would be a privilege if you allow that between us."

Friends? Damn, but she still wanted more. Not that she could have it, and Connie had become used to not having what she wanted. Friends would do. "Very well."

"And I'll devote a portion of every day to helping you."

"Thank you, sir." Exquisite agony to have this man so close, but she'd bear it. Worse that she was liking him more.

"Alex."

She blinked. "I beg your pardon?"

"I want the privilege of calling you Connie. In return, you must call me Alex, especially in private. You do me a great favor, helping me to avoid the ladies, particularly Miss Stobart. She's done everything she can to compromise me."

"What about me? Won't I be compromised?"

"You're a respectable widow, soon to be formally betrothed. You told me so yourself."

He had her there. "And in any case, I'm of an age where I cannot be expected to be on the hunt. Isn't that right?"

"I wouldn't say that." He raked her with his eyes, once, twice, from head to toes.

Every part of her body tingled. How could she bear this? "I'm eight and twenty, sir. I'm far too old to consider husband hunting seriously, even if my arrangement with Jasper didn't exist." He might as well hear the truth. "If it weren't that my godparents had chosen me, I'd be well on the shelf."

"They might consider you decrepit. I certainly don't. But you have my word, Connie, I'll behave. Just don't leave me to their mercies." When he moved back, she caught the scent of citrus and masculinity. He was too real, with her in this room, a man rather than a symbol of power and influence.

"Why don't you just leave?"

He shook his head. "I promised my father I wouldn't. He's an old curmudgeon, but he's the only father I have. In a week, I will be kicking the dust of this admittedly charming house off my heels. I just need help until then."

So he could help the old widow woman sort out the dusty books. The situation appealed to her underused sense of humor. If she could bear his presence, and since he'd dropped his society mask she found him much more agreeable, then she could watch the play unfold and smile. As a widow she was allowed more leeway than others, and even if rumors came her way, she was safe. Jasper would arrive any day now and then her quietude would be at an end. She would be an engaged woman. "Very well, but not for long. Until you leave."

"Thank you, Connie. You do me a great service and I won't forget it."

She might as well make use of him. "Be warned, Lord Ripley, I intend to work you hard collecting volumes from the dustiest rooms in the house."

"Alex."

He must look at all women that way and the gullible thought he did it just for them. More fools they. Connie wouldn't join them.

* * * *

Alex left the library smiling. If Connie Rattigan thought her plain gowns and quiet demeanor had prevented him looking at her with more than usual interest, she was much mistaken.

Her determination to avoid the house party had intrigued him at first. Then he wondered how she could think of becoming betrothed to anyone belonging to the Dankworth family. Of course he was biased, since his mother's family were constantly at odds with the Dankworths, but Jasper, in his opinion, was a typical example of the breed. He didn't deserve her. Glad to find her betrothed absent from the party, he'd looked at Connie and liked what he saw. The more he looked, the more he liked.

Discovering her lair had become an obsession that had lightened the otherwise dull visit. He'd traversed several corridors more plainly decorated and much narrower than the more gracious ones in the main part of the house. But he'd failed in his quest.

So it was ironic that he'd found her by accident. He had been escaping the wiles of Miss Stobart. Running away. He'd wandered into the older part of the house, to explore a little. Like many country houses, this one had been added to over the years. Lower ceilings and narrower corridors than in the modern part of the house attested to its age. He'd ducked into an old library, lined with shelves of books that looked read instead of just for show.

When he turned a corner and discovered the lady facing him full-square, his smile vanished. If he wanted to get past her, he'd either have to retreat or beg her pardon and squeeze past. The narrow corridors that a moment ago had seemed quaint now took on a more sinister aspect.

Another lady chased around the far end of the long hallway, no doubt determined to prevent any tete-a-tete. Good for her.

"Ladies, would you both care to accompany me in a stroll around the gardens?" Acceptable, and he could make an excuse and leave them with each other. Perhaps they'd come to blows. A man could only hope.

Alex considered himself an easy-going man but these two had driven him to distraction. So much that he'd left London and taken up the invitation for a quiet gathering, only for them to discover where he'd gone and follow post-haste. The Downhollands were too genial to turn them away.

Even more reason to pursue the fascinating Constance Rattigan. He'd never met a woman before who drew him as she did. The fact that she was about to be married, or contracted anyway, made her safer than the two women who confidently came forward and took an arm each. Also infinitely better company. She conversed like a sensible woman, and while he tried to be a gentleman, he took note of her luscious figure and her lovely features almost without thinking.

Strange feeling. Must be the Yorkshire air, he decided, as he made the necessary detour to the south entrance, heading for the gardens.